A CASE OF TOO MANY DEATHS

A Mother Calls,
A Daughter's Life Turns Upside Down.
A Mystery of Genetics and The Courtroom.

N.K. Napier

ISBN Paperback: 979-8-9889443-1-7
ISBN Electronic: 979-8-9889443-0-0

Library of Congress Control Number: 2023915526

This work of fiction is based on a high-profile legal case that occurred in Australia. Names, characters, places, events, locales, and incidents have been changed and are the products of the author's imagination.

Author Photo: Uli Schlapka
Publishing Consultant: PRESStinely,
PRESStinely.com

Printed in the United States of America.

TMM Press
N.K. Napier
NancyKNapier.com

For Tony, always.

Chapter 1

Early Sunday morning, April 9, 2006

Anticipating a long run in the eastern Washington foothills, outside of Surrey, Emma Raddell laced her running shoes, tucked her bushy auburn hair under a headband, and glanced at her aquarium. Hildegarde, her magnificent zebra fish, stared at her, because, of course, fish stare. Then she saw Konstantine and choked.

Konstantine, the tiny Neon Tetra, floated on the surface.

Emma scooped the carcass into a Tupperware container, a makeshift coffin for a longtime friend. A quiet, non-demanding friend, to be sure, but for Emma, that was as close as it got these days.

Yoda, her fifteen-year-old rescue, had died three months before, and she shuddered thinking of her weeks-long grief. The scruffy part-schnauzer/part-lab never fit a single breed. Emma knew the feeling of not fitting in. Her law firm job confounded her, almost a year in, as she navigated work, colleagues, and probably office politics, but she felt too naïve to know.

The day Yoda died, they'd run the hill trails on a cloudy Saturday morning. Then the dog slipped into lethargy. By the time Emma reached the vet's, Yoda could barely lift her head.

"Kidney cancer. We can operate, but no promises." Dr. Hanson's sad eyes mimicked Yoda's. "Or, you can say goodbye now."

She still ached for the dog, but the fish had helped, even though they weren't as expressive as Yoda. They half-filled her wish for a companion, someone to talk to.

She opened her worn copy of Emily Dickenson's poems, bought during undergraduate days. Emily D had rescued her before, and Emma needed her now. Poem Number 1121 called to her.

Time does go on—
I tell it gay to those who suffer now—
They shall survive—
There is a sun—
They don't believe it now—

"It's just you and me, Hildegarde. You're the warrior maiden; I'm the one who keeps losing friends. But I've got to connect to humans, too." That could be harder if people knew she talked to a fish.

Running usually quelled her sadness. Emma stopped twenty minutes up one of the hill trails above Surrey and pulled her windbreaker hood up, dodging sprinkles. She closed her eyes, shaking Konstantine's death from her head, and slipped on the glassy rocks. Pain shot up her ankle. On hands and knees, she crawled to a nearby tree and grabbed a branch as a crutch.

Ten minutes of inch-by-inch downhill movement exhausted her, and the parking lot felt no closer. On the trail below, two women in red puffy jackets trudged up the hill, deep in conversation. The one in front carried a walking stick and guffawed at some comment the other made. She pointed at Emma.

The women looked like female wrestlers, stocky builds that could withstand heavy winds. *Probably sisters*, Emma thought.

"Twisted my ankle. Hobbling back down. I'll be fine," Emily shouted over to them.

"Oh no you won't. I'm Riley, by the way." Her ruddy complexion made her white teeth more obvious. "Mom, what was that old girl scout seat we made?" She had pink streaks in her bobbed hair, contrasting with her mom's wispy white.

"And I'm Patty. Her mom." Patty stuck her elbow toward Riley. "Honey, you remember it. What's with your brain these days? That man getting to you? Can't focus?" She chuckled. "But you're right, and we're here to rescue this pilgrim. The perfect Girl Scout sling. Right hand on left forearm; you do the same."

"No need. I can get down," Emma insisted. Even bent over her tree-branch crutch, she was a head taller than the determined mother-daughter pair.

"The hell you can." Patty put her hand on Emma's shoulder. "It'll take you till Thursday night to get to the parking lot. Now just shut up and let us get you there. At least you're skinny."

Riley winced. "Mom was a prison guard. She knows how to get people to do what she wants."

The former Girl Scouts linked arms and crab walked Emma down the hill, stopping every few minutes to rest. They razzed each other and Emma all the way down.

Task completed, Patty stuck her face in Emma's car window. "Give me your phone number so I can follow up. Now get thee to an urgent care or if not that, get some painkillers. And ice now and then. Scoot." She flicked her hand, dismissing the patient.

By the time they deposited her, Emma's mood had lifted. She envied the comfortable mother-daughter banter. Yes, she needed to connect with people. Another fish wouldn't do it.

Still clutching her tree branch, Emma limped into Drugs-4-You and headed for the elder care section. On her way, she glanced down the pet care aisle and put her hand on her chest, fighting a wave of unexpected grief.

She hobbled toward the wooden canes and passed a disheartening set of products—walkers, shower seats, and adult disposable underwear. *Lordy, may I never need these.*

An old man hunched over the canes and winked at her. "We old codgers need to stick together, don't we?"

Emma tried to smile, but her foot hurt, so she grimaced. She grabbed a shiny wooden cane and shuffled toward the pain relievers. As she rounded that aisle, she saw Stan from work, another new lawyer, and stepped back to a parallel aisle. The familiar push-pull of knowing she should make contact and not wanting to made her stomach hurt. She counted to thirty and peeked around to be sure he was gone before snatching a large bottle of Aleve.

At the cashier, she noticed the local newspaper headline: "Woman Who Killed Her Kids Now Has Execution Date Set after Twenty Years in Solitary." She gasped. The photo looked like Mom. *Spooky.* She waffled on whether to splurge $2.50 for the Sunday paper, reached for it, and then pulled back.

"Find everything you wanted?" The cashier's voice sounded like a robot.

"Yes. I did. I'll just grab…some toothpaste." She took a $1.50 travel pack size from the display next to the check out and patted herself on the back for not being sucked into that grisly tabloid story.

Chapter 2

Tuesday morning, April 11, 2006

Back from a court hearing for her teenage client's reckless driving charge (and pot in the car), Emma staggered across the open office of Ivins, MacFarlane, and Donohue, Surrey's most prestigious law firm. She'd passed the Washington bar a year before but struggled to fit into the high-end firm. Sweat beads dotted her forehead as she clomped her way across the room. Multiple eyes darted in her direction.

"Twisted my ankle running," she said, tapping her cane in rhythm with her bum foot.

She hobbled past the administrator's orderly desk, where the Sunday paper, with its execution headline, sat atop stacks of colorful folders. Sherry, the head legal administrator, in her signature St. John's suit and camera-ready makeup, was the only person to give the partners any back talk. Also, she pounced on weakness like a vulture. Hence, her nickname.

Sherry tapped the headline. "Now that was a murder trial." She picked up a red folder and lifted her chin. "Ah, Emma. Got your report. Early. Well done."

Emma stumbled. *No way—a compliment from the Vulture?* "Thanks. You see how fast I can finish what you give me. Maybe something a little more challenging next time?" *Beyond teen DUIs and parking tickets.*

The Vulture crooked a finger and beckoned Emma. "I'd rather have them done right than done early. Don't be a rate-buster."

Ouch. Should have seen that coming.

"Don't push me on assignments. It's not a competition." Sherry flicked her fingers. "Off you go." She grabbed her coffee mug with "World's Best-Dressed Nana" printed on the side. *Grandkids probably couldn't find one that said, "Best Ego Killer of All Time."*

Emma straightened. "I'll keep that in mind."

She plunked her way down the hall, a modern-day Captain Ahab: Tink, tink, tink of the cane tip on the wood floor…trying to conquer a white whale, or in her case, the Vulture.

The law office building had been a county jail a century ago. She imagined hundred-year-old air, flooded with the sweat of inmates. Despite the firm's attempt to soften the ambiance with beechwood desks and Aeron chairs, her office felt antiseptic. Georgia O'Keefe's primary prints hung on the rough brick walls, but the fluorescent lights accentuated the room's dank history. Some employees covered their desks and bookshelves with family photos, but she had none. Not many happy memories there.

She flipped through her cases—two more DUIs, two driving without a license charges, and a person who'd parked in a handicap spot. The most interesting was an indecent exposure suit against a middleweight politician.

Emma hung up her Ralph Lauren jacket and stroked her good luck charm, the blue and white Scottish flag lapel pin gifted by her neighbor, Rupert. She hadn't realized when she took the basement apartment that most neighbors were over seventy and rarely left their houses. Rupert defied the stereotype and spent time in his garden and walked to the grocery store.

Antigone Russell, next-door office neighbor, tapped on the door. Her uniform: crisp white shirt with her grandfather's cuff links and her mother's black pearls. Every day. In Emma's first month at Ivins, Antigone had helped her shop for suits and blouses on her tight budget and offered unsolicited advice.

"Be wary in the office. Don't give too much away," Antigone warned. "Sherry says it's not a competition, but we're all on probation."

Antigone slid into a chair in front of Emma's desk. "You, my friend, could be on thin ice. Another run in with Sherry? Seriously? We all saw it."

Emma ran her hand across right cheek, grabbed a gnawed No. 2 pencil from behind her ear, and tapped the eraser on her desk. "I want more interesting work. She should see—"

Antigone slapped her fingers on the desk. "Stop that. You'll get better work. Just don't push it."

She stopped tapping midair. Antigone was trying to be a friend, but Emma resisted. She'd never opened up much, at home or in law school. *Maybe I should try. Can I trust Antigone?*

A knock at the door jolted her. Sherry stuck her head in. "Sorry. You've got company. Just dropping off some new work for you."

Emma stiffened.

Antigone jumped up. "I'm leaving. Good to see you, Sherry." She made a thumbs-up gesture on her way out and mouthed, "Be nice."

"Thanks, Sherry. What's the case?"

"Stalking. Roy Donohue needs new eyes on it. Thought you might be the eyes. He also assigned an intern to you." Two files, four inches tall, thudded on the corner of the desk.

Sherry pushed the door open and ushered in a fresh-faced lawyer.

"Emma and Jennifer, please meet." And off she went.

"Welcome to the firm," Emma said.

Jennifer grinned, her spanking new pinstriped suit cracking with freshness.

"These files from Mr. Donohue—how about if you review them, get whatever extra files and background materials we'll need from the archives, and let's meet Friday for an update?"

The new inmate scurried off.

Chapter 3

Wednesday morning, April 12, 2006

"Emma! Wait a second!" Antigone called from across the plaza in front of the law offices. Emma slowed as Antigone caught up, mid-sentence.

"My mother…such a piece of work…just got off the phone with her. She wants me to come for dinner this weekend. In Seattle. That's a four-hour drive."

Emma sucked in her breath. *A mom who organizes dinners for her daughter? Like it's a natural thing?* "What's the dinner?"

"Some guy she wants me to meet. He works for a big investment firm."

"Tell her you can't come?"

Antigone laughed. "You don't know her. She wants to be involved in my life…. Usually that's OK, but sometimes…she cares too much. Maybe I should send you in my place?"

Emma slowed her pace as she gazed at the office workers bustling ahead of her. *A mother who cares too much?* She couldn't imagine how that would feel. Antigone turned to wait for her to catch up.

"Ankle still bothering you?" Antigone asked.

"A little…. Sounds like a good mother to me."

"Oh, maybe. But you don't know the whole story. Never mind. Sorry to bother you with it."

Emma thought back to finding Konstantine over the weekend. She'd promised herself then to try and connect, or reconnect, with people, not just fish. That had to include Mom. She couldn't even remember why their relationship had dissolved. Probably since it never fully formed but seemed always on the edge, and then she…or Mom…let something come between them. She wanted some of what Antigone had, some of what the two women on the trail had.

Antigone glanced at Emma. "So, what's your mother like?"

Emma stabbed the ground with her cane. "Not like yours, that's for sure." She yanked open the office door and held it for Antigone, who never looked back.

Chapter 4

Wednesday evening, April 12, 2006

Emma stood in the middle of the humane society lobby, listening to barking dogs: excited dogs, scared dogs, dogs with no sense of their futures.... *Do dogs even think about the future?* Human voices murmured, soothing the animals. Hildegarde, for all of her spectacular striped body, didn't respond much to Emma's comments. A dog would.

Inside the room of caged canines, she chuckled at the names: Dollar, Buddy, Sam, Felicia, Camilla. She stopped in front of Herman, a black and white border collie and lab mix. *Herman? What kind of name is that?* She squatted down to read the laminated sign attached to his cage.

What my friends at the shelter say about me:

> Two-year-old Herman doesn't have much experience with the human world. Before coming here, he mostly lived outside. He bonded with his recent family until they had a baby two months ago and had to give him up. His human dad said he likes to run the trails and loves playing with other dogs, but we don't know about cats.

I wonder how Herman would feel about fish.... She felt a presence hovering over her and looked up to see the bottom of a man's chin—rust-colored beard—and the top of a blue and white flannel plaid shirt.

"Sorry, I didn't mean to hover. Need a hand?"

"Nope, thanks. I can manage," which she did most ungracefully, slapping the cane on the floor and slipping before standing. She noticed his scuffed leather boots as she pushed herself up. Standing, at last, her eyes shut halfway as she looked down into his face. She had a good two inches on him, even in her flats. His bushy hair looked like he combed it with his fingers. *A mountain man?*

"Are you thinking about this one?" He pointed his thumb at Herman, who whined and crooked his whole body as he wagged his long tail. "I am." He stepped back from the cage and grinned.

Her heart sped up. She'd come to get a dog and now faced an argument. "I'm interested too."

"Should we b-bid on him?" He stammered.

"Everything OK here? Want to take him out and play?" A staff person in a fire-engine-red smock appeared. "Ah. Herman. He arrived two days ago, and lots of people are interested. But you two may be the winners since you're here."

"Oh, we're not together." Emma leaned over to read the woman's name tag, "Toni. And yes, could he come outside?" Toni shepherded Herman out and handed him over to Emma, who unleashed him.

Mountain Man squatted and snapped his fingers. "Herman! Herman! Here, boy." He pulled a dog treat from his pocket and held it out.

Herman swished his head back and forth before leaping toward the man. He gobbled the treat and stood in front of him, wagging his body again.

That guy's after my dog?

"I think he's smiling," said the dog thief, moving his hands all over the dog's head, scratching Herman's ears.

Irked at the joyful scene, Emma called out, "Are you trying to horn in on my dog?" She scanned the yard for Toni to help break up this fight. But she'd left. "I don't want an argument, but I want this dog. Mine died three months ago, and I want a new one."

"Forgive m-me for saying this, but that's not long enough. You need to process the g-grief."

She started. "Are you some sort of social worker? I know if I'm ready and I am. And this is the dog I want." Her voice was shrill.

He held his palms toward her. "OK, OK. Please. Take the dog. The last thing I'd ever want to do is put an angry woman on the street." When he smiled, his green eyes, which had yellow streaks in the irises, nearly disappeared into his ruddy face.

Her laugh came out like a cough. Herman looked at her. Instead of offering food, she tossed a ball, and he tore after it. *Now we're getting somewhere.*

Herman dashed back from the edge of the yard and ran to the Mountain Man. He dropped the ball and hung his tongue out.

"Ha. Look at that," he said. "He came b-back."

Emma gritted her teeth. *Enough.* She reached the door to the dog pens and felt a tap on her shoulder. Mountain Man handed her the leash and the dog.

"Rather not have this dog if he means this much to you," he said. "I'll find one. You take Herman."

She turned and placed her hand on her chest, leery of showing how touched she was by this kindness, much needed after her day.

At home, Emma tossed the ball for Herman in the backyard.

Herman. The name's not right. Titus? Elvis? Shakespeare?

Dad had always wanted a dog, but Mom nixed the idea. "If we ever get a dog," he'd said on the sly, "I'd call him Shadrach. Sounds like a favorite uncle."

Her father wasn't especially religious but did use Bible stories for bedtime with her—so she knew about Noah's ark, David and Goliath, and Jonah and the whale. And the story of the brothers, Shadrach, Meshach, and Abednego.

"Shadrach! There you go, buddy. OK, Shadrach? Does that sound good, Shadrach?"

The dog-formerly-known-as Herman sniffed at her. Maybe he'd be the connection she needed, since she wasn't making progress with many work colleagues and certainly had blown it with Mountain Man. She had to admit, though, that she wouldn't mind running into Mountain Man again. He'd made her smile, and not a lot of people did that.

She remembered the ping of a voicemail on her drive home. *Uh-oh. Probably Sherry about something I've done wrong.* She never answered while driving, having dealt with so many clients who had made that mistake. She pulled out her phone and looked at the number, one she didn't recognize. *Not Sherry. Then who?*

She staggered when she heard Mom's husky voice. Eerie, since Emma had been thinking about her on and off all day.

"Emileen. It's Mom. I hope you're well in the new job up there. Please call me. You can use this number…it's a cellular phone I'm using…or you can call on the home number if you remember it. Thank you."

She bit the inside of her cheek. As a child she'd not realized how unusual Mom's voice was, until she watched *Casablanca* in college. Mom's voice sounded like Lauren Bacall—deep, "whiskey sour," sexy.

Also, a little disapproving. *Of course, I remember the home number.* And a little proud at having a cell phone. Hearing her old name flung Emma back to childhood in that house, where she never felt she belonged. She replayed the message three times.

She glanced at the time. 9:52 p.m. Almost ten o'clock. As early risers, her parents went to bed no later than ten. *Should I call now?* It wasn't quite ten but still, it seemed too late. *Am I just stalling?* She'd wait till morning when they were both fresh.

Shadrach stared at her and tilted his head. "Coward," he seemed to say.

"You're right," she said. "I'm dodging."

Chapter 5

Thursday noon, April 13, 2006

At lunch the next day, Emma crossed the street to the small city park, found a bench, and called Mom.

"Emileen. It's nice to hear your voice."

And it's unnerving to hear yours. That gravely and distracted voice, physically there but emotionally distant.

"What's going on, Mom? Is Dad OK?" She could picture her mother at the kitchen table, wiping her hand on her apron, twisting the wall phone cord that stretched from the doorway.

"Yes, he's fine. How're you? I hope everything is going well.... I have something to tell you...but I...uh... I don't know how to tell you this...."

So, Mom isn't actually interested in how I am. She clenched her jaw.

"Just say it."

"I hope you're somewhere private. I'm going to shock you."

Get on with it, Mom. "I'm in a park. No one can hear anything. What's going on?"

"OK. Here it goes. You have an aunt; my sister."

Emma touched her throat.

"Really? In Surrey?"

"No. She's about two hours away."

"Why haven't you..."

"There's so much to tell you."

An unwelcome clump formed in Emma's stomach. She looked up into a Douglas pine. Tall trunk, long horizontal branches, birds flitting around. *Listen to her. Listen. Focus.* "Could you just tell me? Don't be so cryptic."

"Emileen. I'm sorry. I need to say this in my own way."

She could imagine Mom leaning on the kitchen sink, rocking back and forth. She'd have a dish towel slung over her shoulder, and her curly hair would be frizzy if there was any humidity.

"OK. But I don't have all day."

Mom gasped, and Dad's muffled voice surfaced in the background. Mom whispered, but Emma could hear her. "She's on a break. Just hold your horses."

Hold your horses. That was a Mom phrase that she'd thought was a warning not to misbehave but realized much later that it meant "don't get so excited; just slow down." But today, she needed Mom to move faster.

"So, you have a sister. What's her name?" Emma pressed.

"Victoria. Victoria Beringer is her name."

Again, Dad murmured in the background. He towered over Mom and reminded Emma of the scarecrow in the *Wizard of Oz* movie.

"Yes, yes. I'll tell her. Emileen. Your aunt. My sister. She did something terrible a long time ago. To her children. She made a bad mistake."

Is this conversation sliding into a ditch?

Emma gritted her teeth. "Would you just say it?"

"She…Victoria. She's…in prison."

Now a tennis ball bounced in her stomach. She dropped onto the bench again.

"Are you there?" Mom asked.

"Just stunned. More than that. Shocked. What's this about?"

"Maybe you remember, when you were little, we told you I had a sister who lived far away? We'd lost touch with her?"

"Vaguely. I never met her." Another tennis ball moved to her throat, blocking easy swallowing. *How could she have held all of that back for so many years?* She grabbed her No. 2 pencil from behind her ear and stuck it in her mouth.

"Well, you never met her because she was in prison. In Washington state, but it might as well be another planet."

Emma bit down on the pencil, and flecks of yellow dropped to her skirt. "All these years… How long has she been there?"

"I'm sorry. This is a shock. It's been nearly twenty-five years…. Shhh, Jim. I'm getting to that."

"For God's sake! What'd she do?"

"Her children. Her four children died. They accused her of hurting them…. Of killing them. There, it's out."

The woman in the newspaper?

Emma's ribs hurt. She leaned back to look up into the trees. The twittering birds failed to settle her. "Oh, my God."

Bile rose in her throat. She scanned the park for a garbage can just in case. The nearest was by a picnic table thirty feet away, so she moved toward it.

"We couldn't deal with the shame. That's why we moved to Snowville, so the neighbors wouldn't know we were related."

The bile returned to its home base. She swallowed and slunk onto another bench.

"Your father and I decided not to talk about it. We didn't want that on your shoulders. Maybe a bad decision, but that's for another time…. I have to tell you more."

Emma rolled her head around and leaned forward.

"More? You've held this back my whole life, and there's more? I don't want to—"

"You must hear this."

Her fingernails dug into the bench, and one broke. "Ouch," she whispered and stuck her finger between her teeth to bite off the remaining bit of nail. "OK. I'll brace myself."

On the other end of the phone, a kitchen chair scraped on the linoleum floor. Maybe Dad had pulled it to sit at the table, and perhaps Mom still looked out of the window above the sink. In April, the claustrophobic woods likely showed signs of tree buds. As a child, Emma hated going out there alone because she feared some killer would leap out.

Mom cleared her throat. "Well, Victoria wrote me the other day, the first time in years. She's been on death row most of this time. And…she got a date for…for her death, her execution. It's only a few months away. End of June.

Emma checked her watch, wishing she were anywhere but here. One of her law colleagues strolled in front of her, waving and smiling. He mouthed, "You OK?"

She gave a thumbs-up sign and waved him on. The last thing she needed was some office guy nosing in.

"…wants help. She needs help. I don't know what you can do, but you'll know."

"Me? Why could I do anything?"

"You're a big-time lawyer now. Isn't your company the best in town?"

"Yeah, but I'm a nobody. I'm at the bottom of the pile. You spring this new person on me after twenty-five years and ask me to help her? Why would I do that, even if I could?"

"Oh, Emileen." Mom's voice cracked. "She's family."

Her stomach lurched again. *Family? Meaning what?* She'd never felt part of her own parents' family, and now her mother wanted to extend this sense of family to a stranger. "Mom, what you're asking is impossible. How's she family? I never knew about her till five minutes ago."

She could picture Mom holding the phone out far enough so Dad could hear. They probably looked at each other, stunned. "Sorry, but that's how it feels," Emma continued.

"You're confused. Upset. But we have no one to turn to."

Silence pierced the air between them. An older couple sat on a nearby bench.

"Mom, I can't. I just—"

"Please, could you visit? Come see us. Just for an hour? Decide after that?"

She couldn't move.

"I'll think about it."

The phone dropped to her lap. Birds chirped, clouds drifted, and Emma noticed that one of the bushes had early buds. *When had my aunt last seen the outdoors without walls and concertina wire framing it?*

Chapter 6

Thursday evening, April 13, 2006

Shadrach raced after the tennis ball in Emma's front yard, bounding back to her a dozen times without losing a speck of energy. Emma tired simply watching him.

Rupert Singer waved at Emma from his porch across the street and strolled over. "Who's the new neighbor?"

Emma snapped the leash onto Shadrach and asked him to sit.

"Meet Shadrach, forty pounds of never-ending energy. Whenever I lose steam, I remember this terrific running buddy who needs to be exercised, and that gives me a boost. And, in his world, I'm the only person who matters."

Rupert swung his arms around, Tai Chi style, before leaning to tap on Shadrach's head. "Gets stiff, this seventy-five-year-old body. I need to move too. Maybe I should take him out sometime?"

"If you're up for it, sure. But he's a fireball."

"By the way, I've got some articles for you. Old ones. I know you like old law cases."

"That's nice of you. Why don't we catch up? Can I invite you for a cup of tea?"

She led him into her basement apartment. "I'm always curious about what you're up to. You retired librarians never quit."

"Westminster University's reference department would be proud." He tittered. "I found some articles about bones from 78,000 years ago in Africa. A three-year-old boy, in a grave, maybe with a pillow under his head. How do they figure these things out?"

Rupert had been in the U.S. forty years but hadn't lost his Scottish accent, his bushy beard, or his relentless curiosity. He scratched Shadrach's ears, and the dog swooned.

"You're going to become his favorite person, it seems. Should I worry?"

Rupert laughed. "I would like to be his second favorite. I had a corgi as a kid when I lived with my grandmother. Loved that dog. Bess. She played in the barn with our horses and got kicked once. She never recovered. It tore me apart."

Emma's heart sped up. "Losing an animal is brutal." She couldn't tell him about the fish; that would be weird. Better to focus on dogs.

He grimaced as he lowered himself onto her futon. She groped for a folding chair behind the door.

"Sorry, it's low. Do you want a card table chair?"

"No, no problem. I need more friends over thirty years old," he said. He looked at the aquarium. "Only one fish? They do better in groups, you know." He pulled several pieces of paper from his sweater vest pocket. "Here. One's about a man on the run in the 1980s. Bank robber—who camped out to hide in the mountains of Wyoming. The park rangers looked for him for weeks, and when they finally found him, he shot and killed one of them. He disappeared for a long time, then was caught. Escaped and caught again. Controversial, as you can imagine."

His voice was such a contrast to some of the people at work. Soothing. "Thanks. You told me once you trained in engineering. How'd you get into library work, then?"

He scoffed. "There're only so many ways to build a road, and you work with the same fellows all the time. At the university, I saw hundreds of kids, and problems changed every day."

"Like a big family." She handed him a mug, settled on the futon beside him, and grabbed a throw as a bit of armor. *Should I tell him about the call with Mom?* He'd been supportive of her work this last half year, but they hadn't gotten into personal discussions much: his natural Scottish reticence and her unnatural awkwardness. A match made in heaven.

"Yes, indeed. I loved what the kids brought. Everything from finding unexpected relatives to unearthing a new dragonfly species. I may not have biological children, but I felt like I had a huge family. What about you? Siblings?"

Emma rubbed her hand along the throw's fringe. She wasn't ready, so she turned the question into a question, a tactic she used in law work or when she feared others were getting too close. "But how did you come to the U.S.? Family here?"

"No, no. My tribe died out early. My parents passed when my sister and I were young—bad flu season. We lived with my grandmother until she died when I was in high school. Then I was with an uncle until I left for military service. After that, U.S. graduate school and I landed here. Nothing very dramatic. And now back to you?"

I suppose I do have a family. An aunt I never met. Never thought much about it.

"Emma? Are you daydreaming?"

Can he read my mind? He knew she was out of sorts, like a father might. Maybe he could be a confidant. She shook tension from her shoulders.

"My mother phoned—my mother, who I've not heard from for months."

"Blimey. Whose fault is that, my dear? Always takes two to dance."

She scowled. *Maybe it was a mistake to tell him.*

He waved his hands. "Sorry. Out of line. Can you tell me what happened?"

She pulled a news clipping from her briefcase. "It's… I have an… Hmmm. I don't know how to say this. I'm in shock still."

"No urgency. Tell me if you wish…or not. I'm not going anywhere. My ravishing salad for tonight's dinner can wait."

So calming, unrushed. She slowed down too. "OK. Long story made short. My mother has a sister I never knew about—"

"How wonderful!"

"Not what you think. I vaguely remember my parents mentioning this person. But she was never around. I mean, ever."

"How do you mean?"

"For a long time, I thought she lived in another country. And later, I wondered if she'd died." She halted. She was standing on a cliff, a cliff of trust.

"Go on," Rupert said.

Now was the time to jump off the cliff.

"My aunt, she's…in prison."

His head jerked back. "Prison?"

A dull pain spread through her chest—fear that he'd judge her.

His face softened again. "This must be painful to talk about, but I'm a good listener."

"Thanks. Yes. In prison. That sounds strange to say…. She was convicted of killing her four children." Emma unfolded the sheet of paper, a printout of the news article she'd seen in the drug store. "It was over twenty years ago. Here, read this. She's run out of appeals and will be executed in a couple of months."

He scanned the article. "Poor woman. And she never knew you? What a loss." He looked at her through narrowed eyes. "And your mother? What does she think?"

"My mother has the harebrained idea that I can help get her out."

"And will you?"

That felt like a challenge. "Are you taking her side?"

He lifted his palms in defense and rubbed them over his grass-stained khaki trouser knees. "No sides here. This is your family. I'm trying to imagine what both women must be going through. What you're going through…. When did your aunt learn about you?"

"I've no idea if she knows about me." She waved a hand impatiently. "But you don't get it. This is someone I've never heard of…I didn't know she existed. And now my mother—my estranged mother—comes begging me to help this person?"

He stroked his beard. "Could she possibly be innocent?"

She pursed her lips and rolled her eyes. "Who knows? Doesn't every person in prison claim to be?" She sipped her tea. "But don't you think that's out of line to ask?" *Doesn't he see what's important here?*

Rupert's opinions were normally solid gold, but tonight he was ornery. People accused her of rushing, pushing too hard. She had to be patient. "Drop the prickliness," the Vulture might warn.

"I don't know. Just think about it. You now have this aunt—in prison, no less? And your parents said nothing, all that time?"

"We're not a talkative family. And the idea of helping... It'd be distracting."

"Distracting from what?"

"In school, they hammered us to stay focused, not get pulled sideways these first few years. Even though my work is boring, I've got to focus."

"That makes sense. Can you walk away, or is it different because it's your family?"

She scrubbed her scalp with her fingertips and tilted her head side to side, like she was weighing the thoughts. *What does he know about family? Not much, from the sounds of it.* "Maybe. But I've got my career to worry about."

"I see. Career over family. Or career versus family. Yes, good point."

Is he scolding me? "That's what you did, didn't you? Career over family? How can you lecture—"

"Goodness, no lectures. I simply ask small questions."

"It ticks me off that Mom made this ask."

"I understand you're annoyed. But why do you suppose she asked for help?" He brushed invisible lint from his shirt sleeve.

What is he driving at? She wanted something straightforward, not all these blasted questions.

"She wanted me to get the law firm involved, but there's no way I could do this."

"My dear young friend. Please put your proud new lawyer brain on hold for a moment. Are you getting ahead of yourself? What would you have done, had it been your sister in such a situation?"

Why does he ask such messy questions? She couldn't imagine a sibling, let alone a sister. *Is this a trap?*

Emma's phone started to ring, and she grabbed it, welcoming the distraction. "Sherry? Anything wrong?" She grimaced at Rupert. "Ah. OK. This Friday, I should be able to do that. Right, the intern. I'll ask her to help. Got it. Thanks. Yes, good night."

Rupert cocked his head.

"The law firm administrator. She gave me some new work, since I asked for it, but the partner needs information sooner than she'd told me. See? That's what I mean. I've got real work to do. This case would take away from that."

"Yes, yes. I recall those days of overwhelming amounts of work. But let's follow our thread, nevertheless. Would you be more apt to help if this were your sister?"

Does he ever quit? "I don't have siblings." *Or at least any I grew up with. A brother. He died early."*

"Well, even if you cannot relate, can we walk through this together? Logically."

A churning stomach, aching head, and frustrated brain yanked her. She preferred logic, which felt like a superpower compared to emotions.

"All right. Let's walk it through."

He lifted his left thumb in the air. "First, this is family. Granted, it's distant, but I'll bet it was difficult for your mother to ask for help."

She crinkled her nose, like she had smelled rotten vegetables. *Why am I so affronted by Mom's request? Do I resent that she seems to care for a sister in prison more than for her own daughter?* She shook her head internally to blow out the cobwebs that smothered his voice. She missed half of what he said.

"…a surprise to me when I see it. Especially since I don't have that in my own life."

"Sorry, I missed that?"

"I said that I'm not sure why, but blood often ties people together in unexpected ways, even when they don't want it." He stuck out his index finger, perpendicular to his thumb. "Second, I gather you're not close, but would you perhaps like more contact with your parents? Maybe this could bring you together?"

Spooky. How'd he figure that? What did I say to make him think I wanted the family back?

"Aren't you a tiny bit curious about this woman?"

Rupert scratched Shadrach's ears. Dogs offered such a tidy way to pause an awkward conversation.

"Maybe a little. But what's in it for me?"

He raised his eyebrows.

"That's crass, I know." She gazed out of the high window. "But I need to know. My mother wants me to visit. To tell me the story face-to-face. Maybe she hopes I'll cave when I see her."

He tapped his finger on the tea mug. "You know I don't give advice. I just ask—"

"Small questions. I know. You asked me a few that helped at work. So, I appreciate that, but—"

"Let me finish, please. Patience."

"Sorry."

"I certainly don't want to sway you in either direction. But my small question is 'could you hold your mind open for a few days?' After twenty years of knowing nothing about this aunt, why not find out a little more before deciding? There's nothing to fear from information, as we librarians say. Until you do something with it, it's just information."

She felt the hairs stand up on her arms. Fear. *Fear of seeing my own mother? But he's right. I could gather information and listen.*

"And then," Rupert said, "whether you decide to go forward or not, you'll at least have thought it through."

Right. If she decided to help, maybe her parents would appreciate her. And if she refused, she'd have the rationale for her decision. She'd probably decide in the end to leave things as they were. The not-perfect life she had would go on, with no close family, no close friends. Just the dog. And the fish. And Rupert if he would put up with her.

"OK, I'll go to see her. Maybe you're right. It is different to be related to a murderer." She smiled, half-way. "Who knows what mischief that could bring?"

Chapter 7

Saturday morning, April 15, 2006

"I found more articles. About the trial and your aunt." Rupert thrust a manila envelope at Emma as she packed her car. "Drive well. I'll expect a debrief."

She tucked the envelope under her purse on the passenger's seat. Tempted to devour the articles right away, she refrained to prove she had patience. She shoved her MGB-GT vintage red car into gear and reached into the back seat.

"Good boy, Shadrach. We'll have a good first ride for you. Just relax." He sniffed her hand.

Away from the city, the wind picked up, forcing her to grip the steering wheel with both hands, 10–2. She tightened her forearms. When she passed a long truck, it sucked her "toy car," as Rupert called it, toward the rig, and she jerked her arms to self-correct. She wondered if she'd have to self-correct with her parents.

An hour out of Snowville, she pulled into a rest stop and opened the envelope. Three articles. Two described her aunt's trial, and the third detailed the prison sentence: manslaughter for the first child, murder for the other three. Her gut twisted when she studied the courtroom sketches. The charcoal pencil drawing looked like Mom; the likeness was so striking. Victoria Knox Beringer wore a full head of wavy, white-streaked hair, aquiline nose, and ramrod-straight posture. And freckles. Emma touched her nose. Before seeing the sketch, her aunt had been a faceless theoretical character, but the freckles transformed this abstract person into a real one. In the drawing, Victoria clasped her hands, left thumb over right thumb. *Is she left-handed?* And she tilted her head to the right, like a dog trying to decipher a human's babble, like Emma did.

Snowville's population sign claimed 2,415 souls, half of the more than 5,000 when she finished high school. King Street meandered through downtown but offered no majesty. Shops with plywood nailed across the windows and doors, graffiti spread across the wood, and knocked-over parking meters dotted the street. The First National Bank building stood out for its white brick and swept sidewalks. She cruised King Street toward the Calhoun River that separated the town from a former ranch, now dump site.

In front of her house, she squeezed the steering wheel, feeling excitement and fear. *How will they act? How should I act?* She'd been irked at Christmas when they didn't seem as happy to see her as she'd hoped. Both seemed distracted. On the last day, Dad told her his biopsy results had come in a few days before she arrived. Stage II prostate cancer. Serious but treatable. That explained it. *But why hadn't they said something?* When she called afterward, they said Dad was improving but gave few details. She felt baffled and excluded. *They didn't let me in on Dad's health but now they want to tell me all about an aunt I'd never heard of?*

The house, a two-bedroom ranch, with a composite roof and aluminum frame windows, was the only one on the street that hadn't been replaced with a two- or three-story mansion. A sycamore stood by the front door and provided the only shade for a house with no air conditioning.

Dad squatted in the yard, planting petunias. She could almost feel the gritty dirt implanted in her childhood knees when she helped him garden.

She slammed the car door, and he turned toward her.

He set his gloved hands on the ground and leaned into them, pushing himself to kneeling. A couple of new holes in his old, cracked leather belt emphasized how thin he'd become.

Shadrach raced to Dad and put his paws on his thighs, and then made circles in the front yard, so glad to be free of confinement.

"Sorry. He gets excited. Shadrach!"

Dad wiped his hands on his khaki trousers. "So, we finally got a Shadrach? How are you, Lou?"

The nickname had started when he sang 1980s Emmilou Harris songs to her, or rather whisper-sung them, a secret between the two of them, when she was about four.

"Doing well. Thanks. You?" Shadrach sat on the ground in front of Dad. His tail scraped the ground, blowing dust up.

"Can't complain. Getting the garden going takes more effort each year, but I guess that's normal. You're here to see Mom?"

"She wants to tell me about my new aunt, who's been around a long time, I gather. Know anything about this?"

He rammed his hands into his hip pockets. "Best let her explain."

She followed him around the right side of the house. A dogwood tree scraped its branches on her bedroom window. Tiny pink buds sprouted, a harbinger of the green leaves due soon. The tree had always signaled the passing of another long winter and brought her closer to the time she could escape the melancholy of the house. No laughter, chocolate chip cookies, or craft projects for her. Just silence and gloom.

Under that bedroom window stood tomato plant cages, propping up last year's withered crop. In grade school, she'd relished the sweet, ripe, tasty beefsteak tomatoes of August. She made sandwiches with Wonder Bread, a dollop of precious mayonnaise, and one tomato, sliced into five thick pieces. Three slices on the bread, and two on the plate. When her mother wasn't around, she'd sneak another mayo dollop on the plate. She drowned the sandwich and slices in salt and pepper and went to the weathered picnic table behind the house. No matter that the bench gave her splinters and the table was slanted. The taste, smell, and texture of that sandwich and those tomato slices carried her in a cloud for days. As soon as they ripened, they retreated. For another year, she lived on the memories of the raw, ripe tomatoes that became pink and drippy as she bit into her sandwich.

At the corner of the house, Dad turned. "I imagine you're surprised. Maybe upset. But give her a chance."

Mom crouched in front of the vegetable beds. She peered from under her straw hat, exposing her pale face and faded lipstick.

Emma had always thought of herself as the "average of her parents": her 5'9" height split the difference between her 6'2" father and her 5'4" mother. Where his hair was black and bushy, Mom's was stringy blond, now grey. Dad's eyes were dark brown; Mom's were washed-out blue. His skin was tawny; hers bleached out and without sunscreen, could become tomato red. Emma's had curly auburn hair, hazel eyes, and olive skin. Like most kids at some point in their lives, she'd sometimes wondered if they were her biological parents, but she had Dad's squint and Mom's long fingers, so she supposed she was theirs.

"Emileen. Thank you for coming."

Shadrach thrust himself in the middle of the humans.

"You've got a dog!" Mom backed away from Shadrach, who wanted to sniff her rump.

Emma never had a dog growing up, or any animal, even a fish, which contributed to the loneliness of the house. She assumed her parents just didn't like animals, but once, when she was about thirteen, Mom made a comment about not wanting another being that might die. The grief would be too much, she said. Emma had never understood the comment and couldn't change Mom's mind. Maybe that's why animals—even fish—meant so much to her now.

Shadrach moved aside, and Mom pulled her close, immediately giving Emma a whiff of White Shoulders cologne.

"Come on," Mom said. "Let's get some iced tea and sit."

When Emma was young, if bad news or an awkward topic demanded attention, Mom had said, "Let's get some iced tea and sit," and they'd decamp to the back porch's rocking chairs. Silence dominated those "conversations," and when words passed, they were often harsh.

While Mom boiled water, Emma sat at the kitchen table and stared at the long-yellowed Polaroid photo on the refrigerator, held by an apple-shaped magnet. In the photo, her toddler self-smiled at a pudgy baby, about six months old, who stretched his hands toward her. She vaguely remembered the soft baby fat on his chest as she squeezed him.

Mom ignored the photo, which she would since she saw it every day.

The tea kettle sang.

Emma broke the silence. "That yellow pitcher. That belonged to your mother, right?"

Mom patted the tea pot. "Yes, it's chipped but sturdy, like she was. Sorry you never met her. Holds enough tea for a good long conversation." She loaded a tray and shoved the screen door open with her hip.

Mom rocked, four times forward and back. "Victoria and I grew up in a small town about 100 miles from here called Ramsey. Lived on the farm our parents ran. She was three years ahead of me. She got pregnant at seventeen. Married the boy. His name was Wendell Beringer, but we called him Dell. They moved to Clady, thirty miles from Surrey. We did too, before you were born."

Emma stretched to pet Shadrach, who leaned against her jittery legs. *Keep your mind open.*

Mom brushed her hands over her thighs, smoothing her faded blue denim skirt. "In due time, Victoria had a beautiful baby, Darrin. Dell had his job at the feedstore. She mostly stayed home with the baby but talked about finishing high school, maybe secretarial school or even college. But…"

This could take more than a single pitcher of tea. "What happened?" Emma snapped and immediately felt awful. "Sorry. Didn't mean to startle you." She heard Rupert's voice in her head: *"Patience."*

Mom threw her head back. "Not long after he was born, the baby died. He was seven months old. He'd had a little cough but nothing serious. He did have seizures right after he was born, but the doctors didn't worry then. Anyway, he died in his sleep."

This story felt far off, like it was about a long-ago elementary school classmate. Close but not close enough to shake her.

"It devastated Dell and Vic, of course. They took the baby to the hospital, but he was already dead. What they called SIDS. Sudden infant death syndrome. We hadn't heard much about it back then."

"Sounds awful." She put her hand on her mother's forearm. "Why did you never tell me?"

"You weren't even born then. So long ago. But I need to tell you the rest."

Emma's head pounded. Drama wasn't her forte.

Mom cleared her throat. "That was 1971. Victoria had another baby about two years later. Again, we were all thrilled. By that time, Dell was moving up in the feedstore. The owner talked about selling it to him in a few years. Things were good." The porch floor wood squeaked as she rocked. "But then this second baby died. Fast. Twenty-four days. He had trouble breathing."

Emma's mouth opened, but nothing emerged. *What would it feel like to have trouble breathing and not understand anything?* Mom looked like she was daydreaming. And it did feel like a dream, unreal.

"Another one that soon? What the—"

"Yes. Shocking. An autopsy found something wrong with his larynx."

Melted ice diluted her tea, leaving it tasteless. "Sounds unbearable."

"It was, but worse, some neighbors, people we thought were friends, started rumors. Saying maybe Victoria was responsible."

Emma rubbed her upper arms, trying to warm up. *Aunt Victoria would have felt isolated, like I did, growing up in this house.* Two deaths in one family seemed much too odd. *The whole neighborhood probably shunned her.* She pushed her back against the chair to sit straighter. *This isn't your drama. It's Mom's. Keep your mind open.*

"What'd you and Dad do during all of this? Did you help?"

"Of course, we tried. We went over a lot. Both of us at first, but then mostly Dad later."

Emma ran her hands over the rocker's arm rest and met a large splinter. "Ouch." Something like a splinter always got in the way in this house.

"These chairs are old. You OK?"

"I think so, but I need some tweezers." *And some time away.* She hurried from the porch.

Chapter 8

Saturday morning, April 15, 2006

Emma took the stairs two at a time to the second-floor pink bathroom. Same pale tiles, same spots in the grout on the bathtub wall, same white linoleum floor. She pulled open the mirrored medicine cabinet above the sink and found, as she'd expected, the old tweezers. She sat on the tub's edge, slowing her breathing as she plucked out the splinter.

She shoved closed the double-hung window to stop what felt like an arctic air flow. *How did Mom and Dad live with this for all of those years? They must have written her? Or visited? Surely they didn't abandon their own family, Mom's own blood? Or did they?*

Ten minutes passed, and she crept back to the porch.

Mom's eyes squinted.

"I got it out. Please, go on," Emma said.

"OK. Well, as you can imagine, it was terrible. I worried about Victoria's mental state. To be honest, I did something I probably shouldn't have. But I was just trying to help her." She clutched her hands. "No one knows this, not even Dad. I told Victoria… I told her I could take the next child, if she had one, to be sure she wouldn't have another tragedy."

Dizziness overwhelmed Emma, and she squeezed her eyes, hoping the world would be righted when she opened them. *How could Mom have made such an offer to a sister she supposedly loved? Was there some weird sibling rivalry at play? Or could Mom think that her sister was guilty?* She felt whiplash—being pulled toward Mom for what she went through, but this shock pushed her away. "How could you do such a thing? What'd she say?"

"What you'd expect. Brushed me off. She said she could handle her own children."

Of course, she'd say that. What mother would agree to something so wicked? Shadrach nudged his snout in her lap. *Give your bad energy to me,* she imagined him thinking. "What an appalling thing to do."

"It was wrong, but I wanted to protect her. To protect another child." She lifted her glass and shook it. "I'll get more ice. We still have tea."

Emma stepped down to the yard. Shadrach raced ahead, nearly to the small wooden white cross at the edge of the woods. Oregon juncos bounced along the ground. *How could Mom have been so cruel?* Then again, she didn't have a sibling and knew nothing of the rivalries, of the closeness or estrangement, that came with sisterhood. *How could I understand what happened between these two women?*

Back in her chair, she glanced at her watch. "You said she had four children?"

"Sorry. I'll try to go faster," Mom said. "After those first babies, more sadness. Two more children in five years. Girls. Both died. Unexplained." Her breathing sped up as if she too wanted to finish and send Emma on her way.

"Four kids. God."

"Hard to imagine, I know." Mom scrunched her shirt. "But Victoria said over and over that she hadn't done anything."

"You believed her?"

Mom brushed away tears. "I wanted to. But in the end, most people gave up. Dad was the only one who stood up for her throughout the whole ordeal."

Emma was unable to lift her arm to the tea glass. *Aunt Victoria's own sister had given up on her. But Dad didn't, with his decency and belief in people, even if they had bad streaks in them.*

"Why didn't you?" She needed a way through this, as surreal as it sounded.

Mom sighed. "I saw a different side of her.... I went over one day, looking for a recipe. We were in each other's houses a lot. I found her diaries on the cookbook shelf. I didn't mean to read but I saw some words that worried me...about helping little Brian on his way. I told Dell about it later."

Emma's stomach lurched. "Why didn't you talk to her first? Before going to him?"

Mom faced away. "I was afraid she...she might do something....to hurt herself. I worried that she'd done something to those babies—that maybe she didn't mean to, but that she acted out against them in frustration. I don't know.... I had to tell Dell. I hoped he might reassure me that she didn't do anything." She clenched her jaw. "But he was the one who ended up turning them over to the police."

"He what?" Emma's head throbbed, and she stuck her hands between her legs to control the shaking. "He turned her in? You both betrayed her?"

"Dell said it sounded like a confession. That's what the prosecutors used as the basis for their case."

"How? Wh—?" Blood throbbed in her ears.

"It's unbelievable. But it's real."

How could something that horrid be real? There was a dreamlike quality to this conversation—similar to how she felt when she woke and couldn't get a grasp on what had just happened during her sleep. "What on earth had she written?"

Shadrach switched his head back and forth, like he'd done in the humane society when he couldn't choose between Emma and the Mountain Man.

"She wrote that Brian needed help to make his journey peaceful." Mom reached to Shadrach. He looked to Emma for an "OK" and then nuzzled Mom. "She said it was a letter to God. Asking to make her son more comfortable. But the words didn't come across that way."

Emma had trouble swallowing. "Tell me the rest."

"There was a trial. She was convicted and went to prison. And now she'll be executed. She hadn't written me for years, and now this. That's why I called you."

Emma eyed the pink hint of dogwood blossoms in the forest. "And why did you never tell me?"

Mom walked behind Emma's chair and reached down to squeeze her shoulders. Emma grimaced to keep from shrugging. "We should have, but it was too painful. We didn't want to weigh you down with it. Since her name was Beringer and since they lived out of town, we hoped no one would find out."

She wanted to have compassion, but the way Mom acted towards her own sister... *How can I square that?* "When was the trial?"

Mom released her shoulders, and Emma relaxed. "Early 1982. You were about two and a half. Sentencing was November, just after your birthday."

"I can't remember it."

"That's what we hoped. Neighbors didn't know who we were, and we kept it quiet. As you got older, I told you about a sister I wasn't in touch with, which was true. We didn't hear much after her first year in prison."

"Did you visit?"

Mom rested her forehead on the screen door. "You can't understand how it was. Dad visited during the trial and once or twice after. I couldn't. Over time, she didn't want visitors, and we lost touch."

Mom's words sounded blurry. Emma struggled between feelings of pity and anger. Pity for Aunt Victoria and anger at Mom for abandoning her. Pity for Mom to go through such an ordeal and anger at Aunt Victoria for letting those kids die. She'd been inclined to help, but now, listening to Mom, she didn't know what to make of it.

"Newspaper articles say she'll be the first woman executed in the state. One called her the worst serial killer in the state's history. And you kept this for more than twenty years? You betrayed your only sister? You don't even have pictures around. Do you really care about her?"

Mom's face contorted. "I must sound horrid to you but, believe me, I do care. I want to connect with her again. I've been a bad sister, I know that, and I want to help her. I thought you might be able to do that. And bring the family back together… be our savior."

The invisible whack to Emma's chest made her gasp. *A savior? Bring the family together? This couldn't get any harder. I'd hoped to reconnect with Mom, but now this?*

"I can't be what you want." By the time Emma reached the front yard, she and Shadrach were at a dead run. She raced past Dad, who lifted his arm, but she shook her head. She wrenched open the car door, shoved Shadrach in, and dropped her head onto the steering wheel, catching her breath. She revved the motor and tore down the street.

Emma gripped the tiny steering wheel, sending her fingernails into the fleshy part of her palms. Little nail moon indents turned white when she looked at her hands. *How could Mom ask this?* She felt unmoored, with no understanding of this this family.

She forced herself to slow her breathing. *Why should I help? Or not. Logic. Use logic.*

First, how could a baby-lawyer like me, doing low-level misdemeanors, even think about taking on a capital murder case, or whatever kind of help might be needed? Granted, her favorite law course was on capital cases, and she was an assistant to the professor who taught it, but that didn't make her an expert. *Second, I know nothing about this new aunt, or her case, so why, after a long-ago conviction, would there be any hope?* The articles' descriptions made the case sound solid—the diaries, the statistics, and the simple question of how four children could die in one family seemed irrefutable.

And last, how can Mom ask me to be the "family savior"? She wanted a relationship, but this was too much. *Does Mom want forgiveness from Aunt Victoria and expect me to grease the process?* Her own relationship with Mom and Dad wasn't great now, so what would it mean to add this new aunt into the picture? *No. No, I can't do this.*

Shadrach barked at that moment.

"That's right, boy. Decision made."

Chapter 9

Saturday evening, April 15, 2006

At the dog park, after the stress of the visit and the drive back, Shadrach chased the Frisbee and Emma soaked up the sun.

Suddenly, a chill dusted her arms. She froze. *Is someone staring at me?* Shadrach didn't seem spooked, but she couldn't shake the feeling and spun around, looking into the park's heavy bushes. A black mini long-haired dachshund dashed after a yellow tennis ball and dropped it at his mistress's feet. Emma watched for another four tosses but couldn't shake the uneasiness.

"It's Herman! And Herman's mom!"

Mountain Man stepped into the park's clearing and waved. She gave a wan smile and scurried toward Shadrach. *Maybe I can lose him.*

"Hey! I don't know your name, but I'll keep yelling until you tell me!" He jogged over, a dog in tow. "Her name is Harriet. I went back to the p-pound."

From what she could see, Harriet came from questionable stock—bedraggled, mangy even. *Or just a bad haircut?* She held back, shy or scared, but he pulled her forward. "Come on, g-girl."

Fresh from rescuing a yellow Frisbee, Shadrach bounded over to sniff Harriet's rear with a vengeance. She tucked her tail and didn't move, maybe praying for the inspection to end. When it did, Shadrach got into downward dog pose and barked.

"He wants to play, Harriet. G-go for it," encouraged Mountain Man.

Harriet was having none of it.

"She's not used to other dogs," Mountain Man explained. "She'd been an older person's dog for ten years, and when the owner died, her children brought Harriet in. My heart b-broke when I heard that."

Emma stared at Harriet. It was now or never. She thrust her hand out. "Emma. And you already know Shadrach."

"Shadrach! Great name. I'm G-Grant Marconi, like the telegraph. Happy to meet you. Finally. At last. Well, I mean officially, not just as dog parents. Sorry. I blather when I'm nervous." His knit cap came down to his eyebrows, so she saw mostly a big-cheeked smiling lower half of his face.

"Good to meet you, Grant-Marconi-like-the-telegraph. So, you found a dog?" She knew she was supposed to make small talk but, God, she bombed at it. But he'd admitted out loud that he was nervous. At least she'd avoided that blooper.

"Hey, I know this is sudden, but could we g-grab coffee sometime? Or walk the dogs? I'm flexible—"

Ambushed, she stepped back. *Not this. Not yet anyway.*

"Sorry. I've got lots of big cases right now and not a lot of free time. And I had to go out of town today, so that cut into my time."

"I don't want to p-push but would really like to get to know Shadrach, and you can come along for the ride."

She smiled. *Maybe I should give him—and myself—a break.*

"You look completely wiped, by the way. Another one of my bad habits. I say what I see. You b-buttoned your jacket wrong, and you don't hit me as someone who messes that up. You doing all right?"

Inside she wobbled, irritated that she'd shown anything to the outside world. She desperately wanted to talk about her trip but resisted. She hardly knew this man.

She rebuttoned her jacket. "It's been a rough day, but I guess we could meet sometime. Maybe Monday after work, here? I'm a lawyer with Ivins. And that's something I do too...babble. Sorry. We're putting all of our flaws out there, I suppose."

Grant Marconi had a killer smile. She relaxed enough to smile back.

"I'll see you Monday then. I'm a recovering accountant. And I worked on some law cases, mistrials and such. So we have something in common. Now I'm a semi-employed musician. Better hours, but I'm glad I made some money before."

Emma's phone buzzed, and she reached into her pocket.

"It's my dad. He rarely calls, so I'd better answer." She turned her back to Mountain Man.

"Dad? Everything OK?"

"I heard the tail end of your conversation with Mom. I'm sorry things ended like that. I know she wants to reconnect, and I thought you did too."

"You're right." She twisted her head around and saw Grant playing with Shadrach, Harriet lying at his feet. She gave a straight-line smile and whispered, "Thank you."

"But the real reason I'm calling is to let you know I called Victoria to ask if she'd like you to visit," Dad said. "She was stunned to hear from me but said yes. Could you visit her before you make any decisions?"

Emma's jaw dropped.

Grant tilted his head. "All OK?"

She nodded and put her hand around the phone, shielding her mouth. "Wow, Dad." Emma spread her stance to slow her weaving back and forth.

"She's desperate, Lou. Reaching out to the only family she has. Even if nothing comes of this, she'd like to see you before… before the end."

Another blow. Emma shuddered as she studied the park's dense brush, which reminded her of the woods behind the house in Snowville, where she'd always expected a boogie man to spring out.

"Are you there?"

"Yes, still here. OK. I'll go, but it won't be till next weekend. I've got work all week."

"You're already doing some good for this crazy family. I love you. Take care of yourself."

She stared at the phone and then turned to face her new dog-parent friend.

"What's up, if you want to tell me?" Grant asked.

"My dad asked for a favor. He never does, so I need to think about it, but it means another road trip next week."

"Sounds like you're a g-good daughter to do that. But I saw your toy car at the humane society. How does that thing go more than a few miles?" He chortled.

"Fighting words, those." This mountain man had made her smile more than once. "It's tougher than you might think. And fun to drive."

"Well, I hope you're careful. It looks like it could be crushed by any old pick up."

She laughed out loud. "I'll take your good counsel."

"I hope we're still on for Monday, back here? Harriet will look forward to it."

"Shadrach too." She followed the dog toward her toy car, feeling better than when they arrived. Had to be the fresh air. But she knew it was something else too.

Chapter 10

Tuesday noon, April 18, 2006

"Sorry, Ms. Raddell. Until you're the attorney of record for your client, I can't let you in the vault." The evidence vault guard, whose name tag said Overton, hooked his thumbs into his police belt, which strained to contain his stomach. *Surely his role doesn't warrant his overbearing attitude.*

Emma stood at the end of a long corridor in the courthouse basement. As a rookie in the law office, she'd made many runs to the cardboard evidence boxes, jammed into gunmetal-grey bookshelves. Hand-written notes on the box ends made clear the case number, date, and general comments. Documentation inside the boxes revealed who'd looked at the evidence within each plastic bag, when, and for what case. Chain of custody mistakes could send a person to law enforcement purgatory, so lawyers and police officer treated the vault like a sacred site.

The place looked like a mating ground for mildew mites hiding in the cervices between boxes, but every time she inhaled with a purpose, the room reeked more of antiseptics than mold. The room appeared chaotic, but the guards who'd worked there a long time knew exactly where to find a certain case box.

"Where's Mr. Morrat? He's usually on duty during the daytime."

"Broke his ankle. You'll have to deal with me."

Was that a sneer? Still trying to learn to read faces, this one baffled her. She'd need verbal cues.

"I only want to see what's in the vault, for one very old case, not to take anything. What's the harm? Can't I get that very simple information?"

"You're a pretty young lady. I can think of things you could do." Overton leered. "Are you offering?"

She bit her tongue and yelped. "I can't believe you said that. What do you think this is, the 1950s? I could get you into a lot of trouble."

"And you still wouldn't have your information." He tilted back in a card table chair next to the caged evidence room.

She stomped down the hallway and passed a grey-suited man ambling toward the vault. The man stepped aside to avoid her.

"In a hurry," she heard the guard say as she neared the exit. "Wanted something she didn't have access to. And I wouldn't give it to her."

"Ah," the other man said. "Her name?"

She looked back as the guard squinted at the crinkled paper on his clipboard.

"Uh. Raddell. Emma Raddell."

She swiveled back and walked out. *Who is that guy, and why is he asking about me?*

Chapter 11

Wednesday early evening, April 19, 2006

"Oh, by the way, the AG himself was asking about you in their office." Antigone toasted Emma with her wine glass. They sat in Pengilly's, surveying young professionals crammed around the bar. The wannabe-English-gentlemen's club had leather booths rimming the walls and dark wooden tables and club chairs throughout.

Emma had asked Antigone, who seemed to know every young lawyer in town, to arrange drinks with someone who knew about old cases.

Emma squeezed her wine glass stem. "The attorney general? Asking about me? Why me?"

"He saw you at the evidence vault. Ah. Here's my guy." Antigone waved.

Richard Li brushed Antigone's cheek with an air kiss and crushed Emma's hand. *Why do men do that?*

Antigone slid one stool over to Richard's far side.

"I heard you want to know about old cases," Richard said. "What about them?"?

"Thanks for coming. You're in the AG's office, right? So you should know about what happens to old cases. Why and how they are reviewed. What's the process for that? How often are they vacated because of a mistrial, and how does that happen? Any particular criteria? Things like that."

"God, that's a lot of questions. This could take some time. Maybe we meet somewhere else?"

Oh no, is he hitting on me? "How much time do you need? And can you really help?"

Suddenly, Antigone flapped her arms at Emma and pointed her finger up and over Richard. Just as suddenly, she yanked her arms back to her body and stared at the bar.

Richard's eyes widened. He stood up and buttoned his suit jacket. Emma looked behind her. The man from the vault, the one who'd asked the guard about her, sidled up to Richard.

"Simmons. I'm Ed Simmons." He bowed slightly. "And you are…the mystery vault visitor?" His eyelids closed and opened at about half the speed as hers. Like a lizard's.

She broke eye contact first, which was probably what he wanted, what he expected. "Why do you ask?"

He slid his right hand into his suit jacket and hung his thumb on the outside, like aristocrats in old movies.

"I heard from the guard you were looking into evidence from a very old case. The Beringer case. That one probably happened before either of you were born." He turned his torso toward Richard and back to Emma. "Nothing there to look at anymore. I'd recommend you stay away from the vault, and from Officer Overton." He lifted an eyebrow. "He's got a reputation, our Overton."

She counted to five, staring at him. "It's nice to meet you, sir, but it's not really your job to tell me what I should do." She swiped her suit skirt and picked off a piece of lint.

"Spunky. I'm giving unasked-for advice, I realize. Sorry to interrupt your discussion." He grabbed his drink and wandered off.

Richard Li let out a big breath. "My boss. He's the AG."

"Ah, I see."

"Uh. Sorry. Guess that shuts down our time together," Richard said. "I don't want to get on his bad side and, believe me, it's easy to do. Sorry I can't help." He plunked down a $20 bill.

Antigone scooched over. "What just happened? Were you wrestling with the big dog?"

"I'm not sure. But he sure has an aptitude for intimidation, and your friend Richard stepped into it."

Antigone stared after Richard. "And I thought he was a good one. Maybe I should have gone to Seattle after all? But what's this case he mentioned?"

Emma checked around the bar. "It's not really a case. I discovered I've got a long-lost aunt, in Killane."

"The women's prison?"

"Yeah. She was convicted of killing her kids twenty-some years ago and is due for execution. My mom wants me to help her."

"Oh my God. The story in the news? The mom who killed her kids? That's your aunt?"

"Yeah. And I'm going to meet her this weekend. At the prison."

"Geeez, Emma. That's exciting and scary all at once. Can I do anything?"

"I'm fine, thanks. I've got to figure out what to ask her in forty-five minutes after not even knowing about her for my whole life."

"So, you get to go to a maximum-security prison, and I go to fancy dinners in Seattle. You'll have better stories to tell."

Chapter 12

Wednesday late evening, April 19, 2006

Still shaken from her bar encounter with Simmons, Emma dashed through Rennell's grocery store. In five minutes, she'd tossed seven items into her basket—a frozen Hawaiian pizza, two frozen Indian dinners, one frozen Pad Thai dinner, a can of tomato soup, and two cans of Blue Buffalo dog food. She rounded the wine aisle and nearly bumped into Mountain Man, comparing two Shiraz bottles. She pulled back into the salad dressing aisle, not in the mood for small talk.

"Oops. Slow down there. Oh, it's you."

"Busted." She patted the cart.

Mountain Man's basket overflowed with fresh broccoli, lettuce, basil, and mushrooms pushed up against chicken thighs, 2% milk, and wine. "I see you're into efficiency?"

She lifted a Pad Thai box. "No time for the joy of cooking in my life. This is the clue that we could never be compatible. You'd die in a week if you ate at my place."

He chuckled. "No kidding. But your dog eats like a king. How is Shadrach? It was good to see you at the d-dog park the other day. Any chance we could try that again?"

Her chest tensed up. "Sorry. I've got a long trip on Saturday so I'm even more strapped for time. Maybe in a few weeks."

The tension came from nerves, she figured, but also from not being completely honest. She liked this man. *Why am I fighting it?*

"Shadrach can't be happy about sitting in the car all that time. Could I take care of him for the day? Harriet could use the socializing."

She ungripped the shopping basket. "That's awfully nice. I may take you up on it. But it would be all day, so I'd have to bring his million-dollar food." She wouldn't tell him that Shadrach would have a longer wait in the car while she was inside the prison. Then again, it felt easy talking to this man, and that wasn't a familiar feeling. Perhaps she'd let her guard down, just a little.

"I'd love it. But on one condition."

She tensed. *Of course.* She knew she shouldn't have trusted him. *There's always a catch.*

"That you have dinner with me when you get home. I promise to have only weeks-old processed f-food, and we'll eat it from the containers they come in. Then we'll see who gets sick first.

Stifling a laugh, she leaned over her forlorn basket. "Deal."

Chapter 13

Saturday late morning, April 22, 2006

The big red V for "visitor" on the plastic name badge made it clear Emma didn't belong in a prison. Her jeans and faux leather jacket confirmed it. She signed her name next to Victoria Beringer in the "Visitor's Register of the Women's Correctional Institution of Killane, Washington." The guard jotted her aunt's prisoner number—#A4873MD—and the time, 11:32 a.m. Emma dumped her phone, purse, and keys into a plastic box and stepped through the metal detector.

She closed her eyes and counted to ten, calming her neck muscles. In the distance, she heard a heavy metal door clang.

The hefty female guard behind the detector cocked her head. "Well, ma'am, not sure where you'd put anything under those jeans, but let's see what you got."

And she got nothing.

"I need my notebook and pen," Emma said.

"Notebook's OK. You can't take a pen or pencil. Here's the inside of a BIC pen. That way nothing bad can happen if an inmate gets it."

The guard led her along a hallway, with white stripes along each side, about two feet from the wall. "That's where the inmates walk," she said over her shoulder. "Single file." The gleaming floors looked slippery.

Windows revealed a courtyard surrounded by a twenty-foot concrete wall, topped with a spiral of concertina wire. She heard no yelling, no tin cans banging metal bars, and smelled only the aroma of spaghetti. The place seemed almost peaceful. Then she remembered her first semester of law school, when a retired sheriff spoke to the class. The sheriff had talked about the difference between working patrol, where street cops rode around for hours, fighting boredom, which could be punctuated by moments, maybe longer, of intense danger, and the work done by jail or prison deputies who faced hours of constant vigil and relentless focus, with no moments of boredom. The sheriff drew a graph on the white board, with the patrol experience as a spikes of action among long stretches of boredom and the jail patrol graph as a flat line, high on the Y-axis: constant stressful vigilance. The deputy ahead of her swept her eyes right, left, and forward, watching and listening.

The room for visitors contained round metal tables with fixed benches and filigree metal in the frosted glass on the door—nothing to make this place cozy.

"Pick your home for the next little while."

Two pairs of people sat opposite each other at tables in the far corners. One pair seemed to be inmate and lawyer. The second was inmate and partner. Those two reached their hands toward each other but did not touch. Their fingers scratched the metal table between them. Emma chose an empty table in the third corner.

Two minutes later, an older woman shuffled into the pale-green room. She wore a heavy dark red cotton pullover shirt and pants and walked flat footed to keep her slippers from falling off. Her tilting eyes and faded freckles mirrored the twenty-four-year-old newspaper drawing. The woman's washed-out face sagged, devoid of energy.

"Forty-five minutes," said the guard, tapping her long righthand fingernails, painted white and yellow, on the table. A tiny beaming sun decorated her ring fingernail.

Sitting across from this person she'd never known, Emma shivered at their physical similarities. This was an older version of her and Mom, yet she knew nothing about her.

"Thank you for coming," Aunt Victoria opened. "Feels like I'm looking at myself twenty-five years ago. I had no idea you'd look like this."

Emma tilted her head before catching herself. *No need to be a mirror.*

Aunt Victoria's tension melted into a small grin. "You tilt your head like I do." She touched her nose. "And, my God, freckles. Uncanny."

"Aunt Victoria...may I call you that?"

"That sounds strange, but I guess you're the only one who has the right to call me that." Her open smile revealed a gap where her lower right canine tooth should have been. She flushed and covered her mouth.

True, no one else in the world could call this woman "aunt," and she had no one else to call "Aunt." Victoria was so different from Mom. Seemed relaxed even. And more unexpected, Emma felt comfortable.

Emma shifted. *God, what a place like this must do to a person. Twenty-four years. And not much time left.* "Now that I see you, I've got loads of questions about you and Mom, your childhoods. But not now. We don't have much time, and today I need to understand what's going on."

The couple in the corner stared at each other, saying nothing. The woman dabbed her eyes.

Emma opened her Moleskine notebook and grabbed the BIC pen insert from her jacket pocket. She bent the rubber tube and watched it straighten. "Before we decide anything, though, Mom said you wanted help? Why now?"

Aunt Victoria shrugged half-heartedly. "Oh, Emileen. Don't blame her. I didn't ask for any help. I simply told her about the execution date. But it's good to meet you."

Emma's pulse quickened. "You what? I thought you wanted help."

"I did think about it and wanted to try to change the outcome because I'm going to die, and I want people to know that I didn't do it. But it's not worth the effort."

Emma glanced at the institutional black and white clock hanging on the wall: thirty-five minutes left.

One of the visitors across the room raised his voice. "No, you're in here. *I'm* raising the kids and *I'm* the one making decisions!"

How awful to live your worst life in front of other people.

"OK, but I came to learn about your case, so could you just tell me? What's the short version?"

"The short version. I've thought about the long version for the last twenty-four years, and you ask for a short version? Ironic." Aunt Victoria chortled. "Here goes. We had four children in ten years, and all died before the age of two. I swear…" She shook her head. Her baggy shirt dwarfed her so that the V-neck drooped, showing a wrinkly lower neck. "The prosecutor said I smothered them. But they never found proof because I didn't do it. The kids were weak, had coughs…but I didn't hurt them. I'd never hurt them."

"What were their names?"

"Darrin, Brian, Fiona, and Dorothy. We called her 'Dot.'" Her eyes welled up.

The door clanged again, announcing another inmate's arrival; this time a bent-over woman pushing a walker. She looked eighty; being in this place, she could have been ten or maybe twenty years younger.

"I'm sorry to ask these questions but I'd like to know. What about autopsies? And tests? Maybe they found something wrong?"

Aunt Victoria placed her palms on the grey metal table. "Could you slow down? I don't talk to people much. You need to make it easy. One question at a time."

"Sorry. Were there autopsies?"

"Yes. I suppose you could look at the results."

"Did they find anything suspicious?" Out of the corner of her eye, she watched the guard rock back and forth on her thick-soled leather shoes, probably five pounds.

"Nothing like bruises or pin pricks." She reached in her trouser pocket for a tissue.

"Was there testing for DNA?" She silently begged Aunt Victoria to keep it together.

"Nothing like that was used in the trial, at least from what I remember."

"What about your husband?"

"What about him?" Aunt Victoria's pursed lips made her look angry. "He disappeared after I went to prison."

"Did he have anything to do with the deaths?"

"Dell? Of course not. He blamed me and drank a lot because of it. That's what men do when they're sad. He wanted a big family. I failed him." She dabbed her eyes with the well-used tissue.

To avoid looking at Aunt Victoria's tears, Emma flipped a page in her notebook and scribbled. "Mom mentioned some diaries?"

"She would, wouldn't she? Dell turned them over to the police."

Mom had told her this, but it was a blow to hear it from Aunt Victoria. Emma hugged herself to warm up, but the chill was inside of her. "Horrifying. I'm so sorry."

"Yes, it was awful. Dell thought he was doing the right thing. The lawyers thought those diaries offered a confession… that I'd done something to those kids. But I didn't. I never—"

"What'd you write?"

"A lot. About how the children couldn't gain weight, about their coughs and difficulty breathing. I said at one point, and this was to God and not a confession, that little Brian needed help in his dying. He was slipping from this world and needed a push to the other side." She reached her hand to her throat. "I can't stand it. Hurts so much, even after all of this time."

Emma reached for her throat in the same gesture but stopped. The similarities unnerved her. *What had Rupert said about family? Blood ties people in unexpected ways.*

The guard strolled past. "Fifteen minutes left."

"OK, a few more questions. Who was the case lawyer? What do you remember about the trial that seemed odd?"

"Slower, please. It was a public defender. After all of those medical bills, for the babies, for me. With Dell's drinking—there was no money."

"Name?"

"I don't recall. Sorry. But the prosecutors. Lord, help me. One of them. I'll never forget that man's eyes. Evil." She blew her nose. "He used my own words against me. Said four deaths was too many and it couldn't be a coincidence in one family."

"I'd like to look at the evidence, the diaries. I'll need access, but that will happen only if you make me your legal counsel."

"What's that mean?"

"If you want me to help in any formal way, you've got to tell the system that you want me to represent you. I could read the diaries, have access to other information, like autopsies."

"And your firm would help?"

She hesitated. "Let me worry about that. But to help at all, I need to be your official attorney."

Aunt Victoria's face scrunched. "Oh dear. This is moving so fast."

The guard paced next to the couple, who were both sniffling. The man had put his head on the table, and his partner whispered to him.

Aunt Victoria sucked in air. "I don't want to waste your time. We tried appealing for years with no luck. Why would this be any different? I don't want to drag you down too. Especially now that we've talked."

Heat flashed from Emma's chest to her face. *Had Mom known Aunt Victoria might not want to pursue this? Was this, in the end, a wild goose chase to make me feel unworthy, again?* "What did you say?"

"I'm sorry that you came all this way, but I don't have the strength."

Numbness in Emma's feet seeped up her legs, and her heart thumped harder. "You're not thinking right. Please don't give up. Wait till we see if there's something first."

"I've been waiting, don't you see? I've been waiting for years and…"

The lump in Emma's throat kept her from swallowing. Her fury at her mother mixed with sorrow and frustration for Aunt Victoria. She was exasperated—she wanted to do right by Aunt Victoria but felt thwarted by her waffling. Her short visit bonded her in a way she didn't feel with her own mother. But if Aunt Victoria backed away, she'd lose on many levels. She'd never get to know her newfound aunt, reconciling with Mom could be harder, and she'd lose a chance to test her legal skills in a case that mattered.

"Let me push for a while. What do you have to lose? I wasn't sure about this but, after meeting you, I want to know more." Emma stretched out her hand but yanked it back to avoid the guard's reprimand.

Victoria scraped her right index knuckle along the edge of her left eye. "Thank you for your kindness. No one's wanted to help me for so long. But I doubt I'm worth the effort."

"Hey, stop that. It seems impossible but it could be huge if we pull this off." She straightened, strangely calm. "From what I know, if there was anything out of kilter in that trial, we might go for a mistrial. I saw something that said the jury deliberated for a long time. Wonder if something there—"

The guard knocked on the metal table, and Aunt Victoria stood.

"No matter what," she said, "at least I saw you." Aunt Victoria put her hand over her heart.

Chapter 14

Saturday evening, April 22, 2006

Emma strolled up Grant's driveway at day's end, entering his garage, jammed with music gear—drum set, amplifiers, three guitars leaning off to the side, and a Yamaha keyboard.

Grant offered his movie-star smile and raised his arms like he'd made a goal. "Emma! G-Good to see you!"

He pointed to two men. "My band mates, Snake and Tully. Guys, Shadrach's mom. Emma."

Tully pounded the drums and nodded.

"Snake?" She squatted to greet Shadrach.

"I got a nasty tattoo in high school that I'm still trying to remove. I lived in Idaho and thought rattlers were the meanest snakes around. I didn't find out till years later that coral snakes can be equally nasty and are much better looking."

"Good to meet you." Tully, wearing a baseball cap, twisted the bill from back to front. "We're just leaving. Had an awesome jam session for three old guys. G is making dinner, we hear, and that's not something he offers much, so take advantage of it."

Grant reddened and pointed at Tully. "He's got teenage kids who actually think they have a cool father."

"Yeah, they don't like our music, but they still let their friends meet me. Works for me. Have a good dinner. I'm off."

Grant shoved his keyboard against the wall. "Chicken chardonnay pasta OK?" Grant led her into the house. "I do have a confession before we go any further."

She braced. *Here we go, already?* Shadrach plopped at her feet, exhausted. "What'd you do to the dog? He's wiped."

"That's the confession." Grant knocked on the countertop. "I lost him—just for a few minutes—at the d-dog park today. He came back with a scratched nose and stuck with Harriet and me after that. Sorry. But I had to tell you. I hope I didn't do any damage."

She gulped some wine and smiled. "That's good of you to tell me. Most people wouldn't. Thank you."

He flipped his hand over his forehead in relief. "Thank God."

They exchanged small talk, and she high fived herself internally for keeping it going. *I'll get the hang of being around people someday. He makes it easy, though.*

Over dinner and wine, Grant talked about his family, which sounded like a fairy tale. "And you? Tell me about yours."

Still too soon. "Just my parents and me. Not much to tell. Typical small-town kid who wanted to leave for the big city, and I did, after high school. Community college, Cascade University, then Seattle College for law school. Now here." A flippant answer, but she didn't have the energy for more.

"Hmm." He drilled his fingers on the table. "Your law school reminds me of something else. This feels like my night of confessions. My life may have sounded all rosy, but no one's is. And something happened a week ago, and I worry the d-dark side of my family may rear its head."

"Do you want to talk about it?" She stiffened, hating the drama but wanting to be a good listener. *So many skills to learn.*

"I have a cousin. He's in vet school now. But years ago, he got into trouble for b-breaking and entering. The house of a prominent Seattle family. He and some buddies took a computer, money, and some guns to sell for d-drugs. He got caught; his pals fled. No one else in the family stayed with him when he got in trouble, except me. He spent four years in prison, and I visited him several times. Sickening place."

Prison seems to be the topic of the day. "How awful. But he's good now?"

He nodded. "He g-got clean and went to school. But it came up the other day when someone ran a check on him. He's a felon and he worries it will affect his job prospects. I'm glad he's moving forward, but sometimes these things throw him backward, and I worry that he'll relapse."

Grant got up to let the dogs out, and a whiff of evergreen from his flannel shirt dusted over her. "Sorry to unload, but it's been on my mind, and I don't talk to the band guys about this sort of stuff, and my family won't listen."

She stood at another decision cliff. *Should I jump and tell more?* He had taken a risk telling her about the dog and the cousin. This quid-pro-quo balance seemed to be part of what she needed to learn. She squared her shoulders and finished her wine.

"I'm sure that was hard to tell me, and I appreciate it. I guess, with your double-barreled confessions, I need to offer one as well."

"Oh? I'm ready to listen." He leaned in.

"Sure you want to go down this path?" She could feel her innards pushing and pulling.

"You know my secrets. You owe me one." He winked.

"Here goes. True confession." She pointed at Shadrach. "I almost named him Humphrey. Since I love the movie *Casablanca*."

He laughed. "But you know 'Humphrey' isn't much better than 'Herman.' You made the right decision with Shadrach."

"That's what I figured. So, there's my secret."

"I'd say that's about a 3-out-of-10-level confession. Mine was more like an 8 out of 10. You've got to do better than that."

She rubbed her hands down her pant legs. The cliff beckoned. *Go for it.*

"Speaking of prisons, that's where I was today."

He sat back. "Whoa. Big day. AT a prison or IN prison? There's a difference."

She chuckled. "Right. I was at and in, seeing an inmate. A relative I never knew about until a few days ago."

"Now that's almost as good as naming a d-dog after Humphrey Bogart. Tell me more if you want to." He cleared the plates.

She swept crumbs off the tabletop. Grant's green eyes pulled her in. She was sinking, and also relaxing like she hadn't done in a long time. *Open up, give in, do it.*

"First, and shocking to me, we have physical similarities—"

"Really? Had you never met before?"

"Nope, first time. One article about the trial had courtroom sketches of her, but I couldn't tell a whole lot, but it reminded me of my mom. Then when we met…she had freckles." She touched her cheek. "We both tilt our heads to the right. One drawing made me wonder if she's left-handed. I am, but she didn't write anything when I was with her—"

"Wait. How can you tell?"

"You know how people put their dominant thumb on top of the other one when they clasp their hands?"

"No, I didn't know that." He immediately clasped his hands and lifted an eyebrow. "I'll be d-damned. You are full of surprises."

She flashed a smile. "You'll just have to stick around to learn more."

"Don't tempt me because I will." He winked.

"Strange, but I felt a connection. Even more than with my own mother." She gazed at the ceiling. "I came away wanting to help this person I'd only just met."

"That's something. So, what was the prison like? The men's prison fits the stereotypes, believe me."

She giggled. "Here we are—comparing prisons. What a way to get to know someone. OK, let me think." She closed her eyes. "A mix of smells, from cleaning products to food. Dial soap on Aunt Victoria. Sandalwood cologne on the guard at the front desk."

"Great sense of smell. Sounds cleaner than where my cousin was. Did any sounds hit you?"

"Oh sure. The normal TV police drama sounds of clanging doors. But no banging tin cans or yelling. And the constant ticking clock, hanging on the wall."

"Good memory. Is that something you've always had?"

She gave him a once over. He seemed interested, not just making small talk.

"Yes, since I was a kid. It helps in my job. I can remember cases and citations."

"Got it. So, what did you and your aunt talk about?"

She clasped her hands and looked down. "See? I'm left-handed. Proof."

"Good party trick." He squinted when he smiled.

"She gave me a rundown on her four kids who died, over a ten-year period. She wrote about it in some diaries, which she said were letters to herself and to God, not confessing to murder. But the prosecution used them as evidence of motive and confession. The worst part was that her husband turned those journals over to the police. Her own husband."

"God."

He sat next to her on the couch and wrapped his arm around her shoulders. She leaned into him. "Thanks."

"Is there more?"

"Oh yes, and it's a doozy."

"Do we need more wine?"

"Probably best to hear this straight."

He brushed her hair from her forehead and kissed her hairline. "Ready."

Just being next to him, feeling his warmth, made it easier to get the words out.

"My mom found the diaries first. She accidentally came across them in my aunt's house. She read parts and told my aunt's husband about them."

Grant braced.

Is he disgusted at what an awful family I have?

"Un-b-believable," he said. "She told you that?"

"I'm sorry. I'm telling you things out of order. No, my aunt told me only that her husband had turned the diaries into the police. Last weekend, when we met, Mom told me she had found them. Aunt Victoria didn't say anything about Mom. It was almost like she was protecting her sister, my mom."

Grant sat up straight and pushed away so that he could look at her. "Your mom found them and betrayed her sister?" His voice rose, and he grimaced.

Emma's stomach quivered. She'd gone too far. She had leapt off the cliff and now, midair, feet scrambling, she knew she'd made a mistake. *He thinks I'm horrible, or at least my family.* She hung her head and whispered. "I'm sorry I told you."

"Oh my God, Emma. Don't be sorry. I can't believe this happened in your family, to you. It must feel awful. Why are you just now learning about this after, what, twenty-some years?" With that, he reached for her, stroked her head, and rocked. "I'm so sorry."

She wanted to sob but held back, forcing herself to finish the story. "Thanks. That means a lot. I'm still trying to get my head around it. She's got an execution date, and my mom thought I could do something to help. I can't, of course, but wanted to meet her at least. I mean, there she is, in prison, about to die, and yet she wanted to forgive her sister for finding her journals. Amazing. She said Mom and her husband did what they thought was 'right,' even though it pretty much cooked her goose. I suppose isolation does strange things."

She shuddered.

Grant grabbed a wool throw from the end of the couch and pulled it across both of them. "Just let it out…if you want to."

They sat in silence for five minutes, and she felt his body slacken. She twitched, and he jerked.

"What? Did you think I'd gone to sleep?"

She chuckled and sat up. "I did, indeed. Are you with me still?"

"Absolutely. Tell me more. How do you feel now? After a few hours to think about it?"

She rubbed her fingers over the back of his hand. *How does this mountain man make me feel so comfortable?*

"I'm trying to see this from Aunt Victoria's perspective. She didn't think her lawyer, the public defender, did a good job, and I wonder if the jury deliberations were too long. Was something fishy going on? But she's out of appeals. Her execution is set for June 27, just two months. And I feel powerless."

"What does your steel-trap legal mind think?"

"That I'll lose if I take it on and I'll lose if I don't."

"How so?"

She had said so much, she couldn't back out now. "I want to reconnect with my folks…that's part of this. They, or at least Mom, thought I could help bring her and her sister together through this case. Big order. And now I've met Aunt Victoria, and she feels more like 'family' than Mom does right now. If we got a review of the earlier trial, or new trial, it'd be a big deal for the firm, for me. A reputation maker."

He squeezed her hand. "And?"

"This case has emotional heart strings, a high-stakes deadline, and a mystery. *Law and Order* TV stuff. Because if she didn't kill the kids, who did? It would be a real winner."

"Got it. I could be your backup. Remember, I did accounting research on some legal cases. And I've one year of baby-law under my belt. Let me find information for you."

"I'd rather you be a sounding board, since you know a little about law. But more information is always better. We need to at least know more about the earlier trial. The articles about it seemed awfully convincing, about what happened and how she was convicted, but maybe that's not the whole story."

"So now think upside down. Why should this crack lawyer *not* take this case?" He looked at her as if she was the only person in the world.

God. What is this? Her chest felt light, and her pulse moved so fast she could hear it. She wanted to stay the night but forced herself to pull back from the temptation. *Not yet. Not yet. Can't be sure that this is worth pursuing. Thank God he can't read my mind.* "Sorry, what'd you say?"

"Why would you not pursue this adventure? The case?"

Does he mean us? Ah, no. the case. What am I thinking?

"Ah. The case. Why not pursue it? Easy. It doesn't stand a chance in hell." She grabbed one more slug of wine. "Unless there's something unusual, what they did before will hold. And, of course, there's the fact that I've got more work than I can handle, mostly small misdemeanors, but I just got one that has more meat. And Aunt Victoria's case would be high profile, not one for a rookie. The firm would have to agree to take it on; someone who's got more experience. And it would be pro bono at that, which would be a miracle. But there's not much time. Aunt Victoria's clock is ticking. Speaking of clocks, Shadrach and I are about to turn into pumpkins. We 'must away,' as they say."

Chapter 15

Tuesday evening, April 25, 2006

A pounding on Emma's door set off Shadrach's barking. Emma peeked through the window beside her door. Rupert. She let out a breath.

"Ah, glad you're here. I've been edgy since I visited my aunt. Come on in. I need to show you something." She pointed to an envelope on her kitchen counter. "This came today and might change the course of my life."

"My goodness, that sounds ominous. What have you got?"

"A letter from Women's Correctional Institution. This will tell me if my aunt wants help."

"Then let's get to the races. Open it!"

She pulled out a folded piece of formal stationery, which had a few typed lines. Also in the envelope was a page from a spiral notebook. In red ink, Aunt Victoria had written "E, I asked that you be my lawyer. Now what? V."

The folded paper's typewritten letter repeated that Victoria had requested Emma Knox Raddell to be her official representative, her attorney of record. Emma placed her hand over her heart.

Rupert reached out his hand. "Congratulations. I'm happy to do any research you need. Pro bono. What do you think?"

She stared at the letter. "Hmmm. Now I'm not sure what I think. Let's go outside."

Points of light, some larger and redder, some blurry and small, filled the dark, clear sky. She found the few constellations she knew—Orion on the horizon, ready to leave the northern hemisphere for the spring and summer. The two dippers looking over Cassiopeia, resting on her couch, and if Emma squinted, she could make out the Pleiades, a hazy cluster of small blinking lights. During childhood summers, she and Dad had reviewed stars and planets and watched comets zip across the black sky dome.

"When's the last time your aunt saw this?" Rupert pointed to the stars.

When had Aunt Victoria last seen stars? Not for over twenty years. Even if she was allowed outdoors at night, her horizon was limited to the walls of the prison. She probably hadn't seen trees up close for at least as long. Goosebumps leapt across Emma's body, like wind had brushed it.

She turned to him. "I'm in."

Chapter 16

Wednesday, April 26, 2006

Emma collected copies of Aunt Victoria's diaries from the evidence vault and cheered internally that the officious guard, Mr. Overton, was not on duty. But when she looked for the trial transcripts, they'd been checked out by the AG, E. Simmons, the man himself, who was about to take over Overton's position as her least favorite in the courthouse. *Why would he want the transcripts?*

At home that evening, she spread the copies of the twenty-four spiral and bound notebooks on her kitchen table, along with typewritten transcripts of the journals. Aunt Victoria's handwriting resembled a young girl's—loopy, with circles as dots over the I's, hearts around the children's names when they were born, and rectangles with crosses after they died. Coffee mug stains on the pages. Aunt Victoria started the first diary right after Darrin's death and stopped on the day her fourth child died. Nearly ten years. Four lives gone. Or five, if she counted Aunt Victoria.

Jasmine tea's scent filled the kitchen.

March 13, 1972

> I can't believe my darling Darrin is gone. He went to sleep and never woke up. They call it 'sudden infant death syndrome.' Never heard of that before. Maybe if I had been a better mother. I know I was short with him, sometimes even cruel. But I meant no harm.

July 10, 1972

Dell blames me. Darrin had a seizure, but we had him checked. After that, he seemed fine. I should have known something was wrong when I put him to bed that night. I wasn't the best mother all the time. I got angry and frustrated. I shouted sometimes. I left him in his room alone more than I should have. But I never meant any wrong. They say his airway was blocked. How can that be? Dell won't talk about what happened. I'm sure he's crazy with grief, but I am mourning too. Who will help me?

December 25, 1972

We should have been a family this Christmas. But Dell does seem calmer. Me too. I have to hope that God gives us another chance.

March 31, 1974

I'm feeling strong with this one. It will be a perfect birth, a perfect baby. We are so happy. Thank you, God, for your blessing on my little family.

June 3, 1974

Little Brian born yesterday. We are thrilled.

June 19, 1974

How can this be? Brian struggles to breathe. I hold him, feed him—but he doesn't eat—I talk to him, and he cries. Sucks in air but never seems to have enough. I'm at the end of my rope. How can I help him? Take away this suffering?

July 10, 1974

24 days. He was in such pain. He needed a little help on his way to heaven. He was so small, so perfect.

July 16, 1974

Brian's gone. Autopsy showed something called "floppy larynx." He had trouble breathing, but don't all babies? I wanted to make him comfortable. When I knew he was going, I wanted to help him go peacefully.

August 13, 1974

Dell is furious, drinking a lot. That's what men do when they are angry or scared.

August 23, 1974

No one cares about me. Except Jim. He comes over, almost every day. Since Dell stays away or is at work, J. helps with things around the house. Such a comfort for me. He's helping me grieve.

October 22, 1974

The neighbors shun me. Kids point at me in the grocery store. I know I'm responsible. For both children. Stress made me do terrible things.

November 2, 1974

My sister made an outrageous offer. I doubt that J. knows.

The inside of Emma's head was pressing toward the outside. She sucked in four long breaths. Aunt Victoria never had a chance.

May 15, 1975

All seems calm now. Dell is drinking less. We've grieved for Brian. As we did for Darrin. And I pray again that we'll have another chance to be a family. Please, God. Please help me with these babies. Please make me a better mother.

October 1, 1977

Our gift child is due end of the month. I never thought we would have another chance. Thank you, Lord.

October 30, 1977

Little Fiona came early but seems fine. She's breathing, eating. She's wonderful. Dell is happy. I'm over the moon.

February 28, 1978

Oh no. Fiona has a croup cough and is struggling to breathe. The doctor says it's an infection, and we have medication. Antibiotics. I'll keep a special eye on.

July 2, 1978

My luck runs dry. I'm devastated. Fiona died on June 30th. In her sleep. Maybe my shouting when she cried all the time made her nervous and unable to breathe? I'm spent.

July 5, 1978

Autopsy says a heart attack. I've been a bad mother.

August 14, 1979

The children thing isn't happening. We might have to forget the idea. Nature, fate, and the man upstairs

> decided I don't get a fourth chance. And rightly so, I suppose. I would like to make all my mistakes go away and find some way to make meaning. Obviously, I'm my father's daughter.

A slug rammed her chest. *What did Aunt Victoria mean?* Emma snatched up her phone.

"What does Victoria mean when she says in the diaries that she's her father's daughter?" she demanded.

"Emileen? Good evening to you too."

Small talk. That blasted small talk. But tonight, she didn't have time.

"Sorry, Mom, but I need to know something. What happened with your father? You never told me about your parents, but she mentioned your father in her diary. That she was like him. What's that mean?"

Mom waited. "Are you finished? I'm not going to yell back and forth over the phone."

"Sorry. I'm trying to figure this family out, and you don't make it easy."

"I'm sure it seems confusing. I'm not sure what to tell you."

"Tell me what she means. Is there something there I need to know? She's my client now, and I need to know."

Emma heard a scraping sound as Mom pulled a kitchen chair closer to the phone. Her mother heaved a sigh. "I probably told you we had a happy childhood. That wasn't…I wasn't being honest."

Emma's throat tightened, and she nodded encouragement, even though Mom wouldn't see it.

"The awful truth is that our father… He and Mother… He… He killed our mother."

Emma crumpled forward, her pulse speeding out of control, heart pumping hard inside her chest. "What do you mean? In front of…of…"

Shadrach nudged her hand and gave her his question look: "Are you OK?"

"He turned himself in while we were at school," her mother said.

Shadrach sat on Emma's feet, his protection mode. He knew something wasn't right.

"What did you… Oh God, how terrible, Mom."

Her mother sniffed. "I know. Awful."

Emma's mind raced as she mentally retraced the family tree. *My grandfather, who I'd never met, was a murderer? His daughter, Aunt Victoria, convicted as well. How could Mom have held this for so long? This family—my family—is cursed. Too many deaths. So much pain.* "Mom, I'm so sorry."

"We were nine and twelve, about that old. He died in prison." Her mother drew a shuddering breath. "Victoria never forgave him, but I tried. But we never saw him again."

Emma's stomach clenched. Whiplash happened every time they talked because Mom dropped another bombshell. "So, if Victoria writes in her diary that she's like her father, what's she mean? Does she mean because they're both—because they both killed people?"

Mom whispered, "Maybe because she lost her temper like he did."

Gentle rain slapped the windowpane. The warm pool of Emma's reading lamp kept the room from being completely dark.

November 2, 1979

> I have a baby on the way, my fourth, which will mean big sacrifices, again. I hope this time will go well. The last time must have been stress, so this time, I'm staying as calm as I can. I do not want to do awful things again.

November 15, 1979

I know I got angry with the others. With Brian. And I shouldn't have. But when he wouldn't sleep, when he cried all the time. It's hard to stay still and wait. I got so frustrated. Dell wasn't here, and I was alone with them.

December 18, 1979

This baby will be perfect. I know this will bring Dell and me back to some sort of normal happy family. It has to work. I don't want bad things to happen again.

January 5, 1980

Dell came home drunk again and says he's not happy. He's terrified about having another child, that I'll let another one die. I hope he doesn't do anything to jeopardize it. I keep telling him it was me, not the children. I'll handle crying fits better than I did with Fiona and Brian. I'm sure I will. I need to convince Dell not to worry. Even if I did leave Brian in his room for a few minutes…so I could breathe. It helped me cope. With Fiona, I wanted her to stop crying. And one day she did. I don't want that to happen again.

February 8, 1980

I was so stressed and scared, felt so vulnerable with the other babies. I am not sure how to deal with all of this. I don't know if I can go through with this again. I'm using these diaries to dump everything. My feelings and thoughts. My fears. I can't lose another one. I *cannot* lose one more baby. I feel nothing but torture, pain, and fear. I'm trying to figure things out and understand what is un-understandable. This one must live.

March 21, 1980

Dell found these diaries, or rather Elisabeth found them. They think I did something to the babies. I promised them that I did nothing, that I'd never hurt the babies. They can't turn me in. We will have our miracle child soon. They'll see.

May 2, 1980

Dorothy Lee Beringer arrived. All will be perfect. I promise.

July 31, 1980

Dot's good-natured. Thank goodness. It has saved her from the fate of her siblings. Maybe she was warned, somehow.

December 26, 1980

First Christmas with Dot. She seems fine. We've turned the corner. We are a family and will stay together. Dot must stay, I'm desperate for her to stay. I need that to make Dell stay too. I'll do anything.

January 27, 1981

She's perfect and everything is going well. Personality is different from the other three. And there's less going on in my head. She's different. Will she stay because of that?

August 15, 1981

Dell and Elisabeth were wrong. I've proven that. Dot proved it. They need to calm down, but they keep asking me about the others. I might have made some mistakes, but don't all mothers? But now, I'm fine, and so is Dot. I wish they would stop poking around.

November 14, 1981

Dot died.

No other entries.

Parched, Emma reached for the tea kettle. None of this made sense. Aunt Victoria blamed herself. A crafty prosecutor like Simmons made diaries sound like a confession. He took her words and turned them against her. *And what about Mom?* Even she didn't believe her own sister. Even though Aunt Victoria had said she was writing God, not confessing, no seemed to be on her side.

What would Grant think? What questions would he ask?

Startled to think he was the first person to come to mind, she smiled. She'd give him a try, this new man.

And what about the actual trial? If the public defender was competent, shouldn't he have argued for some other reason for the deaths? Did other families go through this? Until now, Emma had no idea what SIDS was, how kids this young could die, unless there was foul play. *What was going on? Bad luck? Or was this actually premeditated murder? Can I even find out?* She had to.

Chapter 17

Thursday evening, April 27, 2006

Rupert had invited Emma and Shadrach for an early dinner and an update on the case. As Emma left her apartment at five o'clock, she scooped up the mail and scanned the envelopes. Fliers for real estate agencies or landscaping services typically filled her box, but this evening, she smiled at a manila envelope with a sticky note: "E, for your reading pleasure, R." Rupert printed and marked up articles rather than forwarding them by email. It saved her time, to be sure, but she winced thinking of the trees that died in the process. The articles covered cases where babies had died of SIDS or experts thought they had. Two articles mentioned genes and mutations. *What?*

Rupert opened the door as she approached. She lifted the manila. "Thanks for these." Then she waved a legal-sized envelope at him. "And I also got this. From the attorney general's office."

He raised his bushy grey brows and ushered her in. "That doesn't sound good. What do you think it is?"

"Don't know. Let's open it together?"

He stirred lamb stew as she spread the letter on his Formica countertop.

Dear Ms. Raddell,

One of the most satisfying roles I have had over the years, as the District Attorney of Surrey County and now Attorney General for the Eastern District of Washington state, is to welcome newer attorneys to our community. Whether they work in the area of corporate, criminal, family law or other fields, I want them to know they are welcome in our region.

I would very much like to meet you and give you a personal welcome. Please contact my assistant, Phyllis Smithfield, to make an appointment at your convenience."

Sincerely,

Edward M. Simmons, Esq.

"Why would he do this? It's a summons, pure and simple," she asked.

Rupert leaned against the counter. "Let's slow down. Why do you suppose he's interested in you?"

"It must be my aunt's case. It seems far-fetched that he'd invite new lawyers to his office, don't you think?"

He reached for his pipe, which sat on the kitchen table's corner. "Do you mind?"

"Not if it helps you figure this out for me."

"All part of the thinking process." He tapped the briarwood pipe on the ash tray, dumping old ashes, and then scooped the pungent Dunhill tobacco from his pouch. He tamped the dark leaves with his thumb, long stained an auburn color, and flicked open a silver Zippo lighter, which had his initials on the side. He sipped a few times, letting the smoke float around him. "Tell me what you think."

"I met him briefly in a bar, and he warned me not to dig into old cases. I wonder if he worked on my aunt's case?"

"I looked the case up this afternoon. The prosecutor's name was Sam O'Brien, who's retired. He'd been in the DA's office for a decade. This was his highest profile."

"But could Simmons still have been involved too?"

"Patience, dear one. Patience."

Moments later, she heard his lightning-fast right index finger racing over the keyboard. Another old-school trait—single-finger typing. But he was faster and more accurate than she was, so maybe the old ways had their purpose.

"You might be on to something," he said, puffing. "Simmons was second chair for the prosecution on your aunt's case."

Emma's phone buzzed. Killane Women's Correctional Center.

"I think Aunt Victoria is calling. Let me see what's up."

She accepted the collect call and heard a click. She assumed all of their calls were recorded, but it still made her uneasy.

"Emileen. It's Victoria."

"Hi, Aunt Victoria. Is everything alright? I'm glad you called because I need to ask you something. Do you remember—"

"Wait, dear. Please wait a moment. Remember. One question at a time. But I need to ask something too.... I found out today that my privileges have been reduced. Do you know what happened?"

"What do you mean? What privileges?"

"Not a lot, but still a change that I don't understand. I can't buy snacks from the commissary. Or writing paper. I can't check out as many library books. As I said, nothing drastic, but annoying. At this stage, what's the point in doing me any more harm?"

"I'm so sorry. Let me find out what's going on. By the way, I want to come down on the weekend to fill you in on what I'm learning."

"Please do come. I'd like that. Now, you said you had a question, and I just sidelined you. What did you want to ask?"

"It can wait, but I'd like you to think about two things, please. You mentioned someone on the prosecution side. Was it Edward Simmons, by chance? And...oh sorry. That's the first question. Do you want to write that down? I know it's hard to remember."

"Just a minute. Yes, I have it."

"Second, did anything about the trial, or before, seem odd to you? Anyone who asked you to do something that you didn't want to? Were the witnesses your defense wanted able to show up? Things like that."

"OK. I'll think about it."

"You have one minute left," said a robot voice from nowhere.

"Emileen. Thank you. For the first time in years, I have an inkling of hope. Because of you. Please don't give up on me."

Her aunt's voice sounded lighter than when they'd met.

Shadrach barked.

"You have a dog? We never had animals when I was a child."

"Someday you'll meet him. Until Saturday, then."

Rupert poured stew into two bowls. "Well?"

"She was distraught. Her privileges have been reduced, all of a sudden. Strange. Would it be possible for Simmons to do that? I asked her to think about him and odd happenings. I doubt that she'll have anything for us, but it can't hurt."

The stew aroma calmed her.

"She also said she had hope, for the first time in years."

"Then we have our work cut out."

"Sorry to call you so late, but I've been thinking about your case," Grant said. "And Shadrach. How is my second favorite dog?"

She stood in the backyard with Shadrach, thinking about the case and, oddly enough, about Grant. "Funny. Me too. What's up?"

"I know you're thinking about a review of the case, but what about a mistrial? If I remember right, several criteria could call for that. Have you thought about that, by chance?"

"That's so nice of you to think about Aunt Victoria. I haven't, but one of my colleagues has done several, so I'll pick her brain on whether that could happen. And yes, I've been thinking about Harriet too. Any chance she'd like to come over for a romp with Shadrach? I could give you a beer, if you brought her. We just got back from my neighbor's and we're not quite ready to call it a night."

In ten minutes, Grant and Harriet stepped through the door. Shadrach wiggled himself silly while Harriet went into downward dog pose.

"She's making p-progress, getting more comfortable," Grant said. "How about you?"

She pulled him to her. "Let's not talk business right now."

Chapter 18

Friday, April 28, 2006

Emma knew what a hangover felt like, and this wasn't that. But her head pounded, her body ached, and her limbs moved like she was slogging through water. As an eight-hours-of-sleep person, she suffered with less, and today showed it. She couldn't sleep after her call with Aunt Victoria and the letter from Ed Simmons. And her evening with Grant.

She waited inside the Blue Angel Deli for Antigone, who had agreed to be a set of outside ears on Aunt Victoria's case.

"You look like you're hungover." Antigone smiled. "Or you're finding some man to spend time with?"

Emma smiled and grimaced, almost at the same time.

"The AG has invited me—summoned me—to his office. Wonder if it's my aunt's case?"

"But that's a cold case, and your aunt's about to be executed. Why are you putting any time on it? And why would he care? Sounds like a dead end to me. Don't let this be a career killer."

"But if there's a chance at a mistrial, or a retrial, I've got to try. You've handled some mistrial proceedings, so I wanted your take." Emma heard her name from the deli counter and went to collect their food.

A burly man in a rumpled grey suit yelled loud enough that Emma, third in the line behind him, could hear him.

"What the hell? I get a sandwich, a REUBEN sandwich, with so little sauerkraut on it I thought it was a BLT. What's with you guys? Fix it." He shoved the plate across the counter.

The deli's owner, June Bee, caught it on the fly. "No need for raised voices." Ms. Bee looked like Mrs. Claus and spoke like a fourth-grade teacher familiar with tantrums. Emma had never seen Ms. Bee angry, even with customers like this irritating man. He accepted his new plate and licked his lips.

Emma wanted to shove the grouch. But Ms. Bee, model of composure, treated him with the same grace she used with all customers and staff. A life lesson for an impatient soul.

The tomato bisque cleared Emma's head as Antigone talked.

"First, please understand that getting a mistrial is like walking up Mount Rainier in sandals. Almost impossible."

"Note taken. I am simply gathering information now. No decisions."

"OK, here's the short version. Mistrials happen for several reasons. First, an important witness or participant was unavailable. Dead, disappeared. And it's someone important for either side. Second, the jury was improperly chosen. Three, some evidence that appeared was, in fact, inadmissible. Fourth, jury misconduct. And last—"

"Wait. Jury misconduct? What's that involve?"

"Oh, the stuff you hear about on TV. They talked about the case when they shouldn't, or they looked at the news, things like that. Last, the jury didn't reach a unanimous decision, required in a murder case. But this one wasn't a hung jury."

"Thanks for the mistrial 101 lecture. For this case, no hung jury. No evidence of missing witnesses. The jury selection also seemed clean. But I wonder about inadmissible evidence and jury misconduct. Since they took so long to decide, could something fishy have been going on?"

"If your emotions are driving this, that's not going to play well. And you're still on thin ice as a junior associate. As the Vulture would say, 'Slip ups shall not be tolerated.'"

Chapter 19

Saturday, April 29, 2006

"How nice. We don't have places like this in Snowville." Mom sat on a bench at the edge of the Surrey dog park, throwing a dog toy for Shadrach. "He seems to like it."

Emma had told her parents about the possibility of a mistrial earlier in the week, and they invited themselves to Surrey to see her and her apartment. Now she sat between them.

She'd had stomach cramps all morning, so she hugged her abdomen to calm it. "Mom, I need to know about what happened if I'm to help Aunt Victoria at all."

Mom's face scrunched. "What do you want to know?"

She could feel Dad stirring beside her on the bench, his long, khaki-clad thighs reaching forward, making a ninety-degree angle two feet in front of him, feet flat on the ground. "Tell her, Elisabeth. Tell her the whole thing."

"Let's walk," said Elisabeth.

Emma grabbed Shadrach's leash. She'd put the choke collar on him since they were doing training—learning to heel, sit, lay down. But right now, she wanted him to stay by her side and not distract them by running around. As they strolled, she jerked his collar. "Heel, Shadrach. Heel."

"It was a hard time, for all of us. You were a colicky baby, fussy, hard to calm." Mom peeked around Emma toward Dad. "And Dad and I were having our own problems. He thought I should be more supportive of Victoria—"

"She's right," he said as he kicked a branch out of his way.

"Everyone wanted something from me," Mom said. "You needed more care than I had expected, and my sister needed attention."

A dachshund and Corgi raced past them, leaping onto each other. Their owners, two women in their seventies, arms crossed, wearing Jackie Kennedy head scarves and huge dark glasses, stood twenty yards away and waved at Emma.

"…And her babies were often sick, and then they died," Mom said. "I just couldn't deal with it all."

How can I square being in this peaceful green park while listening to these awful experiences? Emma felt half-in and half-out of her body, physically there, but her mind drifted above.

"And then you turned her in?" Her voice sounded shrill inside her head, and from the quick turn Dad made, it must have sounded bad from outside too. Harsh, but she couldn't understand why Mom had hurt her own sister like that.

"Yes. I found the diaries, and Dell turned them over. We were concerned she might be doing harm and had to stop it. After all these years, though, I'm not so sure. That's why I asked you to help."

Shadrach yanked her arm, pulling hard on the leash, trying to race after a squirrel. "Stop! Shadrach! Get back here!" She jerked hard on the leash, flipping the dog over onto his back. He popped up again and looked at her. "God, I'm sorry, boy. I'm sorry. Didn't mean to pull so hard."

Mom put out her hand for the leash. "Let me try."

"He's just hard to handle right now."

"Shadrach, come here." Mom squatted down next to him and patted his head. "It's OK, boy. We're all on edge." She ran her hand from his head down his back. "Now, Shadrach, you just sit for a minute. Look at me." He stared at Mom. "Me. Watch me." She pointed to her eyes.

"Now, you know how to heel. We know that, right? Let's take a walk together. A short walk." Mom tugged slightly on the leash, turned sideways, and looked down as he trained his eyes on her. They walked side by side for four steps, and she stopped. Shadrach stopped. "Now, can you sit?" She tapped his rear, and he plopped down. "Good boy. Shadrach, you did it. Good boy."

"Let's try again. Shadrach, heel." They moved forward in sync, eight steps, before stopping. He looked at Mom like she was the only person in his world.

"You're going to make me jealous, Mom. What're you doing?"

"Oh, honey, I wasn't very gentle with you, I realized later. I wish I had been, but I had so much stress and tried to force you to behave in certain ways. I've tried to remedy that over the years."

"I thought you didn't like dogs. How did this happen?"

"I just never wanted another creature that could get hurt. But I've been volunteering with the humane society—yes, hard to believe—and they taught me that being gentle goes a lot further than force." Mom dropped the leash to the ground. "Try it now."

Shadrach came to Emma and sat. "Should we try it, boy?" She held the leash loosely and stood at his side. "Shadrach, heel." She took a big step forward, and he sprang into action, walking in step with her and looking up all the time. "Amazing. Thanks, Mom."

Harriet barreled into Shadrach and jumped on Emma. Grant was close behind.

"Shadrach! Hey, b-boy, how are you?" Grant said. "Oh, sorry, didn't realize you were with company."

Mom and Dad stood to the side, sizing up Mountain Man. Dad's grin outsized Mom's tentative smile.

"Mom, Dad, this is Grant. We met at the humane society, fighting over Shadrach, who was called Herman at the time. Can you imagine?"

Hands stretched across three people, and they mumbled hellos.

The dogs led the four further into the park. Grant pulled Emma back. "They seem great. Give them a break."

She rolled her eyes.

Mom leaned down to pet Harriet and Shadrach. "We need to get back. Nice to meet you, Grant." She pulled Emma to her. "Emileen, please know how much you've already made a difference. Thanks for helping—your aunt and this family. I'm sorry I asked you to be a savior, but you're already helping us understand one another." She leaned in for a hug.

"She's right, Lou," said Dad. "You're making a difference."

Despite still being upset about what Mom had done to her aunt, she saw her softer side with Shadrach. It felt good to be connecting more with her, with both of them. *Maybe I can pull this off after all?*

Chapter 20

Tuesday afternoon, May 2, 2006

Emma slipped out of the office on Tuesday afternoon to go to Simmons's office. She expected it to reek of wood paneling and deep carpets, but this looked more like an engineering office from the 1960s—linoleum floors and gunmetal-grey desks. The fluorescent lights fit the scene.

Richard Li crossed the bull pen in five strides. "We met at the bar. I'm Richard Li. I heard you were due in." His thick black hair, shaped into a crew cut, was sculpted with gel.

"Right. You're Antigone's friend."

She remembered he'd squeezed her hand like he had something to prove. He repeated the gesture, but she refused to show pain.

"Sorry I couldn't help you before. Hope you found out what you need?" His placid face gave no hint of emotion. Then again, she wasn't great at reading faces.

Li led her into Simmons's office, the only one walled in clear glass, out of place in these 1960s surroundings. She peeked into the coffee room, expecting to see a Folger's percolator. Nope. A French press sat next to two ceramic espresso cups.

Earlier in the day, she had turned up an online photo of Simmons, looking like a middle-aged golfer, thick around the middle, in a pink pullover sweater. The office photos revealed a proud law school graduate, a jaunty young man holding a tennis trophy for his Westminster University team, and an honorary plaque. Family mementos included a photo of Ed, wife, and daughter of about seventeen standing on a beach and another of a girls' soccer team with Simmons standing to the side. She leaned into one of a framed child's drawing: a superman character flew through the air, with a note at the bottom, "For Duddy, hero for me. I love you, Zia."

A gold cross pen set sat at the top of his desk with a brass plaque. She read upside down: "To Ed, all my love, Marge."

Simmons's handshake was firm but not crushing.

"You have a nice superman drawing there," she said. "And the soccer team?"

He smiled. "I coached my daughter's team. Fourteen-year-old girls. They went to the state championships four times. Zia's a junior at Westminster now. I hope she'll choose law, but she's waffling. Chemistry, at the moment."

"We need more women in science, so that's good for all of us. I started in biology but switched to political science. Law had more opportunities."

"I'd love for her to meet you sometime. I want her to know successful young women."

How long will this small talk take? This back-and-forth and the timing of it was still a mystery to her.

Applause erupted outside his office.

He cocked his head. "Someone out there won a case. Always a round of applause." He unbuttoned his suit jacket. "Thank you for responding so promptly to my request to stop by."

"Did I have a choice, Mr. Simmons? You made it sound urgent."

Simmons laughed. "The title makes the request seem more demanding, that's for sure."

Self-satisfied chump.

"I try to reach out to the promising lawyers, and we've had a big crop this year."

This small talk seemed fluffy. *Does he have another purpose?*

"And do you welcome all young lawyers to the fold?"

He chuckled. "No, not everyone personally, but we watch for especially ambitious folks. It's partly selfish. I might try to entice them to join us at some point. Or, even if they don't join, I can help nudge careers along, from the outside."

What nerve. She forced a smile. "I appreciate the offer, but I'm quite able to take care of myself and my career. I'll make my way in the firm I've joined for now."

"Oh yes, I thought you'd say that. And you're trying, from what I hear, to pursue cases the firm doesn't even know about. And without much success, isn't that correct?"

She froze and held her breath, holding his stare. *Stay calm. Stay strong. What does he know? How does he know?* She didn't know whether to storm out, sit and take it, or fight back. Any option could be dangerous. The attack felt cunning and vicious. *Answer a question with a question.*

"What do you mean, Mr. Simmons?"

"Working on an ancient case without permission? How much leeway will your good partners grant you before you get caught?"

Simmons lowered his voice. "You must drop this absurd case—or want-to-be case. There's no way you can reopen it after all this time. As you must know, Ms. Beringer used up her appeals. Years ago. It's old, dead business. If you continue, life could become very tough for you."

Simmons closed his lizard eyelids and opened them slowly.

She pushed on her knees to stop them bouncing. "That sounds like a threat," she whispered back. Her phone buzzed, but she ignored it. *Focus. Focus.*

He made a temple with his fingers and tapped the index fingers against one another. "Not a threat. Simply advice from a helpful mentor."

"I appreciate your counsel. But could you tell me, before I go, why you don't want this case reviewed?"

"With all due respect for Mozart, I find his quote about impertinence the opposite of what is proven in life. Supposedly, he said, 'Whoever is the most impertinent has the best chance to succeed.' He never parried with me. And I disdain impertinence, especially in young lawyers."

His lizard gaze unnerved her.

She tried to stare back with the same intensity but failed. "You've not answered my question," she said. "What are you worried about?"

Simmons stood and rapped his knuckles on his desk. "It's time for you to go, Ms. Raddell. Please consider my comments as fatherly advice. Thank you for your time."

Fatherly advice? She seethed at the insult.

As she brushed past the curious junior staffers in the office, Richard Li stood immobile by his desk, his eyes following her across the room. He looked like he knew she'd been reproached because he'd experienced the same.

"Emma! Where are you? The Gleesons waited half an hour and they're leaving. Where the hell are you?" Jennifer, the intern, sounded frantic on the voicemail left twenty minutes earlier, when Emma was with Simmons. Emma stumbled on the sidewalk outside her office as she returned the call.

"Jennifer, it's Emma. Just got your message. I'm five minutes from the office. I'm sorry I missed the meeting. Had another urgent one come up. Hold the Gleesons. I'll be right there."

Jennifer picked up. "Forget it. They left, livid. Where were you? Mr. Donohue's on the warpath too. You'd better get here."

She felt like jelly inside. Roy Donohue was famous for giving people no slack, and she'd messed up. *Will I even have a job after something like this?* She abandoned the intern, had neglected her own work, and now, missed a meeting with some of the firm's major clients. *And what excuse do I have? That I'd been summoned to the attorney general's office? That I was helping a person about to be executed?* She couldn't tell him that. He'd know that this impinged on her work; she'd definitely be out of a job.

On the other hand, maybe he had a heart. Maybe he'd find her efforts to help Aunt Victoria noble, righteous in their own way. *I could say I was doing some volunteer work to save lives. Maybe that would get him off my back? No…he'd want to know more.*

And even worse, she could hear Antigone. *"I told you so. I knew you were going to get caught."*

No, she couldn't admit anything about her aunt yet. She needed another excuse for Mr. Donohue, for the intern. *Maybe a medical problem. Something stress-related… My heart? My joints? Stomach?* Yes, that would do it for now. She'd say she'd gone for a checkup last week and they discovered something questionable. *Just a tiny lie?* That would hold them off for a few days. She'd deal with the Gleesons tomorrow. Tonight, she wanted to spend time with Grant, needed him to hold her and tell her it would be alright.

The next morning, Emma stayed in her office, scrambling to finish documents that she'd pushed aside.

Sherry stuck her head in about 10:30 a.m. "He's calmed down. You should be able to come out now." She scanned Emma's desk. "What's that? Doesn't look like one of the cases I gave you. Are you working on something else?"

Emma went rigid. *Does Sherry know something?*

"This is just background for the Warden case, the stalking one. Lots to consider." She placed her hand on top of the files Sherry had zeroed in on. *Guilty as charged. How did Sherry know to notice those?*

Sherry disappeared just as Antigone slipped in. Emma rolled her shoulders to release the tension.

"Was that Sherry? Watch out. You could get caught, you know, so be careful."

Little does she know. "By the way, have you mentioned my aunt's case to anyone?"

"God no. And I won't since I'd go down with you."

"Thanks. Until I decide how to move forward, I want it quiet." Her nerves felt jangled, but she controlled her voice. "Just so you know, I got a letter from Simmons, almost a summons."

"The AG? The one you dissed at the bar, right? You don't want him on your bad side so be polite, listen, and get the hell out of his way."

"Got it, but—"

"Don't get distracted. Your real work could suffer, maybe already has if Sherry is on to you." Antigone tapped a manicured nail on the desk. "Simmons. I'd have nothing to do with him if I were you."

"But I still want to bounce ideas off you, OK?"

"I'm more worried about the DA than you are."

"But if he wants me to drop this, there must be a reason. Did he do something wrong?"

"Heaven help you." Antigone raised her palms. "Beyond my pay grade."

Chapter 21

Saturday morning, May 6, 2006

Emma sat at a small round metal table in Killane, glass walls on one side of the room, and no wall clock.

Aunt Victoria, palms flat on the table, stared at Emma. "What sort of music do you like? Do you have a boyfriend? There's so much about you I want to know. Tell me."

Emma's arm muscles tensed. *Where'd this come from?*

"Uh, I'd like to know more about you too, but we don't have time right now. You know that, right?"

"I know, but it's just tempting to be normal with you."

Nice sentiment, but not now, alas.

"I asked you to think about a couple of things this week. Did you?"

Aunt Victoria laughed. "The first homework I've had in thirty years! I did what my teachers told me, and I do what you tell me. I wanted to continue with school but never had the chance. But please, two minutes? Tell me how you've been? I like asking someone that question. It's been too long."

Emma slowed down and smiled. "OK. Thanks for asking. Small talk." She was getting the hang of it. Exchanging small—and large—bits of information. It felt good, this small connection for a few minutes.

"Now. Sorry to be so driven, but it's the time crunch." She tapped her watch. "But all's good with me," she said. "Work is overwhelming, and I'm trying to save my aunt." She winked. "I've made progress on your case, and think we should go for a mistrial. But first, what do you know or remember about Mr. Ed Simmons? He was one of the prosecutors."

Aunt Victoria looked at the ceiling. "I remember the main man. O'Brien, maybe? There were others at his table. Simmons was one. All men, of course."

"Any specific memories? He would have been about thirty years old then. Tall. Very confident. He questioned you about the diaries. The other man did most of the rest of the questioning—of witnesses—but Simmons focused on the diaries."

Even though the meeting room lacked a clock, she had a built-in alarm for how much time she and Aunt Victoria had. She glanced again at her watch. *Right. Thirty-eight minutes left.*

"You seem antsy. Have you always been? Or just on this case?"

She shrugged. "Maybe always. I don't know."

"I see. You asked about Ed Simmons. Of course, I remember him…and his questions. Wicked man. He made me sound like a killer in my own words."

"Do you remember anything that seemed odd to you, before the trial, during?"

"I did remember something after you mentioned that. Before the trial, two people visited. One tried to get me to plead guilty and not go to trial."

She felt she'd stumbled over a crack in the sidewalk. *Why didn't I hear about this before?* "What? Who were they, and when did that happen?"

"One was a man who said he'd been a classmate in high school. Wally Newcomb. I did remember that name but didn't know why he would come to see me."

Aunt Victoria could drag out a story, like Mom did. *Just be patient.* But she couldn't.

"Aunt Victoria, please, a little faster. We have just over thirty minutes left."

"Sorry. Yes. Wally Newcomb. But it wasn't Wally. Some Hispanic man I didn't know, so I asked that he leave. I never heard what he wanted, why he had come. And, of course, being in jail, I couldn't very well follow up.… I wondered—"

"And the second person who came?"

"Ah. She wanted me to plead guilty to save the community a lot of anguish. She thought I was having an affair with her husband and wanted me out of the way."

The back of Emma's neck tightened.

"What? Who was that?"

"It doesn't matter since I refused. I was—I am—innocent and wanted a trial to prove that."

Aunt Victoria hugged herself and rocked forward and back to calm down. "Please don't make me think about this. Or talk about it."

"But this could force a mistrial. I must know who asked you to plead guilty." Sweat trickled down her back.

"Please forget I said anything." Aunt Victoria swept her arm across the table. "Nothing to talk about."

Emma's legs twitched, and she crossed them, hoping to calm the jitters. It didn't help.

"Please tell me. Of course, whatever you say is private. But I need to know." She stared at the table's center and counted to ten, then twenty. She feared that if she looked up, Aunt Victoria would dig in more. She glimpsed and saw they mirrored each other's actions: she'd tilted her head like Aunt Victoria and had clasped her hands, left thumb over right. She almost laughed but couldn't.

"Elisabeth." Aunt Victoria's voice lowered. "It was your mother."

Whack. "Mom? Mom asked you to plead guilty? Are you serious?"

She yearned to reach for Aunt Victoria's hands but couldn't risk being cut short on the visit. The guards watched always.

Emma continued, "I…I don't know what to say. But why? Why would Mom do such a thing?"

"She thought Jim and I were carrying on. Of course, we weren't. He was kind and helped me during the troubles. And she…she thought I'd damaged the children."

She's a monster. Every time she tried to get closer, Mom dropped a bombshell, or, now this, someone else did.

"Ten minutes," the guard said.

"I'm so sorry. And…I'm so angry. I'll have to talk to Mom—"

"NO! No, you mustn't. You said it would stay between us. Please, please don't say anything. It's water over the dam, or under, whatever that expression is. Please let it be. I know she wants to reconcile. That would make it impossible. I just want to spend time with you. And her if she'll have me."

When her dog Yoda died, Emma finally understood the physical manifestation of an aching heart. The same feeling crept up her chest. Barely breathing, she pushed herself to standing, staring at Aunt Victoria's downward-facing head, as though she was in prayer. The thirty-second speech was one of Aunt Victoria's longest, and she had to respect her client, even if her heart broke for her. But this could be the key to the mistrial plan, if only Aunt Victoria would let her use the information.

Chapter 22

Sunday evening, May 7, 2006

"Come in, come in. I've something to show you," Rupert held his screen door open. Still spinning from Aunt Victoria's revelations, Emma shoved those feelings down because Rupert had been so insistent. He deserved her open mind, so she plopped onto the couch.

"I've got more articles, eleven of them. From the start of the trial to the sentencing. Even the national press got wind."

He had fanned the news clippings and journal articles on his coffee table. The scent of leftover pasties drifted in.

"You found all of these without interns?" She grinned. "I've got one, and she's driving me crazy."

"Leverage. Use her—and me—for research. You do the thinking; we'll do the searching."

"I didn't think managing other people would be so hard. I have enough trouble managing myself. But let's get to it. What have you got?" She rubbed her hands together.

"You said jury tampering could be a mistrial reason, remember? I found a list of the original jurors in the public domain, although I suspect some wish their names weren't out there."

He tapped his fingers on the table. "The jury didn't reach a verdict easily. Rumors floated, even during the trial, that most of them decided quickly, but there must have been some holdouts, or at least one. It took five days for the verdict."

She flipped through the articles. *Five days?* That was glacier time in a murder trial. *What went on in that room? And what agony that must have been for Victoria.* "What do you make of it?"

"Not sure yet. The joy of research. I searched for anything odd about these jurors for a year after the trial ended."

"That's why you're the detective librarian."

"I found tidbits.... Got my Spidey sense a-tingling."

Come on, come on. He could be infuriatingly slow and deliberate. Maddening. But she channeled his advice, called on patience, and squelched her irritation. He was helping her, for God's sake, and for free.

"Usually, people are motivated by money or power," he said. "In a trial, there's no power to speak of for jurors, but money might come into play. In other words, could they be bribed?"

"Bribed? Are you joking?"

She felt off kilter. The idea that a juror had taken money to change her or his decision on a murder case was outrageous. *How could bribery happen in modern courtroom trials?* It seemed old fashioned, out of another century. They were playing with Aunt Victoria's life.

"Sorry. What were you saying about the jurors?"

He ran his finger down his list. "I wondered about three jurors. One was thirty-eight, left her job as a pediatric nurse after the trial and moved to a fancy resort town in Vermont. She bought an expensive condo...in early January 1983. The trial ended in November 1982, so a few months after the trial. She disappeared six months later."

"Disappeared? What's that mean?"

"I talked to some library mates in New England. They couldn't find her either. If she died, there should be a notice. Or maybe she took a new identity? If that's the case, we'll never find her. It just felt odd."

"That's one juror. She won't be useful. What about the others?"

He coughed. "The second juror was the sixty-year-old wife of a retired long-haul truck driver. They both died shortly after the trial."

"That's dramatic."

"In Switzerland." He arched his left eyebrow. "The daughter posted obits in the Surrey paper, but she lives in Seattle."

"Look at you—quite the detective."

"I have the time, the interest, and the internet. I used to think of myself as a librarian-detective at the university and I guess I still am."

She chortled. "Detect away, then. You've got jury and trial articles, but here's one on…gene mutations? Huh?"

"Tuck that to the side, for now." He rifled his notes. "Here we are. The daughter laid out the story. Her mom was the juror. Her dad had bone cancer. Later, liver cancer. Bad case."

She rubbed the back of her neck, trying to erase soreness and sadness. She knew that all families had pain. And now that she was trying to reconnect with her parents, especially with the scare of Dad having prostrate cancer, she couldn't imagine having to deal with their deaths.

"His disease wasn't life threatening at first. Maybe two years before it exploded. By then, they couldn't check it. He had a lot of pain. Remember, this was in the 1980s, and treatment was still primitive for some cancers." He pulled his fingers down his right cheek, wiped his hand across his lips, and took a long blink.

"Sounds like you know what you're talking about?"

The wrinkles under his eyes stood out. "I'm afraid so. My sister's started as uterine, but…it was so far along before they caught it that it presented as bone and then lung cancer. Gone in three months. That's why I came here for graduate school. Nothing to hold me there," he said with a catch in his throat.

"I'm sorry. That's fast. When was this?"

"The same time as all of this, early eighties."

Always more surprises from this man. She knew so little about him still. The smoke from his pipe filled her lungs. That was one form of smoke that she enjoyed, although it probably wasn't good for either of them, speaking of lung cancer.

"That article about gene mutation you just saw? It's about recent research that's able to find the genes related to uterine cancer, earlier. If only… But back to the task at hand." He moved to the edge of the couch. "The man's cancer spread suddenly, as the trial started. He wanted assisted suicide."

"Assisted suicide? Back then?" She squeezed her fists, trying to send blood to her cold fingers, but they felt stiff.

"I looked it up. Assisted suicide wasn't legal in Washington, of course, but it was in Europe. Switzerland and the Netherlands. They've allowed euthanasia for some time, starting in the 1940s."

"Incredible And awful to think someone could be in such pain..." *How would I react if Mom or Dad ever raised such an idea? How does someone reach a point where that is the only answer?* She hugged herself.

He exhaled slowly. "Two months after the trial, according to the daughter, her parents went to Switzerland. The wife, our juror, died in a freak car accident right after they arrived. Her dad went into depression and postponed treatment until his daughter could get there. Since they'd not told her why they were going to Switzerland, the euthanasia plan took her by surprise."

"She had no clue?" She sat on her hands, still trying to warm them. "I can't imagine."

"Yes, the poor woman was blindsided. Her mother died unexpectedly, and then she learned her dad wanted to die. He went ahead with the treatment. And there she was, two parents dead in a month."

How would I feel if both my parents died suddenly? She wished Shadrach was with her; she would dig her fingers into his fur and get some of his warmth.

"With all of his medical bills, I wondered how they'd managed the money to get to Switzerland, let alone the treatment at a hospice there."

"Where did it come from? Did she take a bribe?"

"Not so fast. The daughter said a high school friend of her father's—big-time entrepreneur—paid for their travel, the treatment, and after both parents died, he brought them back to the States. We'll have to accept the daughter's story about that."

She chewed on her inside cheek, trying to make sense of this. In spite of the ghastliness, the events rang true. The juror was desperate to help her husband get the treatment he wanted, even if it meant losing her life partner. But then for her to die first would have been awful for the husband. No need for bribes, just the funds to get there and be treated. A possible mistrial was losing steam.

"You mentioned three?"

"Yes, good memory. Money seemed tight and then wasn't for that one as well. Juror #8 was a thirty-five-year-old elementary school teacher with an ill daughter, who died in April 1983. She was eleven years old. Cystic fibrosis."

"Really? I thought people lived longer with that disease. Thirty? Thirty-five?"

"You could be a reference librarian," he said. "Yes. The average age of death has increased since the 1980s. It's too bad she was born back then. But, to her story. She was in ICU for two months before the juror and his wife brought her home. They had full-time in-home nursing care. As you can imagine, that's not cheap—then or now. She died five months after the trial ended."

Good God. Two months in ICU. Five months at home. And she'd heard that cystic fibrosis was a painful disease, with raking coughs, difficulty breathing. *How could that man and his wife watch it?* It had to be horrifically expensive to care for her. A teacher definitely would have needed the money.

"Is he still in town? Did you talk?"

"Slow down, now. He does live in town, and I did try to talk with him. But I got too scientific with him, and he shut me down."

Another dead end. Her shoulders drooped. "Is he our last hope?"

"Could be, but if he won't talk—"

"Give me his contact information. I'll try. If he doesn't talk, we're sunk."

Chapter 23

Thursday noon, May 11, 2006

"What can I get you?"

"Coffee. Black."

Coyle Adams, former Juror #8, shuffled to the counter of the Happy Perks Café. The wings of Adams's shoulder blades poked into his Mr.-Rodgers-red cardigan, which had black suede patches at the elbows and a moth hole above his right elbow. Wispy grey hair stuck out over his ears. His right shoulder tilted downward, emphasizing his limp, which he tempered with a cane.

Emma waved her hand through the rising steam. The shop murmured with satisfied customers, an occasional guffaw, and low "pure chill" music.

"Thank you for meeting me. I heard you didn't want to talk with my colleague, Rupert Singer, so I appreciate you giving me a few moments," Emma said.

"Your colleague was too scientific for me," Coyle replied. "I'm an elementary school history teacher so I didn't know what he was talking about. Something about genetics. I never figured out what he wanted." He toasted her with his mug.

"Well, we're doing an informal investigation about the case of Victoria Beringer. You were on her jury twenty-four years ago."

He sat back.

"She's due to be executed in late June, and she still claims she's innocent," Emma continued.

He waved his hand in front of his face. "Why would you help her? It's an old case. She was convicted. The jury decided that."

"I know, but…I learned recently…that she's my aunt. I knew nothing about her until about a month ago when my mother told me. Puts it in a different light for me."

He turned to face the bustle of the café.

She had hoped he'd see the importance of this case to her, but he acted almost defiant, like he wanted nothing to do with her. *Why?* She couldn't read him. Nothing new for her. Just another occasion for frustration.

She continued, "Her trial and conviction happened when I was a small child, and my parents never talked about it while I was growing up. So, I knew nothing. They were estranged from her, and I assumed she lived far away. I was shocked to learn about her."

Straight tight lips stiffened his face.

Is he sneering? Or scared? Or closing up?

"And now she wants help? In this final moment? A bit late, no?" he retorted.

She bit hard on her tongue to keep from blurting something she'd regret. "I agree. It's taken me a while to get used to the idea…but I do want to help. I was never close to my family but…this may bring us together." She stared at him. "I haven't said that out loud before. Feels funny. Sorry. But I guess I've got a wild hope."

Crash!

Shattered porcelain skittered past the booth, and Emma yelped as steaming coffee sloshed over her hand. Customers craned to ogle the poor barista, who apologized and ran to the kitchen for a mop.

Three minutes later, the chaos settled. Composed again, Emma leaned toward Adams. "About the case. We might have evidence for a mistrial. Failing that, perhaps a new trial."

"And how might you go about that?"

"There's scientific information that would help more with a new trial since it would be new evidence."

"Ah. What Mr. Singer talked about?"

"It's complicated. But some research suggests that unexplained deaths can come from several possibilities; one is genetics. My aunt's children might have had gene mutations and underlying medical conditions that led to their deaths. If that's true, it would help exonerate my aunt." She scanned the café and lowered her voice. "So, we're looking into that."

"This is over my head, as I said. But it sounds promising for your aunt."

"The research also might help parents going forward. Maybe save some future children."

"Encouraging indeed. But what's that got to do with me?"

She gulped her coffee and took a big breath. "We're also looking at a mistrial, which means we argue that something happened during the original trial that wasn't right, that might lead to tossing the results."

He took a beat and lifted his chin. "How so?"

"I guess the most far-fetched might be when a prosecutor has an affair with the defendant—"

"Gracious. How does that happen?"

"—or something like jury tampering."

Adams's face remained still.

"So, we're looking for anything unusual about the case."

Adams bounced his cane on the toe of his shoe.

"The press said the trial lasted three days. And the jury was out for five, a long time. Rumors spread that the jury vote wasn't unanimous, until right at the end. Obviously, that means at least one hold out, maybe more."

"That's true, but I can't go into specifics," he said. "As you must know."

She held her tongue. *Let him talk.* She studied her boring black coffee like it was the most interesting insect she'd ever seen.

"But you're right. It wasn't unanimous until the end."

"Mr. Singer found… He's a retired librarian from Westminster—"

Adams smiled. "I was there a long time ago."

"Maybe you overlapped? He started working there in 1982."

"After I finished, then."

"He retired ten years ago, but, once a reference librarian, always one." She chuckled. "He found articles about the trial and the jurors."

His eyes fluttered. "What do you mean?"

"If you…if one of the jurors believed my aunt was innocent, or at least not guilty, that person was likely right. If the gene mutation theory pans out, then we'll know for sure, but back then…maybe someone believed her story, that she did not kill those children. But if that juror was pressured to change his—or her—vote, that could mean a mistrial."

He traced the blue veins on his left wrist. When he looked up, he seemed resigned. "I don't know what you want from me. I won't tell you who the hold out was. I'm probably not allowed to. The vote changed; that's all there was to it."

She felt nauseous in anticipation of her next words. "I heard your wife died a few years ago."

His eyes shot up.

"As I said, Mr. Singer researched all of the jurors." She splayed her hands on the table. "I was sorry to hear about her. But I wondered…what she thought about the trial? You couldn't talk about it during the trial but…after?" She crossed her arms.

He hung his head, shook it, and closed his eyes. "It was a hard time."

Her head pounded. "I also learned that you had an ill child for several years. Even during the trial period…"

"I don't want to talk about this."

She felt mean to push him, but he was the only juror left. She was a lawyer, and lawyers pushed people.

"I'm sorry but I need to say this. And you need to hear it."

"Go ahead then." He rapped his knuckles against the edge of the table.

"It must have been terrible for you both to watch a mother on trial when she too had sick children. Awful to imagine what she went through."

She looked around the room again. The barista, who'd recovered from her debacle, laughed with a table of four men in their seventies, who looked like regulars.

Adams sighed. "It was horrific to have that trial in the middle of Alexandra's illness. She had cystic fibrosis. In those days, life expectancy was about ten years. She died five months after the trial. Eleven years old. So painful."

"Did you have more children?"

"We were heartbroken.... We couldn't risk that pain again."

Her stomach wrenched. *Is that what Mom and Dad felt when my brother died?*

The wrinkles on his red blotchy face deepened.

"It was like a bucket of love had simply drained out. Nothing was left." He put his hand over his eyes.

She gasped. *Is this what Mom and Dad felt?* She'd simply not understood. And hadn't tried.

"But...if you'd had another child, surely you'd have learned to love again?"

"One was enough," he said.

"I thought love expanded?"

"For us, it was fixed, and we used it up on one child. But we're far away from your questions." He reached under the table and withdrew his cane, which had a carved wooden duck head. "I've told you all I can. I need to get on with my day."

She wanted to scream 'no' to keep him at the table. On top of that, he'd shattered any self-worth she'd held onto when it came to trying to understand her parents and grief. *What a morning.*

Her hope for a mistrial seemed dead on arrival.

Chapter 24

Friday evening, May 12, 2006

Emma put the tenth page of her notes onto the copy machine at the local FedEx store. She glanced out of the window and saw Rupert on his way in. *Why would the good Scotsman be here?* When he saw her, he shuffled over at double speed.

"I struck out with the juror, just like you did," she said. "We may be at a dead end."

"Don't be discouraged. At least not yet. You know I collect odd dots when I have no idea how they might find their way together. And the science articles got me thinking. I asked a geneticist from Westminster University for help." He looked out of the window, and his face seemed to soften.

Emma tucked her notes into a plastic envelope. "I'm all ears."

He smiled. "She deciphered some research—in plain English…let me grab my notes…on a gene called CALM2. It's a family of genes, called 'calmodulin.' They can be inherited from the mother. The mutation leads to what's called 'cal-mo-du-lin-o-pathy.' I think that's right. It's a pathogenic gene mutation, meaning it can cause illness and it's rare."

"You've got the lingo. What's it mean? Should I make copies of your articles?"

He handed them over. "Ah. Here's what I learned." He flipped through his journalist notebook. "The children—your aunt's daughters, that is—might have had a gene mutation that may have caused sudden cardiac arrest, or what's called 'lethal arrythmia.' To be sure, a geneticist would test DNA in a lab to sequence the genomes."

"That means we'd need DNA samples, maybe from the autopsies? But did they take blood back then?"

"Apparently. Blood samples came from..." He flipped through his notebook. "...'neonatal screening heel prick blood cards.' That's a mouthful. They did that routinely in infants in the early 80s. Still do, I gather. So, with blood samples, they'd have DNA."

"Touché."

"It's rare for this gene mutation to be in a healthy woman in her late twenties, early thirties. But if Victoria had it, she could have passed it to the girls."

"But there's no evidence that Aunt Victoria had any heart problems—"

"Right-o. She may have had no 'cardiac abnormalities.' But it still could appear. And what's frightening—sixteen families around the world had children who died from this gene mutation last year. Without obvious abnormalities in the parents."

She hung her jaw.

"You heard me. And remember, this is recent research, so who knows if more died earlier because of the mutation. In most of the families, the carriers were the mothers...and they were asymptomatic. Like Victoria."

The FedEx door opened, and a wave of warm air gushed over her. She saw a four-year-old girl, dressed in a light blue smocked dress, walk by with what was probably her grandmother. She wondered what it felt like to have a grandmother. *Maybe I could offer that to my own child someday, with Mom as a grandmother?*

"Now, to the boys. You said they had breathing problems if I recall. Didn't one have seizures?"

"That's right. Their deaths weren't from heart problems; that we know."

"The same types of DNA tests and genome sequencing could help us understand their situation. A couple of studies talk about another CALM2 family gene mutation. It links to lethal epilepsy in mice."

Epilepsy in mice? How does that relate? Sometimes Rupert found the oddest dots to connect. But he'd been right more times than wrong.

"Studies on mice sound far farfetched. What about humans?"

"They haven't looked for it in humans yet, but Natalia's searching."

Natalia? Did I miss something? "Wait a sec.... How'd you find this geneticist?"

He blushed. "She's part of Westminster's genetics department, one of the best in the world. In fact, she helped build it. In our own backyard." He sat back, hands on his belly like a satisfied St. Nicolas, with a beard and dark green sweater to complete the ensemble.

"I see."

"Oh no you don't. I'm simply following the data. If it takes me to a woman of intelligence and charm, who am I to pass it by?"

"Good for you." She winked. "Now what were you saying?"

"She's talking with colleagues elsewhere, since they're more likely to talk to her than to us."

Could this be the start of a beautiful relationship? Gene mutation, a geneticist, and a Scottish librarian?

Chapter 25

Monday, May 15, 2006

"Want to go in?" Emma tilted her head toward the Ring-Around-the-Rosie Pub.

"I'd rather stay out here. Crowds don't suit me." Juror #8, Coyle Adams, slipped into the passenger seat of Emma's toy car. A green minivan cruised into the strip mall's parking lot and expelled four young women.

Maybe moms on a night out? "Fine with me. I can hear you out here." *And not worry about being hit on inside.* Adams had day-old whiskers and unbrushed hair. Rather than a dapper elementary school teacher, he looked like a lost uncle.

"Thanks for coming. I thought talking to you might help me move beyond that grief, for my child and my wife. For the life we never had with Alexandra."

"What would your wife say about you talking to me?"

A tiny smile started on his lips. "I miss her. She thought I should tell what happened, especially after our daughter died. She didn't want me to carry the secret forever."

Her sweating hands wiggled the skinny smooth wood steering wheel back and forth. *Don't break his train of thought.* "And what secret is that?"

He drew a tissue from his jacket pocket and unfolded it. "That I was the juror who turned. And I did it for my daughter."

Wham. She'd hoped for this, but still, shock draped over her hearing him admit it. Staring ahead, she sucked in a bouquet of pub beer and sausage.

He dabbed his eyes. "Sorry, give me a moment…"

She could hear Rupert's voice. *"Don't rush him."* The inside tingling up her arms felt like crawling ants.

"I couldn't believe that your aunt would harm her children." He cleared his throat. "You know that we had a sick child. She suffered awfully, but never could we imagine harming her or, as the prosecutor said, 'helping her to die.' I believed your aunt. Maybe I was naïve, but I couldn't imagine any mother doing something like that. So, I voted 'no.'"

She held her breath, letting silence do its magic. Three couples sauntered across the parking lot, arms slung over each other's shoulders, singing.

He chuckled. "That was a lot to dump on you. Sorry."

"What exactly happened, if you want to say?" She was so close. If she could only contain herself. Excitement mixed with dread that he would stop.

He took a huge inhale. "A man approached me after Day Three of deliberations. He promised if I changed my vote to guilty, so that all twelve of us were in sync, that one month after the trial finished, my wife and I would receive $50,000…for our daughter's care. In those days, that was enough to pay for a year's care, and the doctors didn't think she'd live that long."

She dug in her purse and handed over a travel pack of tissues. He'd have to repeat all of this for the record. He understood that, surely. But now, he needed to talk.

"And…the other jurors? Were they surprised you changed your mind?"

"Of course. On Day Four, I said I was thinking about changing but wanted to hear their arguments for a guilty verdict again. They were suspicious and queried me…I guess, interrogated me…on why I'd changed."

"And what'd you say?"

"That the diaries and the confession sounded stronger than I'd thought at first. I mean, when she wrote that she wanted to 'help little Brian to heaven,' you could interpret it either way.

But then, four kids...*four.* In *one* family? That couldn't have been an accident every single time."

The expert for the prosecution—a pediatrician from Australia—had said more than three deaths, or maybe even two, in a single family couldn't be a coincidence or an accident. That statement must have stuck in the jury's heads. It stayed with her too.

He gripped the door handle. "I'd also read somewhere, about a disease that some mothers have—pretending their child is sick to get sympathy and attention."

She and Rupert had talked about Munchausen's by proxy but dismissed it, since Aunt Victoria hadn't seemed to seek sympathy, only understanding.

"I think it is called Munchausen's. It didn't sound like she and her husband were getting along, so maybe she felt sorry for herself? That's what I told the others. They bought it."

"So, on Day Five, you made it official and voted 'guilty.'"

"Right. And, sure enough, a month after the trial ended, we had our money."

Despite the windows being open, the air inside the car felt stifling. Her back was wet. *From the heat of the late spring evening or the confession?* She squirmed out of her long-sleeved jacket and tossed it onto the jump seat. Part of her was disappointed that this man she'd almost held as a hero, one who could save her case and her aunt, had done something as despicable as take a bribe.

"What about the person who approached you?" she continued.

"He wore a suit, was medium height, Hispanic. He waited for me in the parking garage. It wasn't a threat, more like a compassionate offer of help."

"And you and your wife lived with this for...twenty-some years?" *Aunt Victoria has been wasting in prison for that long....*

Adams scrunched his face.

"Thank you for telling me all of this. Now, you'll need...to state this on the record. For us to use it. You realize that, right? To help my aunt."

His head lurched. "No! I won't talk about it anymore. I wanted to get this off my chest, and you were the right person to tell. I won't carry it further."

He can't say all of this and then walk away from it. What is he doing? "Hold on. You're the foundation of a mistrial, a way to get my aunt out—"

"I'm sorry, but no. This was a confessional. I needed to tell someone but I'm not going public."

She caved into her seat, crushed. "I…I don't know what to say."

"If you say anything, I'll deny it."

What a complete loss. "Better not to have told me at all."

Crossing his arms, he sucked in his cheeks. "What's in it for me if I talk? I'd go to jail, right?"

"For God's sake. You took money to help your child and sent an innocent woman to prison. Doing this, you'd right a wrong."

"What about the other jurors who convicted her? They couldn't all be wrong?"

"But…you changed your vote for an illegal action."

No head rest in these old cars, so she lay her head back on the seat and looked straight at the car ceiling, eight inches from her face. Thumping music from the pub had earlier felt upbeat but now oppressed her. Her mouth gaped, and she snapped it closed. Salty tears seeped from her eyes. *How will I tell Aunt Victoria? Mom? Rupert?*

She'd put all of her eggs—her hopes—in this mistrial basket, and the man had just wanted a therapist.

What other options do we have? Rupert and Natalia had some inkling of gene mutations, but that sounded far-fetched, too blurry to be a clear path. She needed to get this man out of her car so she could get back to work.

He shifted in the seat. "Maybe you're right…." he whispered.

She didn't move. Or more truthfully, she was afraid to move.

"Maybe…I should do this. I'm the only one left. Daughter, wife, both gone. Even if I went to jail, I have nothing to live for.

Maybe this could be my one good deed. . . ." He began weeping, gulping in air, but no sound emerged.

She felt his hand on her forearm, shaking her as though she was sleeping. She lifted her head as he dragged his fingers across his face, wiping tears. He straightened as she sat up.

"I'll do it."

Lifted by Adams's change of heart, she knew it was time to go to Donohue and argue for the mistrial and for the firm to take the lead. She needed to prep for a few hours in the office that night. She walked through firm's parking garage at the end of the evening and saw a number on her phone that looked familiar but she couldn't place it.

"Emma Raddell speaking."

"Ms. Raddell. Ed Simmons."

She froze.

"Mr. Simmons. How can I help you?"

"Thank you for answering. This will be quick. I hear that you're still looking into that old case, the Beringer case. You need to leave that alone."

"You've told me that before and yet you've never told me why to leave it?"

"Just take my word for it. I'll let your boss know of your adventure if you don't stop. He won't be happy that you're shirking your firm's work."

Her pulse quickened as she stopped in the middle of the shadowy parking garage. She forced a laugh, more to boost her confidence than to give him any indication how she felt.

"Thank you again for the fatherly advice. That seems to be a hallmark of how you and I interact. But I don't need it." She didn't do snippy especially well, but she tried.

"Watch your tone. Don't stick your nose into places it doesn't belong. I told you I have influence on careers in this town. I can make or break people." He hung up.

She stubbed her toe and tripped. Her briefcase went in one direction, her purse another as she scraped her palms and her nose in the fall. *I've already stuck my nose into a place it shouldn't have been, looks like. So much for his advice.*

Chapter 26

Wednesday morning, May 17, 2006

At 10:58 a.m., Emma followed the Vulture to Roy Donohue's office. She was 20 percent excited and 80 percent nervous about asking for something she probably shouldn't. But if she failed, Aunt Victoria's life would be gone.

Sherry handed a coffee mug to Roy Donohue and lifted an eyebrow at Emma on her way out.

Roy Donohue, senior partner for Ivins, MacFarlane and Donohue resembled a pirate with his black eye patch. She admired his creativity in finding colorful patches: glittery green for the holidays, orange for Halloween. They'd had little interaction—just the additional work on a stalking case—but she'd heard he was a stand-up guy.

"Thanks for coming in, Emma. Sorry we've not had much time together. Hope you're doing well? Getting into that stalking case?" His teeth gleamed. "But that's not why you're here, I gather?"

"No, thanks, Mr. Donohue...."

"Oh, please, call me Roy."

"Roy." She gave a half-smile. "Thank you for letting me visit. I have a proposal you may find interesting."

"Already? Don't we keep you busy enough?"

"Oh, sure. But this is something unexpected. Could make a big splash for the firm and help a lot of people."

"Ahhh." Sunshine drifted through the mesh back of his Aeron chair. "I'm listening, but get to the point. We have fifteen minutes. You know how lawyers bill."

“Do you remember the case…long time ago, of Victoria Beringer? Convicted over twenty years ago of killing her four children? They thought at the time, at least for the first child, that it was SIDS—”

“Of course. The type of case that all defense attorneys want a piece of at some point in their careers.” He stopped, caught in a memory. “The prosecutor was brutal. I think it was…Sam O’Brien. Old battle axe.”

She squirmed, counting down the minutes in her head. She had a hard enough time focusing and now she had to get him to do it too.

“But what if it wasn’t SIDS that killed those kids? Or what if it wasn’t murder?”

He put his arms on his desk, leaning toward her. “What’re you trying to say?”

She hesitated. “Some recent research makes the argument that a gene mutation might be behind some cases of unexplained deaths in children so young.”

He fixed his eye on her, which disconcerted her. “I don’t get what you’re telling me or why.”

She willed herself to remain calm. “I’m saying that the case deserves another look. That maybe some new evidence could put the conviction into question.”

“Speculation, sounds like,” he said.

“But if you’ll let me explain—”

“I remember the conviction was solid.”

She looked out of his east-facing window that spilled in morning light. Her north-facing, high-window office felt sterile while this one yelled positivity. But she felt anything but positive now.

“Well, maybe. You’re right that the prosecutor was Sam O’Brien. His assistant was Ed Simmons, who we all know. He used Victoria Beringer’s diaries as circumstantial evidence and claimed that she confessed in them. But what if—”

Roy held up his hand. "Whoa, you have a lot of 'what ifs' and 'maybes' in there. We don't pursue cases based on speculation. And it's a done deal, from twenty-five years ago."

Twenty-four years ago, but who's counting?

"But what if a judge was willing to review, to reopen it? Turning over a case like that could be huge for the firm. Don't you think?"

"What evidence do you have beyond wishing to boost your own reputation?"

Heat flooded her face. She wanted to put her hands on her cheeks to cool down but dared not show weakness. *Does he think I'm grubbing for my own glory? Then again, isn't that what young lawyers are taught to do?*

Roy peeked at his watch. "Eleven minutes."

Embarrassed, she noticed people outside of the glass office walls looking in at them. Her breath caught in her throat. "I see two angles on this case. First, there's recent scientific research that a certain gene mutation may link to heart attacks, especially in children. Ms. Beringer's two girls died from heart attacks."

"I'm still not following. You're saying the case should be retried? Reopened? Using science research? You'll have to speak English if you want me to understand you. And where'd you get this information?"

"A colleague who used to be the reference librarian for Westminster found one of the key genetics researchers at the university."

"So…some research that may link deaths to a gene mutation. Flimsy."

She despised and envied him at the same time: he could summarize what she'd been trying to say with such dispatch but he dismissed it just as fast. She had to get better at the former, she knew, but at this moment, she had to get beyond the dismissal.

"But the research was done by twenty-seven scientists, in seven different countries," she said. "They collected data from four of those countries—"

"Spare me the details. Get to the facts."

"—It's all over. Legal cases… Tried in Australia, U.K.—" She sounded shrill in her head and assumed he picked it up as well. *Not a good look or sound.* She was slipping in the mud.

"Tough to argue," he said. "We don't commonly draw upon cases from outside the U.S."

She looked at the bowling trophy on his desk. *Is that a joke? He doesn't look like a bowler, but what do I know?* And now her mind was scattered, wandering. She was not doing what she'd set out to do.

"Seventy-four scientists sent a letter supporting this research. They said the case should be reviewed."

He scooched back in his chair and studied the ceiling. "What you argue wouldn't stand up. If I recall, during the trial there was a question about how one family could have four children die unexpectedly…and so suddenly? To the expert who testified, it seemed like too many deaths in a single family. I don't remember my Oscar Wilde precisely, but the expert used *The Importance of Being Earnest*, where Wilde said something like 'to lose one parent is a misfortune but to lose both looks like carelessness.' It was funny in the play. And the expert used the same logic: for four children to die in one family was preposterous. And the jury and most of us watching remember. So that says the prosecutor did a good job."

She slid forward on her chair. "It was a good line. But there's more. Maybe something that could mean a mistrial. I talked with a juror from the case who claims the prosecutor's office bribed him."

Roy slammed his tilting chair straight up. His single eye glared at her.

"Mistrial? Dangerous—outrageous—assertion. You could get in real trouble for peddling something like that."

The microseconds between her heartbeats shrank. Once again, she noticed lurkers outside the office. Sherry waved at Roy, who stepped to the door. They whispered for a minute.

"Go ahead. Finish up," he said. "You're on the edge, though."

"I talked to the juror last night. He's willing to go on the record." She brushed her hair stubs behind her ears. "He said he was offered money to change his vote to guilty. Sure enough, after the trial, he and his wife received money to help their ill child."

Roy shook his head. "Speculative, nothing firm, nothing that directly challenges the case. Even this juror. From twenty-five years ago, hard to prove. Maybe the juror has a grudge for some reason. Who knows. Far too tentative. And the science. You know science is never 100 percent sure on anything. Relatively new research, sounds like. What do we know about it?"

"But—" She broke in.

Roy pointed a finger at her. "Let me speak. Assuming a judge was willing to review it, assuming the firm took it on, and assuming the firm took on the case…again, a lot of presumptions there, why are you so interested anyway?"

She counted to five before responding and lowered her chin, like an elephant about to attack. She'd read that elephants used ear flapping and loud honking to threaten but they meant business when they became quiet, lowered their heads, and tucked their trunks. Then an attack was eminent. She channeled that strength.

"Victoria Beringer is my aunt. She's the one who was convicted and now she's about to be executed, end of June."

His palm banged the desk again. "Oh my God. It's *personal*? Bad reason to consider a case. You lose that logical brain power when emotions take over."

"I know that. That's why *you* should take it on, carry it forward." Words tumbled out, too fast. "I'll stay in the background, do whatever grunt work you need, give you my notes—"

"And who pays for all of this?"

His voice was barely over a murmur, forcing her to lean in to hear him. She'd heard about veins popping out when people lost control. Watching him, she had a front row seat.

"I…I thought pro bono? Because of the great publicity for the firm?"

Roy placed a fist on the open law book in the center of his desk, tightened his jaw muscles, and slowly unbuttoned his left cuff to roll up his sleeve.

"Absolutely not. I'm stunned…that you'd even ask me. This whole thing has too many red lights. First, you're a new attorney in our firm. That you even thought you could take this on while you've got a job to do smacks of bad judgement. Right now, do your work and let nothing else distract you."

She opened her mouth, but he held up his hand again and shook his head.

"Second, you're overstepping the bounds of what the firm does. We do not do pro bono cases, and certainly not for a personal vendetta. You should know better. We are here to make money, not to be bleeding hearts."

She licked her lips and bit the insides of her cheeks. He was on a roll.

"You're making me question why we hired you. So, the answer is no, obviously. I don't want to hear about this anymore, don't want to hear that you're working on it, and don't want to have any complaints about you not getting your work done. Are we clear?"

Mortified that the office staff had watched this discussion through the glass, she struggled to stand without wobbling. Sweat pooled in her armpits and trickled along the back of her neck as she closed his office door.

Not even Mom had spoken in such harsh terms. But she knew she was right, even if Donohue couldn't see it, with only one eye. And she was on her own.

Chapter 27

Thursday evening, May 18, 2006

Grant, Rupert, and Emma sank into plastic booths at Marvin's Good Time Diner, which served breakfast all day.

"I bombed with my boss on the idea of a mistrial. At least Round One. But Grant might have information for us."

Rupert smiled. "Well, well. Emma tells me you've been doing some sleuthing yourself. What's going on?"

Grant could perform music in front of a raucous crowd but squirmed in front of the two of them. "Quick b-background. I did a business/law program. In five years, you could get a bachelor's in b-business, or accounting in my case, and a law degree. I did the business part and a year of law school before I realized I'm too stiff for either profession. I can't talk in front of people easily, but I can p-play music because the focus is on the music, not me. Anyway, I did accounting, for several years. Mostly forensic accounting. Good money."

"Bless your heart, my boy," said Rupert. "And that comes into play for this case how?"

Grant tossed her a look.

She felt exasperation creeping in. *Why are people so slow in telling their stories?*

"Take your time," Rupert said, winking at her.

"Thanks. I worked as an accountant for five years and then at Amazon for three. I made a b-boatload of money, but again, accounting wasn't my thing. I started in the music scene…"

Her legs jiggled.

"After Amazon, I moved here and worked for the county. In the process, I made some contacts in the accounting and county government world."

Rupert turned to her. "Please give him a chance."

"I called three of my contacts from the old days to see if there were any whispers about Simmons. Two refused to talk. These are guys with their ears to the g-ground, and they dodged my questions. Both are married with kids, though, so they'd be easy to bully with threats of losing their jobs, if that's what happened. But I wondered what could cause such fear?"

Janice, in a white uniform and full pink apron, dropped the heavy pottery plates in front of them, eggs and bacon, Eggs Benedict, and eggs and grits. "Hot plates."

Emma leaned into her plate, whiffing the bacon.

Grant continued, "The third guy did talk. He'd heard that Simmons kept a g-group of fix-it guys who helped convince people to do things. Apparently, once, or twice, Simmons coerced a juror into changing a vote. All rumor. Nothing confirmed."

She held her breath. *It's one thing to have doubts and suspicions, but could this lead anywhere?* "Jury tampering." She put a fist on the table. "That's what the juror said. Corroboration. This could be the reason Simmons wants me to stop."

"There's more." Grant spun the straw in his iced tea to mix up the lemon and fake sugar.

"Pray tell. What more could you have?" Rupert said.

"My buddy knew a little…again, rumor…of Simmons's background. He grew up in a family business—machine parts for farm equipment—and he may have used the family business as a b-bank account for himself. He borrowed from the firm, maybe every couple of years, and usually repaid within a year."

God. What would this mean if it is true? But its flaws might drown it. How can I let him down easily?

"Let's not get ahead of ourselves." Rupert's voice lowered.

"Right," she said. "Good effort, Grant."

He looked at her like a lost puppy. "But you have doubts?"

"Let's think this through. What you did was noble, but it probably won't get us where we need to be. How would a prosecutor rip this up? You went to law school, so you can imagine, right?"

Grant bowed. "I guess I c-could."

"You talk about rumors and 'friends' who did you a favor, but where's the solid evidence that Simmons did any of this? So, we're still in the dark, basically."

Grant's face fell. "Yeah, you're right. I wanted to find something, anything, to help you, but you're right. It's hearsay. Are we sunk?"

She shook her head.

"Sunk. With just forty days to go. Now what?"

Chapter 28

Friday afternoon, May 19, 2006

At 3:00 p.m., Emma pushed back from her desk in her jail-cell office and stretched, glad she'd completed the brief she'd focused on for the last two days. She needed to get back into Donohue's good graces, and this would do it. And she could justify working on Aunt Victoria's case tonight.

Her phone rang.

"We're waiting. Where are you?" Interns should never screech, but Jennifer used that as her default gear. Everything was an emergency.

"The Gleesons are here early, and they're upset by the documents you sent. Some pages are missing."

As promised, Emma had finished the testimonial documents for the Gleesons by the end of last Tuesday. Six months earlier, she had handled their teenage daughter's DUI case for them, got her off with a fine and no jail time. They'd been so grateful they had asked for her help with other parts of their lives, so she'd stepped up. And they had been happy. Until now.

On Tuesday afternoon, she had passed the documents to Jess, another intern, to deliver by Thursday morning. When she checked with him Thursday noon, he swore the documents were with Joyce, the senior partner, and that the Gleesons were due in on Friday.

But something had gone terribly wrong. She phoned Jess to ask once again what he'd done with the documents.

"I turned them over, like you asked."

"Did you go through them? Was anything out of place?"

"Well, two pages were reversed, so I fixed them before making the copies. But nothing else."

She flipped through the document. Twenty-three pages, all there. So, what had happened with the originals? She scurried to the conference and found the couple, along with Joyce, a senior associate who looked like a micro-version of Sherry in her matchy-matchy suits and brooch. *Who wears brooches these days, for heaven's sake?* Roy sat off to the side, glowering.

The Gleesons, owners of the convenience store franchise that spread throughout Washington, Montana, and Wyoming, contrasted with Joyce in their rugged leather jackets and Western hats. They had matching apple cheeks and silver belt buckles. She was jolly, he was a terror, and together they played opposite roles in any negotiation. She came across as the good cop but wasn't. He came across initially as the bad cop but in the end gave up more than the other side expected. But today, they were on a parallel warpath.

"A second slip up," Lila Gleeson said. "We wanted these documents weeks ago, and Ms. Raddell didn't perform."

Roy Donohue waited for her to stop ranting. "I'm sorry. No excuses, but I think Emma has had some medical issues. We're trying to sort that out."

"That's too bad. Maybe we jumped the gun." Harry Gleeson fingered his hat rim. "Don't want to get her into trouble."

"Like hell we don't," his wife said. "If this is delayed anymore, we miss out on all those tax advantages."

"Perhaps Emma can explain what's happened." Roy gestured in her direction. His voice was even colder than when they had last talked.

Sharp pangs in Emma's stomach made her want to double over. "I'm so sorry, Mr. and Mrs. Gleeson. I finished the documents on Tuesday, as promised. Somehow, two pages went missing between then and now. I have a copy of the missing pages."

"But we need the original."

"Which we can create and get the signatures again. No problem."

Lila Gleeson tapped a long navy-blue fingernail on the table. "If you're under the weather, I'm sorry about that. But, young lady, that should never interfere with your work. In fifty years, I never let being a touch ill harm my work and I had a business and five children to raise. Toughen up."

Emma quashed her desire to let the woman have it. She heard Rupert's voice in her head and lowered her shoulders from her ears.

"Thank you for the advice, Mrs. Gleeson." She hoped she didn't sound as snarky as she felt, but Donohue's quick head turn proved she'd missed the mark.

He stood to end the meeting. When the Gleesons left, he closed the door and turned on Emma. "Once again, you've created a mess. Insulting some of our biggest clients is unacceptable. I had hoped after our talk, you'd focus more on your firm work. I made it clear that you are not to pursue side gigs, not your aunt's case or others, without my or one of the partner's permission."

She went slack. No support from him, from the firm, and yet, she had to try to help her family. She was committed, even if she couldn't let anyone else know.

That evening, Emma made chicken soup and wallowed in her fast-slipping world. When the phone rang, she considered letting it go to voicemail, but the phone said, "Police Department."

"Is this Ms. Raddell? This is Officer Stanton from the Surrey Police Department."

Probably one of my DUI clients or a parking ticket?

"Do you know a Mr. Coyle Adams?"

"I do. Why?"

"Do you know his next of kin?"

She grabbed the edge of the sink. "I'm not certain he has any. His wife and child are both deceased. What's this about?"

"Is anyone with you right now, ma'am?"

"No. What's going on?"

"I'm sorry about this. We found your business card in his wallet and thought you might be his attorney. I'm sorry to tell you that he was in a car accident two hours ago. His car went off Turnberry Road by the river. It's totaled. And Mr. Adams is dead. We think…it was suicide."

Chapter 29

Saturday, May 20, 2006

Emma woke to Shadrach nuzzling her. 6:00 a.m. She'd spent the night replaying Coyle Adam's confession and the police call and finally got to sleep about 3:00 a.m. She forced herself out of bed to take Shadrach out, feeling sluggish—*from the late night or my queasy stomach?*

"He never quits, does he?" Grant sauntered up to Emma in the dog park.

"Ah, Mountain Man. You're up early?"

"You look like a wreck. Are you missing me?"

She shrugged. "Some bad news last night, and I didn't sleep. What's your excuse?"

"I've got a gig tonight so wanted to get Harriet out since she'll be cooped up later."

Ten minutes of chat passed before Shadrach lumbered toward her. He sat, sucking fast short breaths. Suddenly, he collapsed, and his limbs shook.

Emma shrieked and dropped to the ground. "My God. What's happening? Come on, Shad. Come on, boy." Her voice quaked. The whites around Shadrach's irises got bigger, and he looked terrified, pleading for her to do something. She rubbed his shaking legs. "Calm down. You're OK."

But he wasn't. Shadrach couldn't get his breath. She felt helpless.

"Oh my God!" She rubbed his belly. "What's wrong? Shadrach? What's going on with you?"

Grant squatted.

"Has this happened before?"

"Never. I've never seen him like this. His eyes are rolling. Oh God, he's slipping."

Grant scooped up Shad. "Might be a seizure. Let's get to the vet. Grab Harriet."

She climbed into the back seat of his Jeep and sat with Shadrach's head on her lap.

"Shadrach, buddy, please hold on." She stared at the back of Grant's head. "I shouldn't have taken my eyes off of him." Her mind raced through the minutes in the park. She'd talked to Grant, they'd laughed, she lost track of how many times she'd thrown the ball. And then, boom.

"Hang in there," Grant shouted from the front seat. "Going as fast as I can."

"He's fading!" She blamed herself. Shad was such a great companion; he had to come through this. His legs had stopped shaking, but he didn't seem able to move. She caressed his head, but he didn't react. "Oh, my God."

At the High Desert Veterinary Clinic, Grant rushed Shadrach inside. A vet tech yanked open an exam room door and rammed the group in. Dr. Hanson laid his hands all over Shadrach, who dry heaved three times in two minutes.

"Did he eat anything new?"

Emma shook her head and stroked Shadrach's ear. "He was fine until twenty minutes ago when he collapsed in the dog park. My fault. I let him out of my sight."

She felt gob smacked. *A disaster of a week and now this?* She pleaded to the dog higher being if there was one.

"Don't beat yourself up," Dr. Hanson said. "Dogs get into mischief and, I have to tell you, those dog parks can be the worst. There's been poisoned meat in the bushes lately." He looked at Grant. "Was yours there too?"

"Yeah, but Harriet doesn't wander."

"Let's keep him overnight," Dr. Hanson said. "Call me in the morning."

Emma leaned over Shadrach. "Please don't be scared, buddy. They'll take good care of you." She looked into his eyes. "I don't think he believes me."

"I'm sure he does. We'll monitor him. Please trust me."

When Grant and Emma clambered into his old Jeep, Harriet sprang from the back seat to the front, nuzzled Emma for a moment, checked on Grant, and was snoring in under a minute. The drizzle had turned to rain, sounding like pellets on the roof.

Emma's emotions fluctuated from jealousy that Harriet jumped around like normal to gratitude that at least one dog was healthy. Harriet always seemed so docile, while Shad was lively, curious. *Am I a bad dog parent, letting him get into danger? Shadrach will be OK. He has to be.*

"What do you suppose is wrong?" she asked Grant. "His comment about poison was horrifying."

Grant gripped the steering wheel and put his key in the ignition but didn't turn it. "I'm sure he'll be OK. But what's with you? You look like you've been hit by a truck, and it's not just Shadrach, is it?"

How can he read me like that? In the middle of a crisis? Do I look that bad? Mountain Man kept surprising her.

"I can't believe how bad this week is," she said.

"Hit me."

"I blew it with some important clients—some pages went missing from their documents. Now I'm paranoid that someone's trying to sabotage me."

"That's strong. Who—and why—would someone do that?"

"No idea. And I think the partner doesn't like me."

"It can't be that b-bad."

"You've forgotten the politics of big organizations."

He pulled the key out and faced her. "And I don't miss it. So, what else?"

"I told you that Roy Donohue, the partner, refused to take on the mistrial. Then came the client flub up yesterday, and that didn't help. I thought he'd fire me. To be honest, he still could."

Grant reached to the back of her neck and massaged it.

She moaned and leaned into it. "Had no idea I was this tense. Thank you."

He smiled. "Anytime. I'm sorry you're going through this."

"I have to tell you the rest."

"Oh man, there's more?"

Her brain sorted through her next comments. She needed to be clear, so he understood how devastating this was. She reached her hand back to her neck, squeezing his hand. "Even though everyone tells me to drop this case, I can't give up. I just can't. It's only thirty-eight days till the execution. She needs me. And I now see…I need the family. But I'm on my own. No support from the firm on this—no interns, no copy machine, and…"

She put a fist against her lips.

"What?"

Her head buzzed. "I'm still in shock."

"Tell me, for God's sake. Did something happen to Rupert?" He removed his hand from her neck and turned to face her full on.

"No. Not Rupert." She looked at the peonies in the vet clinic's yard. *How could so much beauty exist in a world of such sadness?* She slumped, unable to lift her hand to brush the hair out of her eyes.

"I feel completely spent. No energy. All of this work stuff, and now Shadrach." She leaned her head against the window and closed her eyes. "I just want to sleep."

"EM! Look at me!" He grabbed her forearm. "What's going on? If we know what you're d-dealing with, we can figure it out. I've got your back, so let me help. But you've got to tell me. We're not leaving till you do."

She panted, like Shadrach had, and felt she couldn't get a full breath. "I'm trying. Sorry. The police called last night. The juror…my juror who was going to testify and give us the mistrial… He took a bribe and was willing to admit it. That juror."

"OK. Yeah, the possible bribe? Can you use that information I found out about Simmons? To nail him?"

She'd love to nail Simmons, to put his head on a stick. But Grant's search for information wouldn't help now. Nothing would help the mistrial now.

She gripped the door handle and doubled over, from cramps. She sat back up and stared through the blurry windshield. "The juror. He was in a car accident. He's dead."

Grant's head jerked toward her. "What the—"

"No brake marks, so it could be suicide. My card was in his wallet. Did I make him do it? By admitting what he did? And now Shadrach? I feel like a jinx."

"Damn. I hate to be so crass, but…" He lowered his voice. "What's it mean for the mistrial?"

"God, Grant!" She threw her head back. "Don't be so naïve. It means there is no mistrial. There is no case. There is no hope."

Harriet jumped to the front seat and landed on Emma's lap. She brushed her hands through the scruffy fur.

"So you really can't use any of what I found? About his likely bribing? His threats?"

"Nope. I'm sorry you wasted your time on it. But without a juror, there's no mistrial."

Two cars roared past them on the street, and thunder blasted. They waited for the noises to pass. Harriet swished her head back and forth between them.

Emma's phone buzzed. "The vet clinic. News already?"

She put the phone on speaker mode.

"Emma Raddell speaking. Grant's here too."

"It's Dr. Hanson. I'm so sorry, but Shadrach had another seizure. His heart stopped for a minute. He's slipping. If you want to see him, come back now."

The phone skittered to the floor mat and disappeared under her seat. Dr. Hanson's tinny voice continued. Grant swooped down and snatched up the phone.

"We're outside your office. We'll be right in," he said.

Shadrach lay on a shiny metal table, panting hard.

The smell of ammonia and antiseptics mixed with damp dog fur from a large Newfoundland and a Golden Retriever in the lobby.

"He had another seizure, hard one," Dr. Hanson said. "I don't think it will be long now."

Emma stumbled next to the table, and Grant grabbed her.

"But what…what happened?" Her voice was husky.

"It definitely was something he ate. He acts like he ate some cyanide, straight."

Emma screamed inside her head. *Poor baby.* Shadrach's watery eyes opened, and he looked happy to see her. "So sorry, buddy. I'm so sorry to let you down. My fault—"

"Please, Emma. It wasn't your fault," Grant said.

Dr. Hanson put his hand on her shoulder. "Grant's right. Not your doing. I've seen too many dogs in the last few weeks like this. They've got to find the awful person doing it. But please, don't put this on yourself."

"What happens now?" She held back tears, barely.

"If it is the end, this normally takes about forty-five minutes, if he goes on his own. So, you might consider helping him on his way."

She shuddered at the words, so similar to Aunt Victoria's diary entry. But she had to focus. For all of the love Shad had given her, asking nothing in return, the least she could do was let him go in a peaceful manner. But what a decision. Along with work problems, the double whammy of losing two dogs so close together slammed her. She felt like giving up. But Shadrach wouldn't approve.

"Of course, it's your call," Hansen said. "I can't say it's over; some dogs do come back. So, let's hold some hope for a while."

"Give me a few," she said, turning back to the dog.

Hanson stepped out of the tiny room, and Grant moved aside to give Emma space.

She rubbed Shadrach's nose and scratched his rump. She thought of him leaping for the Frisbee and snuggling with her at the end of long days. He deserved better, and she wished she'd been able to give it. She would never take a dog to the dog park again.

Shadrach licked her fingers.

"Thank you, for being with me. You've been a great friend." Her chest hurt from missing Shadrach already.

Grant reached for her. "Come here. I've got you." She sank into his hug, smelling his shampoo. This mountain man came through for her over and over. "You can count on me."

She heard a whimper and a thud. Shadrach's tail beat the metal gurney with rhythmic plop-plop-plops. He tilted his head upward and looked for her.

"Dr. Hansen! Dr. Hansen! Is he reviving?" She yanked open the tiny exam room door to let him in.

Hansen leaned over Shadrach, lifted his eyelids, felt around his torso. He leaned back against the cabinet and watched the dog's chest move up and down. "We'll watch him, but I'm optimistic. I think he might be beating the odds." He stepped forward again, leaned down to listen to Shadrach's heart, and stroked him. "Yes. Yes, I'd say it looks like he's coming back. He's a fighter."

"Harriet will be relieved," Grant said. "Me too."

Chapter 30

Sunday afternoon, May 27, 2006

"I'm anxious to hear about the case," Mom had said when Emma phoned to say she'd come to Snowville over the weekend. "And I've got something to tell you too."

After Emma's wretched week, dealing with clients who wanted to tear her apart, a dead juror, and a nearly gone dog, the last thing she needed was Mom drama. She wanted comfort from her.

Snowville's late May air hung still and humid, a prelude to grueling summer heat. When she was a child, Dad had insisted they didn't need air conditioning.

"It never gets that hot," he'd said.

But humid summer days over 95 degrees Fahrenheit clogged her nose, and as she arrived at her parents', familiar congestion filled her head.

In the kitchen, a tray with two glasses sat on the counter. She braced. *Not another heavy, life-changing conversation. A month ago, it was an unknown aunt in prison. Now what?*

They settled into backyard lawn chairs, with a tattered umbrella and wrought iron table next to them. Newly mowed grass scent filled what little air entered her stuffed nose.

Sitting in those chairs rekindled memories of hours of silence in the house, on the porch, and in the backyard. Whenever she returned from school, bursting with news of learning to read, completing a geometry proof, or mastering a dance step, her enthusiasm melted when she barged through the door and ran head on into the reticent melancholy of the house.

"What's been going on?"

"Oh, Mom, I've had a hell of a week."

"I'm sorry. What's happened? Is it the case?"

"Yes, and I'm on my boss's bad side, and Shadrach almost died."

Mom gasped. "Oh no! He's the first dog I've really liked. I'm so sorry. What happened?"

"The vet thinks someone laced meat with cyanide and left it in the dog park. Who'd do something like that? So, yes, it's been hard."

"You're right. Why on earth would someone do something so cruel? To an innocent dog?"

"The vet said it's been going on in other cities—a terrible prank, if that's what it is. No one has been caught, yet."

"We have to hope they'll find whoever did it. How upsetting. How're you doing? And what's it mean for the case? Are you able to concentrate?"

"We failed. No mistrial. The juror who was going to testify cannot anymore." She held her iced tea glass against her forehead and slapped her ankle.

"I'm sure you did all you could. I'm so impressed with how you're handling the case, your aunt, your shock at finding out about her. Dad and I are proud of you."

She felt lightheaded, hearing those kudos. *Maybe we are turning a corner?*

Mom's old-fashioned pale-yellow shirtwaist dress looked cool and wispy. She fiddled with a silver charm bracelet on her wrist and massaged her collar bone. "That's so sad about the case. Is there any other way?"

The humid air melted the tension she normally felt being around Mom.

"Well, some research points to genetic reasons that may unravel unexpected child deaths. I'll tell you more when I know. But you wanted to talk about something?"

"I did," Mom said. "I want to tell you about your brother. Some history."

The moment of connection passed, replaced by the familiar stiffness when they were together.

Emma leaned back into the chair, hoping to make the likely whack she expected less jarring. "Should I get more tea? How much of a surprise will this be?"

"Emileen. Nothing bad. I just want to tell you more about him."

Emma rocked. "Please, then."

"We wanted several children, maybe four or five, and started with you," Mom said. "When a second one came about a year after you were born, we were thrilled. Joshua. You know that."

The invisible brother—his photos and toys remained in her room long after he died.

A dog raced through the back yard, and Emma gasped, for a flash, thinking it was Shadrach. But he was with Grant and Harriet. Out of mischief. She hoped.

"The neighbors have a new dog," Mom said. "She's still a puppy and gets out."

So glad Shad can run like that. How awful to think I almost lost him.

"...healthy infant. But when he was almost six months old...you were about eighteen months...he died. In his crib. At night. You were in the same room."

She flinched. *What did she say? That I was in the room when my brother died? Is that creepy or just bad luck?*

"He died when you were sleeping. Did you hear me?" Mom's voice rose.

Emma pressed her fist to her lips. *Was Mom accusing me of something?* "I heard you."

"We thought you might have called out to us. But you didn't."

Emma wiped perspiration from her clammy cheeks and pulled air through her blocked nose.

"You normally slept only fitfully, for short stretches. You called to us most nights to help you get back to sleep. But that night, you didn't."

Is Mom blaming me for my own brother's death? She peered at the small white cross by the side of the woods, tilting into the weeds around it. The words etched into the wood—RIP Joshua—had nearly worn off.

"He died from SIDS; that's what they told us. Like Victoria's children. The grief devastated us. We couldn't get over it. Never really moved on."

Her stomach flip flopped. "Is that what this is about? Is this why you never could love me?" *Did they want him instead?*

"Oh no, Emileen! Please don't think that. We simply never got over what happened. It's like our lives stopped. The grief overwhelmed us."

She stood up, knocked the table, and her tea glass fell. The brown liquid dripped through the wrought iron tabletop onto the grass. The insects buzzing in her ears sounded like rain. She always felt she didn't matter to them and this…this admission proved it. No matter what, she'd never measure up. "I was never enough," she said under her breath. She stood in front of her mother, ready to run.

Mom reached out for her hand. "Oh, sweetheart. Don't think like that. We were so young, so damaged. Watching my sister's children die like that and then to have one of our own. We didn't know how to pick up the pieces."

But they chose to be parents. Not to just one child but to any children. And they still had one. Coyle Adams jumped into her mind, the juror who'd taken the bribe. He'd said that when their daughter died, he and his wife never wanted more children, that they could never love another as much. *Is this how Mom and Dad felt?*

She pulled her hand from Mom's grip and sat down. "And you never talked about it. Why now? Why tell me now?"

"I wanted to be open with you and…I thought it might be related to Aunt Victoria's case."

The case was dead, or on life support. "Forget the case. How could you hold that against me? For my whole life. I'm leaving."

She'd let down her guard, and another bomb hit her. She stalked off, yanked open the toy car's door, and pulled the door handle off. *Of course, this is the time the car acts up.* She couldn't even manage a proper getaway.

She pounded the steering wheel as she drove off, yelled at Mom, Dad, her dead brother, Aunt Victoria…but mostly at herself for thinking she could restore a relationship that was never there to begin with. They'd never bonded; now she knew why. She was never enough. No wonder she'd always had to prove to people that she was good enough, smart enough, worked hard enough. *I wasn't enough for my parents, why should I be for anyone else?*

She sped through the dusty brown land along the highway. *Did I overreact? Probably. Surely a mother—even Mom—couldn't blame a sleeping child for the death of another child….*

As she entered the city's outskirts, late evening, a lit-up billboard of a baby and mother, an advertisement for the local children's hospital, caught her eye.

"We're here for you anytime, day or night. That means research, treatment, and support. For you. For your child."

She pulled into her driveway, put the car into park, and screamed.

"NOOOOOO!"

Emma jerked upright at a tapping a few inches from her head.

"Emma!" Rupert called, his voice muffled through the car window. "My God, what's happened?"

She pushed her hair back and rolled down the window. "I'm OK. Just give me a second." She gathered her purse and stepped out of the car.

"I visited my mother again. I'm trying to reconnect with them and also wanted to update them on the case, on the dead case. But…every time I visit, she drops a bombshell. And this was the worst."

She replayed Mom's words in her head, *"…in the room with him…he died…you didn't wake up."* She teetered between the heat of fury and the chill of betrayal.

"Let's go to the house, and you can tell me."

She held Rupert's elbow to be sure he didn't trip as they walked up his driveway and realized he might be thinking the same about her, as he gripped her hand. "I'm sorry you found me like that. I'm still in shock."

"Here, sit by the bergamot candle. Or do you need lavender? That's a calming scent…. Later maybe."

Fussy Rupert. Caring Rupert. The men in her life seemed softer and more compassionate than Mom.

"Now tell me. You went to see your parents and…"

She released a big breath over four seconds. "They had another baby, a boy, born when I was a little over a year old. I knew that. Photos and toys were all over the house. But he was invisible to me."

"Invisible?"

"I never knew him because I was too young. It was like I was an only child except I wasn't."

"Only child? I'm not following."

"He died. Before I was conscious of him."

He gasped. "Oh my word."

"And the worst was…they blamed me for his death." Her voice rose an octave. *How could they have thought such a thing?*

"Take another breath in. Out. Now explain yourself. That's a harsh statement."

Her restless leg jiggled. "She said when I was little, I didn't sleep well. My parents came to check on us—"

"Us?"

"My baby brother and me. Joshua. We slept in the same room. But that night…the night he died…I slept through. I didn't call for them. He died, and I never knew. How could I have known?" She stifled tears. "Sorry. I'm upset still. Obviously."

He tugged his linen handkerchief from his trouser pocket.

She gaped at it. "You and your old school handkerchiefs. Such a gentleman. I can't take that. I'd mess it up."

"Whiskey then?" He went for glasses and liquor.

A coffee table book on deep sea creatures lay open to pages describing sea worms. "Sea worms?" She chuckled.

"Now, now, my dear. Sea worms are almost as fascinating as eels, which we know almost nothing about. I could tell you...but I digress. Back to you. Did they find out why your brother died?"

"SIDS. Like Aunt Victoria's kids. That's why she told me. She thought it might relate to the case since I had told them about the articles on gene mutations. It stuck in her head."

"She may have a point."

Was there a point? She gazed at the fresh daisies on his coffee table, in one of his antique vases.

"I thought this case might bring us together, as a family. But I'm going backward. How could they blame me for Josh's death?"

"Um-hm."

She guzzled the whiskey and coughed. "Maybe more than I should have taken," she said, her voice husky from the liquor.

"Now that you're fortified, let's talk this through. It's hard to imagine a mother blaming her daughter for another child's death. So, let's review exactly what she said. Use your worthy memory. Did she really use the word 'blame'?"

Is he taking Mom's side in this? She needed support, not a challenge. But she'd humor him, for now. Woozy from the drink, she shut her eyes to recreate the scene.

"She said he died in his crib at night, and I was in the same room."

"Keep going."

"They thought I would have heard something and called for them." She squeezed her jaw to steel herself for the rest of the story.

"She said they were overwhelmed by grief and didn't know how to get through it. That their lives stopped when he died."

"Did she ever use the word 'blame'? I don't hear it in your recounting."

She could have sworn her mother used the word, but if her retelling was accurate, "blame" hadn't been said. But she'd felt it.

"Maybe you're right. I must have had the impression, but I don't recall her using the actual word."

"You'll need to talk to them again about this," he said. "To be sure they and you understand this was no one's fault. If you want that family connection, you've got to get through this."

She'd landed at the bottom of a big hill that she needed to climb. Again. *Do I have the energy?* She could have used that handkerchief now but didn't dare ask. She excused herself to fetch a tissue.

"On my drive home, it hit me that if there is a genetic connection, for Aunt Victoria and her kids, could the same be true for my brother? Maybe his SIDS death was something else?"

Her logical brain whirred, and it felt good. Emotions drained her. Problem solving energized her. "If my cousins had the mutation, maybe my brother did too. And then, could I?"

He grimaced. "I was afraid you'd make that leap."

She pulled a throw pillow toward her, like protection, and squeezed it to mask her shaking.

"This is a lot to take in." He started for more whiskey, and she waved him off. "What if we take things a step at a time? Let's both reread the articles. I don't remember if they said how the gene passes down the line. Your aunt had sons *and* daughters. Your parents had you and a son.... Were there other children? Did she say?"

"If there had been, I'd remember them. But at eighteen months, they reckoned I was too small."

Moths batted against his screen door, and chirping crickets buzzed outdoors.

"Should you take a pause on this case? To be sure this doesn't overtake you?"

"How could you say that? I'm spent, exhausted, yes, but I'm also driven. It's only thirty-two days till the execution. I don't have time. She doesn't have time."

"Then I'm with you and might have something to show you on those mutations."

"God, I hope so. If these mutations explain the deaths of Aunt Victoria's kids, maybe others? And wouldn't parents want to know? Those who've lost children and those who might have them? Like me? This is bigger than me, than us, than Aunt Victoria."

"Then you need to meet the geneticist. She may be the answer."

Chapter 31

Sunday morning, May 28, 2006

Emma stood in front of Dr. Natalia French's colonial house.

A tall man in his thirties, wearing a maroon pullover and grey slacks, opened the door.

Rupert, standing behind the man, beckoned her inside. "The Marvelous Marty here set up a projector so we can look at the children's autopsy pages. Thanks for getting them."

Marvelous Marty? The darkened living room revealed a standard beige couch and chairs, tapestry throw pillows, and genetics books scattered on the coffee and end tables. Dr. French sat across the room, a small woman with wiry short grey hair and black rimmed glasses. *An older Ms. Frizzle?* She reminded Emma of the teacher in the *Magic School Bus* books for children who whisked her students away on many adventures. Some of Emma's few happy memories were when Mom read those books with her.

"Dr. French, I'm Emma Raddell. I've heard a lot about you." She stretched out her hand.

"Nice to meet you." Dr. French exhaled as she spoke and didn't move her hand from her lap. "Sorry. I'm not able to greet your properly. ALS."

Emma blinked hard and made out the shape of a wheelchair with a head piece holding Dr. French's head steady. Not what she'd expected.

"Call me Natalia."

Shocked, Emma looked at Rupert for help.

He stood next to Natalia, hand on her shoulder. "But her mind's like a wolf trap…steel trap? One of those traps. She's driving this search for information about the children. I'm just the errand boy." Natalia turned up one edge of her mouth.

Emma saw clues she'd missed—oxygen tanks, a reaching device, remote controls, and medication tucked into a shelf next to the fireplace. Above the mantel hung large photos of African wildlife. A cheetah, next to its baby replica, a herd of seven elephants with two small offspring, and three giraffes, one of whom was half the height of the others. Crystal clear, almost humanlike expressions on their faces, the photos drew her in.

"I was an amateur photographer. I miss it," Natalia said.

Emma leaned toward the giraffes. "You're very good." She stepped away from the mantel. "I've heard about your research and am anxious to learn more."

"I can give you the overview, but for the details, for the recent research…you must meet my colleague in the university. Dr. Simon Albrecht. He's the man you need to see."

Rupert smiled. "She's modest. She knows all of it as well as anyone. Now let's hear about this."

Marty hung a sheet in front of the curtained windows and turned on the projector. Rupert clicked through the DNA results, page by page, for Aunt Victoria's two girls. When he needed help, Natalia clarified.

After thirty minutes, Rupert sat back. "All yours, Counselor. We're excited and hope you see why. Any thoughts?"

"Thanks for all of this. It could be very helpful, especially since the mistrial fell through."

Rupert nodded to encourage her.

"So, what you and Dr. Fre—Natalia—found…if I understand you, was that Aunt Victoria's children had underlying conditions along with a genetic mutation, making them especially vulnerable. And the boys and girls had different conditions and different specific mutations. The boys had a mutation related to epilepsy and blindness in mice; we don't know if it's the case in humans. On the other hand, the second son, Brian, had epilepsy and he was blind."

Natalia raised her hand. "Also, son number one had floppy larynx. Likely triggered by epilepsy."

"So, the boys had similar underlying conditions, and the girls had a different gene mutation and died from respiratory and heart conditions, leading to heart attacks. Equally dangerous but different. Did I get that right?"

"Correct," Natalia whispered.

"Let me take a side path. Is there a chance another, distant, relative could have the mutation?" She darted her eyes toward Rupert, who made thumbs up.

"Perhaps. What are you thinking?"

She gulped and leaned against the mantel. "What if I had the mutation? Is there any sort of test?"

A line formed between Natalia's eyebrows. "Ahhh. This is personal. Rupert didn't tell me."

"I didn't want to bias you, of course," Rupert said.

"And you were right not to." Natalia twisted her chair to face Emma. "Yes, there is a test. I can help you get it, when you want."

Emma's legs felt like Jell-O, and she sank into a chair. "Thank you. I'm so relieved. Now I can focus on our case."

Rupert chimed in. "I'm glad that's resolved. Natalia has also found a directory of incidents around the world. An Italian pediatrician tracks cases of children who died from unexplained deaths. Like your aunt's children. He estimates that about half were related to a genetic mutation."

"That's big. More evidence unavailable twenty-four years ago. That means a new trial, which we need since the mistrial is dead." She clapped her hands. "If this is true, it might be enough to convince a judge…but it's our, or rather, your, research and word only."

Rupert bristled and glanced at Natalia. "We've thought about how someone could challenge it." He turned to Natalia. "Did you think of any who might support this?"

"Yes. A friend in England. Conal Olson. Works on gene mutations." She stopped to take in a big breath.

Marty pecked on a computer keyboard in the corner of the room.

"…Researches SIDS and SUDC—"

"Sorry, what's that stand for?" Emma said.

"Excuse me. I use jargon and should not. SUDC means 'sudden unexplained, unexpected deaths in children, under eighteen.' Lots of research. Europe. North America. Japan. Decades of data."

"Uh-oh. I'm sorry, Natalia," Marty said. "He's dead. Conal Olson, Head of Genetics at Warwick Research, died not long ago. Pancreatic cancer. He was fifty-eight."

"Confound it." Rupert pounded a fist on the mantel.

"Oh no. He's such a good man. And friend." Natalia's eyes welled up.

Marty brought a tissue. "I'm sorry. But there must be someone else you know, right? You know the top geneticists in the world."

Natalia's head fell forward, and Marty moved it back into the brace. "Want to close my life with a good deed," she said.

"You'll have many more good deeds and time to do them," Rupert said. "Let's stay positive here."

Emma's mind hustled. "Maybe there's a way to get this information out for scientists to review. Some people will know about the research; others not. If they say it's valid, their reputations carry more weight than ours."

She stepped in front of the photos again. "Do you two know about LinkedIn? Clusters of people in the same field, like these elephant herds. Maybe LinkedIn could help us contact other gene mutation experts? You have a LinkedIn account?"

Natalia nodded. "Started when it came out and I could type…2002, I think. But I haven't kept up."

Rupert looked from Natalia to Emma. "What are you talking about? Remember I left the tech library world in 1995. Lots has changed."

"LinkedIn's like a professional Facebook. You build networks. People in your field."

"Ahhhh," he said, raising his eyebrows at Natalia, who tried to wink, but both eyes closed.

"There are subgroups like people who study genes," Emma said. "I looked last night. Natalia's in it. Instead of us pushing this case, maybe scientists could help push it from the outside? What if Natalia asked scientists to review peer-reviewed research. If they think it's legit, would they support the request for a new trial?"

Rupert stared at the articles in front of him. "Ah. Bring scientists into this discussion? Your aunt was convicted because of her diaries, not because of scientific evidence. But we've got it now. If the gene mutation was responsible, why not try to get others to see it?"

"And…the underlying conditions weren't identified as something related to the deaths," Natalia said. "That's what Conal found, and others did as well."

Rupert sat back, stunned. "Could this LinkedIn…could it generate interest?"

"Worth a try."

Natalia dictated, and Marty typed a letter. Two hours later, the letter swooshed its way to twenty-one of Natalia's colleagues around the world.

Emma's phone rang at 2:20 a.m. Her throat caught as she reached for it. She and Grant had spent the rest of the day together biking and they were both exhausted. He turned over in his sleep, or what she hoped was sleep. *Is something wrong with Rupert?*

"Emma, it's Marty. Natalia insisted I call you. She doesn't keep track of time since she is awake most of the night. She woke up about thirty minutes ago and wanted to check LinkedIn. You're not going to believe this."

She pressed the phone against her ear even harder.

"Something like sixty comments! She knows most of these researchers, but there are also pediatricians who deal with unexplained deaths. Their comments are consistent and supportive that the gene mutation, with other medical conditions, could cause SIDS-type deaths. We did it. Or rather, you and Natalia did! And she says now you must go see Albrecht. She'll arrange it for later Monday…or rather, today."

Emma made tiny jumps in the air, like she had as a child on Christmas mornings.

"Wake up! Grant! It's time to hit up a judge!"

"What? You want to get married? At this time of night?"

Chapter 32

Monday evening, May 29, 2006

"I am pleased to introduce you to my colleague, Dr. Simon Albrecht."

Emma and Rupert had joined Natalia and Marty in her lab at the university. Yellow-tinted sunset light landed on top of the lab tables. Simon Albrecht, in his early seventies, bowed in an old-fashioned European way. He wore his white lab coat like a freshly pressed military uniform and clasped his hands in front of himself, showing a gold family crest signet ring on his right pinkie finger.

Natalia continued, "Dr. Albrecht and I worked together for twenty years. He came from East Germany; I am from Poland. We fled extreme governments and are happy to be here."

Albrecht placed his hand over his heart. "She speaks the truth."

"Please question him about the research," Natalia said, "since he is your key witness. I've told him you hope for a new trial, based on our research."

"It's an honor to meet you, Ms. Raddell and Mr. Singer. We are grateful for your interest in our work."

Albrecht spent forty-five minutes reviewing the genetics of the case and details of the gene mutations that affected the girls and the boys. He ended by emphasizing how important it was to get the father's DNA.

When he finished, Emma asked a question she had heard her firm's partners ask when they first met a potential witness. "If this does go to trial, Dr. Albrecht, do you anticipate any surprises…from your possible testimony? What might the other side bring up that we've not thought of? We always ask this." She looked from Natalia to Albrecht.

"The research is solid," he said. "Many other labs around the world have replicated it. We've published in the highest-level academic journals."

"Nothing to blindside us?"

Albrecht sniffed. "Nothing. The research has been road tested, as you say. Nothing for you to worry on."

Chapter 33

Tuesday, May 30, 2006

Emma popped a Pepto Bismol for her woozy stomach and studied the stalking files. She jolted when Antigone knocked on her office door.

"How's it going? Any progress on that mistrial?"

Emma's pointed Antigone to a chair.

"Oh God. I haven't seen you for a while. Unfortunately, the juror who I thought would help died. Unexpectedly. He had led me to think there was bribery during the initial trial."

"What? Died? Are you kidding? And bribery? That's hard to believe. Does that put Simmons in the middle of it?"

"We're back to square one. But there may be another angle. Gene mutations might have caused the children's deaths. We're interviewing experts in the next few days."

"Good work. What've you got?" Antigone shoved the office door to close it. "No need for Sherry to hear about this." She winked at Emma.

"Right. I'm on her hit list again after the Gleeson incidents. Basically, there's research from around the world that's supportive. I still need DNA from the father to test whether a different mutation affected the boys."

"How will you get that?"

"No idea, but I have to."

"What about the previous trial evidence? Didn't you say it was your aunt's diaries?"

"Yeah, but those are circumstantial. Not objective. What we've got now is the science part of it."

Antigone swiveled her head to find a tapping noise.

Emma pointed. "It's a bird, up there, at the high window. "It must see its reflection and comes to greet the other bird about three days a week." She craned her neck to look at it. "Almost feels like a friend, now."

"So, what are next steps?"

"I have an appointment with Madeline Mason to lay it out and get a reaction."

Antigone's right eyebrow lifted. "Madeline Mason? The defense attorney? She's legendary. Didn't she work here a long time ago? How do you know her?"

"Remember that reception we went to last year for young lawyers? The one where the older women lawyers said they'd be mentors for us? I met her there, and she said if I ever wanted to bounce ideas off of her to call. So, I called."

"That's gutsy. I never take those comments people make at receptions seriously. I've heard she's a tough bird but also a straight shooter. Team player for women. What will you give her? Other than the gene mutation research?"

Queasiness tickled her stomach. *Had I misread Mason's offer? And what's with Antigone's probing?* She seemed more interested than normal. *Why, all of a sudden?*

"Well, a physician in Europe keeps a directory of families with these sorts of deaths. Especially families with more than one death."

"Good for you. You said something about an expert on the diaries?"

Another pang of apprehension. Something nagged at her to slow down, to be careful.

"Uh, yes. We found a content analysis expert to help with the diaries."

"Well, good for you. I'll be anxious to hear what Ms. Mason says. But in the meantime, what about the Hampstead project? Isn't that one up for some TLC?"

"You'll never let me forget. The intern's on it. When this thing is in the bag, I'll be full time on my Ivins work."

"Good to hear." She stood. "By the way, have you had any more interaction since your visit with Mr. Simmons? Or is he out of the picture?"

The hairs on her arms rose. She'd not spoken to Antigone about her visit to Simmons's office.

"Uh, no. Where did you hear that?"

"You told me, remember?"

"I don't think so."

Antigone turned to the door. "Well, I could have sworn you did. Sorry. Keep me posted."

Emma rubbed her arms to get those high-rising hairs to lay down. *That was spooky. Is she saying my memory is slipping? Never.* Antigone knew about the DA's letter summoning her, but she'd not said anything after the visit. *Maybe Richard Li in the office is still in thick with Antigone?* He'd been there when she went to see Simmons. *Or someone is watching me. . . .*

Chapter 34

Wednesday, May 31, 2006

At 6:45 p.m., Emma zapped the screen to close down her latest interview with an expert for Aunt Victoria's case. Professor Clinton Yee would make an excellent witness. His folksy speech pattern meshed with his scientific knowledge, without making him less academic. The University of Texas professor's lab used state-of-the-art content analysis technology to determine profiles from written documents. He had briefly reviewed Aunt Victoria's diaries and offered a tentative conclusion: she was agitated but not capable of murdering her children. He'd grown up in Taiwan, moved to the U.S. for university, and built a reputation that she couldn't find any holes in. No surprises. *Yes, he'd be great.*

Just as she closed her computer lid, Sherry poked her head in the conference room.

"Who was that?"

"What do you mean?"

"On your screen? Who was that man? Looked Asian."

"A possible expert witness."

"For a case I gave you?"

"Uh, it's a potential witness."

"After hours? I hope you're on the up and up. I wouldn't want you to do something that could cause trouble—for us or for you." Sherry closed the door and strutted off.

Rupert joined Emma for an evening stroll.

"I had a great interview with the content analysis expert today. But I almost got caught."

He looped his arm through hers. "My dear, you can't let this jeopardize your career. Be careful or be done with it. But do tell me what you learned."

"Professor Clinton Yee works in psychology and linguistics. He uses technology from the FBI and CIA to analyze text—written, spoken—to generate a 'psychological state' of the author. He analyzed more of the diaries, not just the thousand or so words Simmons used in the first trial."

"And what did he find?"

"Briefly that she's, and I quote, 'self-reflective, anxious, and honest.' And not a murderer."

"So this wasn't something a mother would do?"

She slowed. *Not what a mother would do? What do mothers do? How would I do as a mother? Where are these thoughts coming from?*

He heaved a sigh. "That's wonderful news."

Her stomach churned. *Geez. Why can't I seem to shake this bug?*

"Anything else? Emma? Are you with me?"

"Sorry, thinking about something else. Ah yes, Professor Clinton says that Aunt Victoria didn't try to hide her thoughts. Remember, that's what the prosecution said before, that she covered up her misdeeds by using fuzzy words. He thought she exuded grief, not cunning."

"Good work, young counselor. You've earned your wine this evening. We have one more expert to check, right?"

"Yes, I've arranged for a Skype interview, but we should avoid my office. And how's your search for the father coming?"

Rupert stopped midstep. "Not good. I've found nothing. He vanished after the trial."

"Oh. And you're the best there is with internet searches. Unless we find him, the rest of the research is moot. And we have no case."

"Let's talk to this last possible witness, and I'll keep looking for the father," he said. "Don't give up yet."

Chapter 35

Thursday, June 1, 2006

Rupert and Emma sat in Natalia's lab's conference room, waiting for their final potential expert, a pediatrician in Italy. He would appear on a video screen in the courtroom, so they wanted to check how he came across.

"I'm feeling confident about our experts."

"They seem solid," Rupert said.

Inside, Emma patted herself on the pack. If she could pull this off, she might be way back into the graces of Roy Donohue and the law partners.

"If we're able to get a new trial, they might use the same main witness—that Australian pediatrician with the catchy phrase that people seemed to remember too well. He's the one who said—"

Before Emma could finish, Rupert jumped in. "To lose one child is a tragedy, to lose two is suspicious, but to lose more than two is impossible. Something like that, right?"

"That you remember it, all these years later, speaks to the power it and he had then," Emma said. "I worry that they'll play that card and it'll have a similar effect."

"Well, it was the trial's tagline, all over the newspapers at the time. But think about it. The man will be twenty-plus years older now, making him, what?"

"Oooh. Well into his seventies, maybe even eighty."

"Do we know how sharp he is? Can he be rattled? Discredited?" Rupert stroked his beard.

"I asked Dr. Albrecht about that. He disagrees vehemently with Packerton's approach to statistics. So yes, his testimony could help discredit Packerton."

Voices came from the screen. "Just push this, and they should see you."

"Ahh. Grazie, Anna."

"We're here! Dr. Busso? Rupert Singer and Emma Raddell are here," she said.

Dr. Silvio Busso popped up—long eyelashes, wavy hair, along with a smile that made Emma lightheaded. She chided herself. *Would this be an advantage with the jurors or a disadvantage?* She'd read his writings and his directory and hoped he had as much substance in his testimony. *What are you thinking? So judgmental when you accuse others of the same.*

"Dr. Busso, we want you to tell the courtroom about your directory—why it's important, what it contains, and how it affects the current case. Can you do that?" Emma leaned toward the screen.

"But, of course, Ms. Raddell. Please let me explain." And he did, in simple terms, beautifully shaped sentences, over the next fifteen minutes.

"You look skeptical, both of you." He laughed. "I studied at Stanford, in California, and married a West Coast artist. So that's why my English is better than the average Italian's."

Emma relaxed and made a thumbs up, low against the table, so Rupert could see it but not Busso. "Thank you for that, Dr. Busso. We'll be sure to bring out your credentials during the trial."

When they hung up, Rupert clapped. "Well done. Three good experts. I think they're ready. Good job. You must be close to going to a judge? But what about the DNA?"

"God, Rupert. Would everyone get off my back on that. I know we need it. Why haven't you found him yet?"

"Hold off, now. I'm on your side."

"I'm sorry. It's getting to me, I guess. My head aches, and I can't seem to nip some stomach bug I've had. I'll ask Aunt Victoria, but I think I've got enough to convince a judge."

"I'm sure you do. We're getting there. What could go wrong?"

Chapter 36

Wednesday late morning, June 7, 2006

"Please come in, Ms. Raddell. I hear you're doing well at Ivins so far? Congratulations."

Emma marched into Madeline Mason's office, wearing her lucky pearls.

Mason gripped a pink fountain pen and fuchsia-colored notebook, which matched her suit.

Talk about gutsy. What woman overdoses on pink? Is this a reverse intimidation tactic?

"It's nice to meet you," Mason continued. "So how can I help?"

A bucket of ice water wouldn't have surprised Emma more. *Mason has no idea who I am. Doesn't remember we've met. Maybe this isn't such a good idea.* Emma touched her briefcase for courage. It overflowed with the most recent LinkedIn comments that Natalia and Rupert had received from scientists supporting the idea of reviewing the case.

"You may remember we met at the reception for new lawyers last year? You offered to let me run case ideas by you sometime? I want to take you up on the offer."

Mason's face remained blank.

"And to ask what it would take to get a new trial for an old case? One from twenty-four years ago. You might even remember it."

"I see. Retrials demand quite a high bar. It's hard to imagine a rookie pursuing something like that." She flipped a page in her notebook. "Not in this town, at least. Tell me more. What case?"

Emma's ribs pressed into her chest, pushing air out and restricting it in.

"Victoria Beringer. Accused of killing four children. New evidence makes it seem it was a wrong conviction. Do you remember the case?"

Mason's hand stopped midair. "Sensational case. Well argued. She was convicted. I read recently that her execution is coming up soon? Is that why you're interested?"

"Yes. It's coming up in twenty days."

Mason closed her notebook and stared at Emma. "You've not told me why this should happen? I said retrials are rare."

The pressure on her chest felt like a twenty-pound dumbbell. She touched her throat and gave her pearls a quick stroke for luck.

"I'll explain. And I won't take too much of your time."

"I'd rather you took none of my time, but get on with it." She tapped her Rolex watch face. "You have ten minutes."

What did I think was going to happen? Why is she such a jerk? She was sinking and not sure of the way out. But she had to press on.

"Thank you. First, a colleague and I found scientific research suggesting that the deaths might have stemmed from a—or maybe more than one—gene mutation. And seventy scientists agree. They wrote letters of support." She fumbled in her briefcase, taking precious time she didn't have, and after several seconds, lifted out a yellow file folder.

Mason held her kabuki face, motionless.

"We also found law cases in other parts of the world—"

"Let me stop you there. I had dinner with a colleague recently. I asked if he knew you when I saw you on my calendar."

Emma's pearls felt like an anchor on her neck.

"I did a little work on my own." Mason looked at her notebook.

Antigone had led her astray on this one. This woman was nowhere close to being willing to help her.

"Although you claim to have some seventy scientists behind this research, or supporting it, that's from an informal online survey. LinkedIn doesn't count as an official source of backing or support."

Emma dropped the folder back into her briefcase, but one piece of paper slipped to the floor, so she leaned over.

Mason ran her pen down her notes. "Yes, Ed Simmons found the LinkedIn letter from a geneticist he knows in England."

Emma went limp. *Simmons? Him again? Ed Simmons has known every move I've made and tipped off Mason? Such a rookie mistake to be blindsided like this.* She'd not considered that Mason might know about this case before they talked. She felt she was underwater. Mason's mouth moved, but no sound came out. *Focus. Focus.*

"...found ten scientists who discount this new research," said Mason, glaring at her over her fuchsia reading glasses. "When the reactions by research experts seems so split, how can we accept one side over the other? Defense strategy 101."

"But the gene mutation, the law cases—"

"To be clear, a judge would never allow these scientists' support letter into evidence. Even expert testimony is hard to get admitted, and this is hearsay, anecdotal, not legitimate. And another thing. You claim other countries have legal cases that support your argument—we do not subscribe to law outside of this country as being applicable for the State of Washington."

Prickly nettles filled Emma's chest, pushing to find a release. *What is this?* She felt a weird tickle in the back of her mind. *Something Antigone said about Mason. What was it?*

"Ms. Raddell? Does your firm know you're here? I can't believe Roy Donohue would approve of you approaching me like this. He's a hard nose and keeps his attorneys close to the vest. You're way out of line. " Mason took off her glasses and scowled. "My curiosity got you a few minutes, but it was a mistake...and hugely inappropriate. Now, please leave." She leaned over to write in her notebook, revealing her grey roots.

Emma closed the door to Mason's office, disgraced, and sank onto the bench next to the door, her arms and legs shaking.

She'd come looking for mentoring, for a friendly older woman to learn from, and got…clobbered.

Mason was worse than Roy Donohue. And Ed Simmons was behind it. She'd been outflanked, outfoxed, and outmaneuvered. He kept winning.

She pressed herself against the wall and felt ghostly, like she didn't exist. She'd lost. Mason and Donohue, but mostly Simmons, had stripped her will. She allowed herself ten minutes of full-on self-pity, but she had to get back to work. But she had no idea what to do next.

As she left the building, she phoned Ed Simmons and got his voicemail.

"This is Emma Raddell. You've done it again, one step ahead of me. Madeline Mason read me the riot act, and it's your fault. You should lay off me and this case because, so help me God, I'm not going to let you win, or intimidate me. Leave me alone."

As she hung up, she stubbed her toe and nearly stumbled to the ground. Patience had lost this round, and she'd overreacted. And now there'd be consequences.

Ah! Mason had worked with Ivins. That's what Antigone said. Something must have happened. Is that what made her so vicious?

After stopping by the pharmacy, Emma arrived home at the end of the day, still bleary eyed from her encounter with Mason and angry at herself for the outburst at Simmons. All she wanted was a hot shower and a frozen mac 'n cheese dinner.

Even her bones hurt from exhaustion; she flopped onto the futon and curled into a fetal position. But she had one more task before crashing, and it was the worst—or best—of all. She'd finally admitted to herself, after missing her period, that she might be pregnant. And she didn't know what to think about it, let alone feel.

She lumbered to the bathroom, ripped open the strip, dipped it into her urine. She followed the second hand on her analog Timex watch for an agonizing three minutes and closed her eyes to avoid peeking at the strip during the countdown. She lifted and lowered her shoulders to loosen and relax. No dice. Tik, tik, tik.

Positive. Numb, she grabbed hunks of her hair and pulled. False positives were possible, she knew that.

Two tests later, and nothing had changed.

She howled like a hurt animal from fear more than anger. Shadrach nosed his way into the tiny bathroom and crinkled his brow at her. Her mind raced so fast she couldn't track the thoughts. Her chest ached, her head felt it would burst, and her stomach writhed in pain. *After this week from hell, now this?* She had no energy to think. She and Grant were still so new, and they hadn't spent that much time together. But it was enough. *How could I have been so lax? Now what?* She wanted children but not in the middle of a case that was on life support. *Grant might have promise, but I'm not—*

Her phone rang, and her thoughts skidded to a halt. Roy Donohue. *At 7:30 in the evening?*

"Emma. Madeline Mason called me about your adventure in her office. I should say lack of judgement."

She gasped. "I'm so—"

"And I heard from Ed Simmons. He said you threatened him. What were you thinking. Such unprofessional behavior. Verging on illegal. You should know better. I can't believe you did something like that. Especially after our last unpleasant encounter."

She closed her eyes and wanted to slip away, to become invisible, to disappear. She slid down the wall, hitting the bathroom tile with a thud. She put the phone on the floor and her head between her knees. "I can expl—"

"No explanations. The partners and I decided to suspend you. We will discuss possible termination, but for now, stay away from the office and any cases you're assigned."

"But we must get a new—"

The phone went dead.

Now she'd done it. Mason had crushed the idea of a new trial case. Her boss was livid. She had no job. She was pregnant and didn't know how to even think about that, let alone what to do, especially if there was a possibility she had the gene mutation that Aunt Victoria had. *When will something go right?*

Chapter 37

Friday, June 9, 2006

Emma pulled into the Killane prison parking lot at 9:47 a.m., dreading her upcoming meeting with Aunt Victoria. Since she was out of a job, she could make the trip on a Friday. *Just get it over with.* This was her latest failure, but she had to tell Aunt Victoria.

Before leaving the apartment earlier in the morning, she'd pulled Emily D from the bookshelf to search for a poem that could help with all that was wrong—suspension, no case, humiliation—all of it. Number 1455 helped:

Opinion is a flitting thing,
But Truth, outlasts the Sun—
If then we cannot own them both—
Possess the oldest one—

Could she ever believe in herself?

Aunt Victoria's feet never left the floor as she scuffled in, like she was too tired to raise them. Her grey stringy hair fell in front of her face, her shoulders slumped forward more than before, and her wrists looked abraded from the metal bracelets. She sat down, staring at the table for a full half minute before acknowledging Emma. But when she looked up, she smiled. Insincere, maybe, but at least she tried.

"Aunt Victoria, you look like you haven't slept in a week. What's going on?"

"Nothing. I'm happy to see you."

"You may not be in a minute. I've got bad news." She reached her hands out toward Aunt Victoria's but was careful not to stretch too far. She searched Aunt Victoria's face for any flicker of hope. Emily D came to mind again: "Hope is the thing with feathers—that perches in the soul." She wanted to feel a feather, but nothing stirred. She felt the invisible clock ticking, no longer inching toward the final day but galloping. She clenched her jaw.

"I doubt we can get a new trial. My fault. I went around my boss for advice, and he found out."

Aunt Victoria gasped. "Oh no. You did all of this for me, and now it's hurting you. I'm so sorry, child." She also moved her flattened palms toward the table's center so her hand was an inch from Emma's.

But that inch felt like a canyon.

"It's not your fault. I wanted to do this, but I went about it wrong. I'm still too impatient, I guess. But the result is the same. I failed you. I failed Mom and Dad. I failed myself."

"No, no, no. Please don't be so hard on yourself. The fact that you worked so hard, and you made the time and effort to come to me. I'm overwhelmed with gratitude. I'm sure it wasn't easy. I'm proud of you."

"But it's all for naught. I'm so sorry." Emma wiped a tear from her eye.

"Don't be upset. Go back to your folks. They need you. You did bring us together. In small ways. I can't tell you how much that means."

"But you're all alone."

Aunt Victoria chuckled. "I was alone for so long, so being around you has been strange. I'll get used to being by myself again."

"I'll keep coming."

She patted the table and pulled her hands back to her lap.

"I will. I mean it."

Aunt Victoria nodded, looked toward the guard, and lifted her chin. "It's time. I've loved spending time with you. Please don't worry about me anymore." She stood and waited for the guard to touch her elbow and usher her out of the room.

On her drive home, Emma rethought the evidence, the argument she should have made, the experts. She had presented it all in the wrong way. She knew now what to do and had to get Roy Donohue to agree. *Surely, he'll give me one more chance.*

Chapter 38

Saturday morning, June 10, 2006

"Emma Raddell speaking." She half-recognized the phone number when she answered at 6:14 a.m. She'd been awake since 2:00 a.m., but this still felt like an intrusion.

"Ms. Raddell. This is Warden Matthews of the Women's Correctional Center in Killane. I'm sorry to call this early. But you are the attorney for one of our inmates, Ms. Victoria Berringer, are you not?"

She swung her legs to the side of the bed and squeezed her eyes.

"That's right. I'm her lawyer. What's this about?"

"I'm sorry to tell you that your client attempted suicide early this morning."

"Oh God!" She tilted her head back and opened her mouth, wanting to scream it all away. She had to remain outwardly calm even though everything inside had gone sour. Time slowed with every excruciating word he said. "Is she OK?"

Warden Matthews blew into the phone. "I wish I could say yes, but that would be inaccurate. She did not succeed, but she is in the hospital. Serious condition. Meadow View General."

"What happened? She seemed fine yesterday."

"She hasn't said anything since the attempt. Was pretty doped up from the meds they gave her. She tried to cut herself and lost consciousness. But she'll pull through."

Her wrath toward Simmons, her humiliation with Donohue, and her fear about the pregnancy all had to wait. First, she had to save her aunt, or at least go down trying. And she needed Mom to help.

Chapter 39

Saturday late morning, June 10, 2006

"It's my fault she gave up. I caused it," Emma said. "I failed her." She looked at Mom in the passenger seat. "And I failed you."

"Be reasonable," Mom said. "You didn't cause this. She did it to herself. You tried to help her. It's not your fault." She put her hand on the dashboard. "Please drive carefully. We don't want to end up in a ditch."

Emma and her mother pulled into the hospital parking lot at 11:45 a.m. and rushed to the intensive care unit. The nurse drew the privacy curtains but left open the sliding glass door. A deputy from the correctional center sat right outside, and Emma suspected he could hear every word.

Aunt Victoria's left wrist was handcuffed to the hospital bed's metal railings. Five inches of gauze wrapped her uncuffed hand.

The sisters glanced at each other before looking away. *Was that some secret communication?* Emma shoved her curiosity, anger, and fear down and waited one of them to speak.

"Emileen. As I told you the other day, I appreciate all you've done," Aunt Victoria said. "I'd given up hope. No one believed me. You did, and I'm obliged to you for that."

Emma's tucked-down feelings rumbled with pity. "I had hope…have hope. I've got some new ideas. But what were you think—"

Aunt Victoria raised her right fingers and swished her hand back and forth. "I have to ask you to stop. No more work. Nothing more for me."

An invisible anvil fell on Emma's foot. She pulled away from the bed and turned toward the open door. *How can this woman be so ungrateful? After all I've done?* "I know you're depressed, but—"

Her aunt balled her fist. "No. Stop, please. Let me finish. You don't understand."

Emma's mind raced. Despite the awful setbacks, she'd revamped her approach. She knew what to do.

"So, what changed? You said nothing yesterday, for God's sake. And now we've got the science evidence and DNA, and I'm sure we can get a new trial. I came up with a new plan on my drive home. You wanted help; I'm giving it to you. You can't stop now."

Aunt Victoria's eyes bored into Emma's. "I'm sorry, but I can't do it anymore. I should have taken some advice long ago"—her eyes veered toward her sister—"and agreed to a guilty plea. It would have been over sooner. This way was harder, trying to convince people and getting nowhere."

Dark circles under Aunt Victoria's eyes contrasted with her pale complexion. Her cheeks, already wrinkled, showed deeper vertical lines than they did a couple of weeks ago, and her mouth, framed in rough red skin, barely moved when she talked. Even her freckles looked paler.

"It's time. I've told God I'm ready. I don't want this ordeal to continue."

Emma's muscles went slack, and she felt lightheaded. She grabbed the arm of a double wide chair and tugged it toward the bed.

"But we're so close." Even though she'd been shot down by her boss and Mason, she had hope; she felt that feather again. She looked at Mom across the hospital bed. "What do you think about this? You begged me to do it in the first place."

Mom reached over Aunt Victoria to grab Emma's wrist. "I'm sorry, dear. I don't like it either. But it's her life. We can't force her to do something against her will. Maybe even against God's will."

With that, Emma felt a burst of...*anger? Annoyance? Frustration?* "Have you both lost your minds?" She shook Mom's hand from her wrist. Aunt Victoria flinched, and Mom recoiled at her sharp rebuke. "You simply can't stop this. It's not only—"

"If Victoria feels—-"

"I've put so much time and effort into this. You—"

Aunt Victoria jingled her cuffed wrist, trying to reach Emma's hand. "Stop. Both of you. Please listen. You don't know what it's like in prison. I want it to end." Aunt Victoria's shoulders caved forward.

Emma leaned over her knees to get some circulation back and to keep from fainting. No one spoke.

"I'm tired of waiting, of fighting," Aunt Victoria said in a whisper. "I have no one left, except you and your mother, doing what's a duty. I have no husband, no children. God urges me to die, to come to him, even though I might go to hell."

Emma peeked at Mom, who met her gaze and shrugged.

Abandoned, once again. Mom had so often turned away and never made her feel loved. Emma had clawed her way through school, made something of herself, and when Mom needed something from her, she'd come through. She'd been there, not just for Mom but for this aunt she'd never known existed.

And now that she was in neck deep, risking her career for them, they left her.

Again.

Her voice came out raw. "I agreed to help Aunt Victoria, even though I wasn't optimistic. But I did what you asked. And in the process, I learned I *did* want to fight for this family. You wanted me to be a savior. I tried. And now you both want to chuck it all?"

Aunt Victoria shut her eyes.

Tears slid down Mom's cheeks. "Dad and I want you in our lives, if you'll have us." She looked at her sister. "But if Victoria wants to step away, it's her decision. Not ours. Not yours."

Aunt Victoria opened her eyes. "Thank you, Elisabeth."

Maybe they're right. Her shoulders slumped. *Maybe I should quit. After all, with no job, legal support, or a boss who wants me, what do I have to look forward to?*

Emma shoved the heavy chair backward. "You want me to quit this case? One I've given up so much to be part of? I can. But it's way beyond either of you now. Someone else, somewhere in the world, will pursue it, will help those families facing this awful disease. And do some good for them. But it won't be you, and who knows how long it could be before that happens?"

"Oh no, Emileen," Aunt Victoria said. "Don't use me as a symbol of something. It's only me. Not worth the fight anymore."

Her throat clenched. *Did they even think about the idea that I might have this gene mutation? That they are hurting me?*

"You're being so self-centered. You think this is all about you. It's not. Not by a long shot. So much more is at stake than one person, one case, even one family. It's bigger than you, than me, than us."

Emma stormed out of the room.

Chapter 40

Tuesday, June 13, 2006

Despite demands from Aunt Victoria and Roy Donohue that Emma stop working on the case, it was under her skin, and she couldn't help herself, especially since she'd been suspended from the office. She spent hours reviewing documents, articles, and running with Shadrach, one of the only bright spots in her days.

After Tuesday's run, she stared at the Bluebird BLT sandwich she'd just ordered—three inches high, chock full of tomato slices, thick bacon, and slathered with bleu cheese. Signature sandwich. And now it turned her stomach. She asked for a takeaway box.

As she left, her phone rang. Roy Donohue. She rolled her eyes in anticipation of another dressing down.

"Thanks for taking my call."

What is this?

"Could you come to the office in an hour? I'd like to finish our conversation from the other day."

"Are you sure I'm allowed?" *Oops, too snarky.* But she couldn't help it. "Sorry."

"Just come to my office."

Steel yourself for the final firing.

"You know Madeline Mason called me after your visit," Roy said. "She said you'd asked for advice about what it would take for a new trial in the Beringer case. That you offered sham evidence from scientists off of an informal online poll of some sort? Then she told me Ed Simmons had tipped her off."

"That's sort of correct…if you want—"

"Just a minute. Let me finish, and I'll tell you what I need from you."

Where is he going with this? Called me in and now won't let me explain? This man makes no sense.

"When I called you about the suspension, I was peeved and overreacted. I'm sorry for that. But later, I thought about my conversation with Madeline, and it smelled funny. I want to hear more details from you."

Stunned, her energy level dropped and then surged. But she called on patience to understand the situation before making assumptions.

"What sort of details do you want?"

"Tell me what you found that makes you think there's something here."

"Well, first the idea of a mistrial is impossible, since the juror I'd banked on to testify that he was bribed is dead." She shuddered to think she might have been the cause.

"God. What happened?"

"Car accident. Suicide. During the trial, he had a very ill child and took the bribe for her care. But in the end, he never believed my aunt could kill those kids. He admitted he'd changed his vote and, when we last talked, was ready to testify that he'd been bribed."

"That's different—and would have been explosive and probably enough for a mistrial. Since that road closed, is that why you've moved to push for a new trial?"

Emma was surprised by the change in Donohue's perspective since their last meeting about the case. "Right. And there's evidence that didn't exist during the initial trial. Information about gene mutations, new ways to analyze evidence—some diaries—and information about other families facing similar deaths."

He swiveled to look at his bookshelves before spinning back.

"All right, tell me more about this evidence."

She spent twenty minutes walking through the evidence, the likely reactions from the prosecution, and her counterattacks.

"But what role does Ed Simmons play in all of this? I was surprised that he was in touch with Madeline and knew what you were doing."

"I was too. He must have a mole somewhere…in our office. Sorry. Your office."

He registered no emotion at the jab.

"Why does he care about this, do you think?"

"If he was behind the bribery, he'd want the case to stay closed."

"That's reasonable…. You know we have history, he and I?"

"No. What happened?"

"It was maybe twelve, fifteen years ago. When he was a prosecutor, long before he made AG. I faced him in criminal case against a woman accused of trying to kill her husband. They were in the middle of a nasty custody battle. He'd abused her for years, and finally, she moved out. He was furious, threatened her, and raced off one night in his old Volvo, down those windy hill roads. He slid off the road and lived, but the police found that his brakes had been tampered with, and he accused my client."

Brakes? Was that what happened to Coyle Adams, my juror? The police said there were no brake marks, but could someone have tampered with them? She jerked back to Donohue.

"Sorry. What'd you say?"

"If you're not with me, then how do you expect me to be with you?" His eyepatch stared at her as well as his steel-grey eye.

"I'm sorry. I was thinking about brakes and tampering and wondered about the juror…but that's a tangent. Tell me what happened with Simmons."

"During the trial, a story came out in the paper about my wife. She's from one of Seattle's founding families. Big timber barons. Lots of money."

He went to the wall and leaned against it, slid down to sitting position. "Strength training. Squats. Hard to find time… Back to my wife. When she was in college, a sorority sister accused her of stealing. It was a major scandal. My wife didn't do it, was cleared of charges, but it was traumatic enough that she dropped out of school. The news articles, of course, shouted the accusation part and went silent on the clearance part. Especially since her family was such a pillar."

He slid back up the wall.

"Bad enough with the publicity, but the other woman hounded my wife, and we learned she'd done this elsewhere. She would move into a sorority, accuse the richest one of theft, and get something from the family—like a payoff."

"And…what's this have to do with Simmons?"

"He found the initial article and spread it around town to embarrass me, to put me on edge. It worked. I was distracted, worried about my wife, and lost the case. I've never opposed him since. And, since I'm doing full disclosure, I think Madeline fed him the article. She was working at Ivins and didn't make partner. She was probably using that as a way to get back at me."

So that's behind her prickliness.

He stared at her without looking at her, thinking about something else. "Now, give me your best courtroom pitch for this case. Once more. But short. Two minutes."

She reached in her pocket for the Scottish flag good luck pin.

"Because the defendant has exhausted her appeals at the county level, we are filing a motion for a new trial, based upon evidence unavailable at the initial trial. This case addresses a terrible mistake: a woman falsely accused of a heinous crime. We will prove that she could not have killed her four children, all of them under age two, over twenty years ago, by offering new scientific evidence, new methods of document analysis, and scientific data that together show that biology and genetics are behind the deaths, not willful murder. There was no crime, just a terrible tragedy."

"Ah. *Habeus corpus.* She shouldn't be in custody."

She slurped her last drops of coffee.

"Please also understand that this case is bigger than a single woman and four horrible deaths in one family. The evidence will help vindicate other families around the world who have faced similar unexplained, unexpected deaths of children. This case may help them, the mothers especially, find closure in knowing what caused their children's deaths—genetic mutations, not wrongdoing by any person. What mother wouldn't want this peace of mind after such trauma?"

He tilted his head slightly, in what she hoped could turn into a nod, but she was afraid to spend time hoping. Someone knocked, and he dispatched them with a wave. The whirr of the air conditioning unit kicked in.

"Finally, this case is personal. This woman on trial is my aunt…" She gestured toward an invisible courtroom table. "Victoria Beringer carried the fatal gene mutation that killed at least two of her children, my cousins. I am also the sister of a child who died under similar circumstances, an unexplained death of a boy under age two."

His eye widened in surprise.

"The prosecution may, or most likely will, argue that I am too close to this case to be part of it, to argue for it; that there is a conflict of interest. I challenge the assumption. I'm the best person to be involved. Yes, I am related to the defendant, but I didn't know of her existence until two months ago. I've maintained the distance needed for a case like this. On these grounds, we ask for a new trial for Victoria Beringer."

She dropped into the chair across from Roy and maintained eye contact.

"You are serious about this."

"It's a life-and-death matter. Of course, I'm serious."

"And how do you see the firm benefitting?"

"What's not to like about this case? Motherhood is on trial, it's got a mystery, it's got new evidence that simply wasn't available, and if Simmons tries it, it brings back one of the earlier trial's key prosecutors. If our firm took this on, and won, what a coup. I want to be part of something like that. Something big. That's partly why I studied law."

"If you don't get to work on cases like this, what would you do?"

"I might have to find a place where I could. In this case, I've learned about families, my own included, and how fragile they can be, especially when something goes wrong. And how the law can help."

"So idealistic." He grinned. "If we take this on, it'd be our first pro bono in years. I told you we never did but I was wrong. We did have one about ten years ago. A hit and run of a child. So maybe once in ten years won't break the bank." He stood. "I'll file the motion—since the appeals were used. This will go to district court. Let's fight this and win. For your aunt. Against Simmons. For the good of lots of women and mothers. I like your spirit. But tamper down the personal angle. You can mention your aunt but hold on the rest. . . ."

She felt blood rush to her face.

"One more thing. You mentioned a gene mutation in the daughters. Weren't there two sons? What about them? If we get a new trial, we want to get your aunt off on all four murders, not just two. That doesn't take us anywhere."

"Ah. That's the one piece missing from the puzzle. We don't have DNA evidence—yet—for the boys. We need that from their father."

"OK, then. Go get it." He looked down at his papers. "I'll work on getting a new trial."

The magical moment passed. Back to the grind.

Chapter 41

Thursday, June 15, 2006

"We may have your trial back on track, but I need your help."

Band aids had replaced the gauze bandages on Aunt Victoria's right wrist, but she rubbed it with her left thumb. *Is she wishing away the scars or wishing she'd succeeded?*

"Aunt Victoria, did you hear me? This is good news." She tilted her head as well.

"I thought we settled this in the hospital," Aunt Victoria said. "No more work. I'm not worth it."

She leaned back, exasperated. "We've been through this before. Stop trashing yourself. And yes, we did talk about it at the hospital, but I'm not ready to stop. This firm is on board. Help me out here."

Aunt Victoria stared at her, unblinking. "Why should I? I want this to end, not to start up and then throw me down again. I'm tired."

"Will you give me ten minutes? After all we've been through, can I get your attention for a few minutes?"

She gaped at Aunt Victoria's band aid. *Say yes. Say yes.*

"I'll give you that. Make your argument."

Emma touched her right thumb. "Point one, this case touches people across the globe. Some ninety families have lost children in unexpected and unexplained deaths. Many of their situations were similar to yours. If we have a chance to find out what caused the deaths, shouldn't we?"

She stuck her index finger in the air. "Point two, in the last two years, research has come up—research that wasn't around twenty-four years ago—that suggests that gene mutations, compounded by underlying illnesses in these children, caused their deaths. Not you, not God, not chance. A scientific reason.

"And last," she held up her middle finger, "your diaries convicted you. We can counter that argument now by looking at those same diaries with new methods and reach more accurate conclusions."

"That sounds better than what you've told me before."

"I didn't have a clear picture earlier. Now it's shaping up. But there's one missing piece where I need your help."

Emma glanced at her watch.

"We have the DNA for the girls—gene mutation and their heart conditions caused their deaths. Not you."

Aunt Victoria nodded without energy. "I understand that."

"The boys don't have the same mutation, so we need to find out if theirs came from your husband's DNA."

"Dell Beringer. Haven't thought of him in years. I have no idea where he is."

The visitor's room clock, old fashioned analog, white face with black numbers and a red second hand, sounded louder than she had recalled. Tik, tik, tik… Time was slipping.

"Anything that would help me find him? Anything? We're empty handed on internet searches." She put her hands in a praying position, but that seemed weird, so she placed them in her lap.

"He disappeared after the trial. Within months. No word until I got divorce papers two years later." She sucked her cheeks in.

What a place, this prison. Emma couldn't imagine spending a night, let alone twenty some years. *I have to get Aunt Victoria out.*

"Please think. Did you know his parents? Did he have siblings? Any friends to follow up with?"

"I don't want to think about him. I can't help."

Tik, tik, tik. Eight minutes. The guard rocked back and forth. The visitors and inmates at other tables raised their voices and spoke quickly. The room felt hotter than when she'd entered.

It reminded her of a summer job in high school when she'd proctored math and science tests for her fellow students; the room heated up over the couple of hours, from body heat, fear, and hope, as fifty to one hundred students poured their futures into those tests. The prison room had the same feel of body heat and fear, but not much hope.

Emma continued, "Please. This is for you. For your children. For other families who face the same mutations and don't even know it."

Aunt Victoria's eyes darted around the room, and she shook her head. "He had a brother, in Seattle. Strange name. Something like barley…maybe Farley? Met him a couple of times. I don't know if they stayed in touch, or if he went there."

Emma scribbled in her notebook. "That's good. Anything else? Any friends? Relatives? His parents?"

"Time." The guard rapped on the wall.

"Farley Beringer. That was all she gave me," Emma raced to her car as she talked to Rupert. "See what you can find."

By the time she pulled into her driveway in Surrey, Rupert had found the brother in Seattle.

Chapter 42

Monday, June 19, 2006

Finished with her run, Emma wiped her phone with her sweaty palm.

"We did it, Emma," Roy Donohue said. She heard the plunk of his briefcase onto a desk. "We have a new trial. July 12. Not long."

She made a fist pump. "Congratulations. That's fast. How'd you do it?"

"I used your elevator pitch, without the heartstrings.... We're arguing for a new trial, given the new evidence. Simmons asked for that date."

"I don't follow."

"I assume he thinks we won't have enough time to prepare. I suspect he'll use a retread of his former case so that doesn't take much. He'll argue the diaries showed motive and confession. We have so much more now. But it all depends on the DNA. Otherwise, we have half a case, which is worthless."

DNA. I have to find Dell.

"...was Lincoln Black, now retired, so we can't go before him."

"The original judge?"

"Yes. Aren't you listening?"

Touchy Roy. What'd they call him in the office? Roy Rogers, because he was trigger happy, anything could set him off? "So not him, then who—"

"We got Andrew Masco. Five years on the bench. Good man, some background in health care, not that it will help or hurt. We've got three weeks to prep. We also have a stay of execution until after the trial. I've heard rumors that Washington state may declare the death penalty statute unconstitutional soon, but for now, she could face the gallows if we don't pull this off."

"Oh God. Don't remind me."

"The genetics evidence is the cornerstone this time around, and we have to be watertight. Oh, and you'll be second chair."

"So…am I no longer suspended then?"

Dead air space.

"No promises. But the case needs you, obviously. And don't forget, we still need the father's DNA. Any progress on that?"

"I'm going to Seattle this weekend to look."

"Find him."

He hung up.

Chapter 43

Thursday, June 22, 2006

"I should get frequent flier miles for all the trips I've made here," Emma chortled.

Aunt Victoria pushed her eyebrows together. "Huh? What are frequent miles?"

"Sorry. You've been away too long. Big news. We have a trial date. July 12. Three weeks and a couple of days, so not much time."

"Why so soon?"

"The district attorney, Ed Simmons, the man with evil eyes, wants it. My boss, your new lawyer—Roy Donohue—thinks he wants to limit our prep time. He's right. It will be a stretch to make it. But we've got most of the pieces in place."

Victoria gave a washed-out smile.

"And we did find an address for Dell's brother, in Seattle. Farley. So, thank you for that. I'm going this weekend."

"Why is all of this so important to you? It seems like it's more than it was at the start."

Now or never. She had to tell someone, and why not the person who was the core of all of this drama? She paced in a tight circle before sitting down.

"What's wrong, Emileen? Something's eating at you."

She looked at Aunt Victoria's drooping grey eyes. Her hands were clasped.

"I never asked…are you left-handed?"

Emma could see the whites all the way around Aunt Victoria's eyes. "I am. How would you know?"

"We both clasp our hands the same way."

Aunt Victoria looked puzzled. "Whatever you say. What's going on? The clock's ticking."

Indeed. Tik, tik, tik.

"Remember that I had a brother who died? Mom thought it was SIDS, but what if it was a gene mutation? And…what if I have it?"

Aunt Victoria's mouth fell open. "Oh, Emileen. I'm so sorry, I never considered that. Oh my God. Of course, you want to find out. I'd hate to think you'd picked this up too."

"And there's more. I'm pregnant."

Aunt Victoria's wheezed. "Oh, dear God. Now I'm terrified for you. It doesn't matter what happens to me, but—"

"Don't you see that they are tied together? If we get your case back on, we could find out more about what might happen to other families, other kids, to me."

"No, no. You must not have the baby. You can't imagine the horror of having a child die. You don't want that, believe me. Tell me you'll not go forward with this."

The slam of a baseball bat couldn't have shocked her more. *How could Aunt Victoria think—and say—such a thing?*

Aunt Victoria continued, "You've been too kind to me. Whatever happens, I'm grateful that we met. You've changed our family forever."

She stretched her hand toward Emma's but did not touch it.

"But you must promise not to carry this curse any further. No other children, no other families must suffer what I went through. What your mom went through. Please, no more children.… Deputy Alders, I want to go now."

Emma sat at an empty table. *Now what?*

Emma's mind raced as fast as her car on her drive to Surrey. Aunt Victoria's outburst, rather than causing her to dither, clarified her thoughts. She definitely wanted the gene mutation test. But the bigger question was whether and when to tell Grant. She hadn't known him long, but her gut told her he was the one. He was a man she could count on, the one who made her wobbly, the one she wanted to have children with. She had to tell him.

Chapter 44

Friday, June 23, 2006

Emma hadn't heard crickets this loud since she was a child, in her parents' backyard. But Grant's yard held an orchestra, along with the shadow of a barn owl in a large spruce tree. She sat at dusk with him on a metal glider, a love seat for two people that slid forward and back on metal runners.

"What a great yard you have, Harriet." She bent over to pet Grant's scraggly dog, who looked no better after a bath than before. Harriet was no slave to fancy dog salons or fashionable grooming techniques.

"I'd love to have you spend all your time here, if you want," he said. "You and Shadrach c-could move in?"

Her insides felt buttery, a good, smooth, warm feeling. "Hmmm. Maybe. Let's talk more, but not tonight."

"OK, Ms. All Business. How's the case going?"

"Pretty well, but a few things niggle me."

"Niggle?" He laughed, which she also loved hearing, along with owls and crickets. "Is that an official lawyer-type word? I missed that in law school."

"Sometimes you have to create the right one."

He gave her butterfly kisses and then a lusty real one. "What's the official word for that?"

"Not sure. Maybe we should work on it though?"

"Sure thing. But first, tell me what's niggling you?"

How can I drop this on him? She needed to ease in, to avoid scaring him off. She heard Rupert in her head. *"Don't rush this."*

"You know that I had a brother who died."

"You told me. Also, that your mom blamed you."

"Well, I might have jumped the gun on that. She never used that word, but the implication..."

"That's tough for a kid to hear, or think she heard. I'm sorry for you. How're you thinking about that these days?"

Without knowing it, he was leading the conversation in a direction that she didn't want to go. She could let it continue down this path and never get to what she wanted to say, or she could haul it back.

"I'm back in good standing with Mom. But..."

"Yes, niggler, what else?" He winked at her and wrapped his arm around her.

"I...I worry that there might be a risk to me. That I might have it, a gene mutation. What would you think about us being together if that's the case?"

The glider stopped.

"Oh God, Emma, what a thing to say. I'm with you, for the trial, for whatever health stuff you may have, including some weird gene mutation." He hugged her, pushed the hair from her face, and kissed her, long and hard. "I've got your back; don't you know that by now? What else do I have to do?"

She whimpered and sank into his arms. "You're a good one, Mountain Man. Thank you."

Several minutes passed as they soaked in the evening-turning-to-night sounds. He sat up straight. "But back to the mutation. Didn't you say there's a test?"

"I—" Her ring tone warned of Donohue calling. "I'm sorry, I should get this." She punched the phone. "Roy? Everything OK?" She walked into the kitchen.

"I've just read the transcripts of your meetings with the experts, the ones you did before there was a case..."

"Yes, I can expla—"

"No need. They were great, but it's even clearer that we need that DNA. Sorry to keep harping on it, but we only have nineteen days till trial. Where are you on that?"

Does he know that it's 10:15 p.m.? Does the man never sleep?

"I'm on it. Going to Seattle tomorrow. I have the brother's contact information and hope he'll know where the former husband is. I'll keep you posted. Now I should probably get—"

"You should get some sleep. Sorry to call so late, but I was excited about those transcripts. Good work." He rang off without waiting for her to say anything more.

The man's as rushed as I am. He needs a good talking to from Rupert.

Grant stepped in from the dark. "I just heard the end. It sounds like you're working yourself back into the firm and your job. Good for you. But I gather he's on you about the DNA?"

"Yes. Seems like everyone is on me about that. Don't you get started, please." She chuckled and kissed him.

"Never. You've got a long drive tomorrow. Best get some shut eye."

The moment had passed.

Chapter 45

Saturday, July 1, 2006

At least I'm alone. Emma had pulled into a rest area on the highway to Seattle the next morning, opened her car door, and spewed her breakfast, an orange and dry toast. Nothing tasted good. This was the part of pregnancy women joked about in public but screamed about in private. She'd slept little, after her unfinished talk with Grant, and slipped out of the house before he woke.

On the drive, she replayed the conversation, such as it was, before Roy's call interrupted it. After that, she hadn't the energy to lead Grant back. He'd have to wait, or rather, she'd have to wait to let go of the pregnancy news. But now, she needed to find Dell Beringer. And that started with his brother, Farley.

Emma found Farley Beringer in a high-rise condo on 12th Avenue in Seattle, four blocks south of Volunteer Park, home of the city's Asian Art Museum. The refined neighborhood made her expect a professor, an accountant, or a lawyer. She lurched back at the grizzled man who opened the door, wearing sweats, a Green Bay Packer's t-shirt, and two-day old beard. He stood in the doorframe, unmoving.

"Hello, Mr. Beringer, my name is Emma Raddell. I left you a message yesterday?"

"I got it but don't know why you're here."

"Ah. I'm trying to find Wendell Beringer? I believe he is your brother?"

"Now that's a name I've not thought about for a while." He crossed his arms and completely filled the door space.

"May I come in and tell you? I promise to be quick." *One, two, three...* She would count to ten, and if he didn't budge, she would leave. *Nine...*

He stepped aside and waved her in. "Make it snappy."

A huge picture window faced west, overlooking Puget Sound. The interior design was more Pottery Barn than back-woods cabin—fluffy pillows and throws over an upholstered couch. Artificial roses sat on the glass-topped coffee table.

"Beautiful."

"My daughter's place," he said. "She's out of town for the month. I live in West Seattle, nothing fancy like this, but it's nice to have the view for a few weeks." They stared at a ferry chugging toward Bainbridge Island. "What are you after? Do you want coffee?"

She lowered to the couch's edge, bracing herself for this conversation she'd planned on the five-hour drive from Surrey. She had one chance to get it right.

Beringer returned from the kitchen, coffee mugs in hand.

"Mr. Beringer, I don't know how much you know about the trial that your brother went though. Or his wife—"

"I know that she murdered his four kids, and he was devastated. Never got over it. He was glad she was locked up but...he never got over losing those young ones." He looked at his palms.

"Right." She let a few beats pass. Her pacing needed to be spot-on. "Well, new scientific evidence may show that his wife did not kill those kids. That gene mutations did."

He recoiled and narrowed his eyes. "What're you saying? But she was convicted. All four. That's what Dell said."

"I know. He was right. Then, in 1982, twenty-four years ago. A lot of research has happened since then."

"Research? I thought it was an open and shut case. She confessed. In her diaries. That's what he told me."

"I understand. The way she wrote the diaries *could* sound like a confession. But she said she was writing to God, asking for his help, not confessing."

"I don't know about that. When I saw him, after it was over, he was so mad and hurt, he could hardly talk about it. He stayed with me for a few months. Cried a lot, drank a lot. The place smelled like sadness."

"That must have been hard. Where'd he go, after he left?"

Farley shrugged. "I heard that he got married again, but that didn't last. A friend of his, Adelson...Abramson...called me once and said that Dell had tried to do himself in. He was so depressed. I imagine it just got to him."

She put her hand over her heart to slow it down. *Dell, suicide? God, this family has nothing going for it.* "How awful."

"Yeah. He came back to Seattle later. I saw him a few times, but then he disappeared. Homeless, I think. It's been ten, maybe twelve years?" He ran his hand under his nose. "Sorry. It still makes me mad, and we weren't even that close. Just bothers me."

"I'm so sorry. But I need to find him."

"What the hell for?"

"We know the girls died from a specific gene mutation that comes through the mother's side. Their mother...Victoria...had it, and so did the girls. It caused heart failure in both of them."

"What's that got to do with Dell?"

"The two sons died of something different—they had seizures and problems with their breathing. And maybe another gene mutation."

"Dreadful." He picked up a piece of pink quartz and tossed it from palm to palm. "My daughter says it brings good feng shui, good energy. Who knows. I need some in my place, I guess."

"I've heard that...but back to the kids. If the boys had this other gene mutation, we have to prove it came from the father, from Wendell, or not. That's why I need his DNA."

He rubbed the top of his head. "Damn."

"So, I need to get him tested—to know if he had that gene mutation, which could have been passed to the boys. And caused their deaths, not Victoria."

The quartz stopped moving, trapped in one palm. "Did Dell cause them to die? Because he had a bad gene?"

"No, no. It's not his fault, but if he had this gene mutation, if he passed it on, that plus the kids already being weak could have led to their deaths. The gene mutation is the cause, not my aunt, not—"

His head jolted up. "Your aunt? You said your aunt. That murderer was your aunt?"

"Uh. I didn't want to bring it up in case…what just happened."

"You were trying to trick me. That's not right." He stood, gripped the quartz. "You should go."

"Oh please. First please tell me how to find him, and then I'll leave."

"If you think I can help you find him, you're crazy. I told you, he's gone, dead or drugged out. I have no idea."

"Can you think of any places? Or people who might have an idea of where he could be? I'll take anything."

"You're wasting your time. He's a bum if he's still alive."

"Well, let's start with that. Where would bums go in Seattle? Used to be Pioneer Square. Is that still a hang out?"

"I never go downtown so I don't know. Or care."

"What about homeless shelters? Where are they?"

"I've heard homeless people go to the library because it's warm." He chuckled. "That would be a laugh, Dell in a library. He hated school."

She watched the ferry boat inch its way toward the dock below Pike Place Market. During college, she had ferried across the Sound and biked around Bainbridge Island. She tugged her attention back to this contrary man.

He shook his head. "Probably best for you to leave."

"All right. Thanks for your time. I'll let you know if I find him in case you want to make contact again."

She stood and moved toward the door. *Hold on. Maybe this isn't a dead end.* When she and Rupert examined the family tree, hoping to find some kind of link for the gene mutation, she hadn't known about Farley Beringer.

"Mr. Beringer, maybe you can help me in another way." She cleared her throat.

"You don't give up, do you? One more question, and then I want you out of here."

How testy people can be.

"You could help so many families who want to know how their kids died; that it was a gene and not chance or their own doing. Don't you see that?"

"But what do you want from me? You want Dell."

"Let me be clear. If I cannot find Wendell, you're the closest relative he has. We use your DNA instead. It would be a huge help, would go so far in clarifying this—"

Farley laughed. "Well, Ms. Raddell, you've got this all wrong. You're barking up the wrong tree."

She tilted her head. "What're you—"

"Dell and I were adopted. Three years apart. From different parents. No common DNA with each other. Or with our parents. So, you're out of luck."

Chapter 46

Sunday, July 2, 2006

Emma shrugged out of her prissy lawyer uniform—grey suit and white shirt—and donned a Seahawks sweatshirt and jeans she'd found at a thrift store in downtown Seattle. She stuffed her work clothes into a plastic bag and walked toward Pioneer Square. Thick trees darkened the square even during mid-afternoon. Clusters of two or three people sat under trees or slept on benches. Two drank from paper sacks. She approached the least scary person, a woman about sixty, wrapped in a dark green plastic poncho.

"Excuse me. Ma'am."

The woman looked up with glassy eyes, one of them clouded. "Eh?"

"I'm looking for someone. Wendell—or Dell—Beringer?"

"Did he win the lottery?" The woman chuckled. "Otherwise, no one here wants to be found."

Emma squatted. "May I pet your dog? What's his name?" She reached out her fist.

"Grover. He's a drooler, so watch out."

Grover, some boxer mix, turned his thick head toward her, sniffed, and turned back. Not interested. He reeked of fish and cheese.

"And he doesn't like strangers—"

Grover growled, so she jerked her hand away.

"Are you sure you don't know anyone by that name? It's important that I find him. Last name's Beringer." Drizzle fell along with the temperature.

The woman pointed her chin toward a man sitting ten feet away, under a sycamore tree. "Ask him. Knows everybody." She reached for Grover and pulled the poncho over her head, dismissing Emma.

Sycamore Man's face was brown with dirt, and he lacked most of his top front teeth and stunk of bad bourbon.

Emma leaned in to hear him mumble, "Who are you after?"

She wrapped her hands in the bottom of her old-new sweatshirt and crossed her fingers—superstitious, but she'd try anything. "His name is Wendell, or Dell, Beringer."

"No one here named Dell. Beringer neither. Sorry."

He snapped his fingers in a lazy sort of way. "But there is a Berry. He's usually here, but I haven't seen him. Could be sick. Could be dead."

Sycamore Man passed a paper sack to his neighbor.

She shoved herself up from squatting and stretched, relishing the rain mist. *This might be all I get from this trip. Rain.*

She traversed First Avenue, walking eight blocks to Pike Place Market, stopping to ask people lying or sitting on the ground if they knew someone named "Berry." No luck. She spent nearly an hour trekking north on the sidewalks, going from one side of the street to the other. As she approached the market, she gagged on fish smells and sat to catch her breath. *Am I fighting a lost cause? What if I never find Dell? Or what if I find him by some miracle but he's unable or unwilling to talk to me? What if he's dead?*

She faced a group of men, most sitting on the ground across the street. One held a cardboard sign, handwritten and fading: "Veterans. Grateful for help." He wore a baseball cap with a First Infantry Division Big Red One emblem and an army fatigue jacket ripped on the right sleeve.

She knew the of Big Red One because her father had told her that was his father's division during WWII. At the vet's feet, a flat metal tray held several one-dollar bills, coins, a couple of twenties, and what looked like a five Euro bill.

She dropped a twenty into the tray and asked how he was doing.

"Not much business. Not many tourists yet."

"They'll come. Could I ask you something?"

He slapped his thigh. "You already did." He chuckled. "But go ahead. Ask something else."

His response sounded like something a grandfather would say, some love behind it and a little joking. These men may have had normal lives, with grandchildren, but now they were on the street.

"Do you know anyone named Wendell or Dell Beringer… or Berry? A man from eastern Washington."

The veteran looked sideways at her, wrinkles framing his eyes. "Berry? You want Berry?"

Did my luck just change?

"Try the guy with the old black parka with a Cavalry patch." He stuck his elbow out. "Earmuff hat. He can't stand the cold here. Wet cold…. Berry! Berry, wake up. You've got company."

The man with the black earmuffs grunted, fluttered his eyes open, and stared blankly.

"Come on, old man," Big Red One said. "A pretty young lady wants to talk to you. Maybe you won the lottery." He winked at her.

She shook her head. "No lottery, sorry. I only want to talk."

Berry hoisted himself up, pressing against the brick wall behind him, digging his fingernails into the crumbling mortar. He brushed his jacket and took off his Arctic earmuff hat. "What can I do for you?" He wobbled, and she reached forward, ready to assist, but he raised his hand. "No need."

Not what she'd expected. He needed a shower, but she sensed no alcohol or weed. "Hello, Mr.—"

"Call me Berry. My friends do." He chuckled. "Should we go somewhere more private? My calendar is pretty open today." He wobbled to another bench at the end of the brick building.

"Do you want a coffee or something?"

"Bad for you. Tea drinker now."

"Well, tea then?"

She wasn't reaching him and feared he'd cut her off before she had a chance to make her case.

"Nah, I'm good."

"Thanks for talking to me."

"I don't know what we're talking about, so no need to thank me. What's on your mind?"

"I think…I'm a relative of yours." She looked at him straight on.

His eyes sharpened, and he pulled his head back. "That's not possible." He put his hands on his thighs and leaned against the wall.

"You're Wendell Beringer, right?" She watched for a reaction, but he had a poker face. "You were married a long time ago to Victoria?"

He closed his eyes, soaking up the mist. "Never heard of such a person. You must have mistaken me for—"

"Your brother told me you might be here."

"I have no brother. Once, I had a wife. She died a long time ago. No reason for us to talk."

She gritted her teeth and forced herself to slow down, but she felt the internal "tik, tik, tik." "Will you hear me out, please?"

He shook his head, eyes still closed, and shrugged. "Go ahead. But I'm not your man."

"But you may be, sir."

"Don't call me that. I'm not in the army. And I'm not the person you think I am. Say your piece and leave but don't expect me to answer your dreams."

He had to be the guy. He was the right age; his brother had thought he'd be on the street.

Across from their bench, a fish monger behind a glass counter tossed a two-foot-long steelhead to his colleague in front of the counter. The second one waved the fish around, showing off for customers. Tourists, in skimpy sweaters and no rain gear, clapped. The man tossed the fish back to his buddy.

She balled her fists. "Let me tell you a story about a family many years ago…a man and woman, in love, and they wanted a big family. They had a child. A boy. Perfect. But he died, unexpectedly. Suddenly. The doctors said it was something called SIDS, sudden infant death syndrome. Not common. But it happened to this couple. They were devastated, grieved for months."

His face went slack. *Had he fallen asleep?*

"Hmph," he said.

A response! "They wanted more children, so they tried again. Another child, another boy, came along after a couple of years. Sadly, he died too."

He rolled his head back and forth along the brick wall, loosening mortar pieces that dropped onto his shoulders like dandruff. The veins in his neck popped out. "Not sure I want any more of this fairytale."

"You promised you'd listen to me. Just a little longer."

His jaw muscles pulsed.

"Life was tough for the couple," she continued. "They tried to move forward but couldn't. He worked harder, drank, and stayed away from the house. She prayed, gardened, and they avoided each other for a while. But luck found them again. Another child. This time a girl. The little family had Christmas together, and life was good. But then—-"

"No. No more." He lifted his head from the wall and stared at her. "You don't know what you're talking about. Nothing happened like that…. Time for you to—"

"Do you mean nothing happened that way? Or it never happened at all?"

"I mean I want you to stop. What are you telling me this for?" His lips became a straight line, and he scraped his palm over his mouth.

Her shoulders shook. *Can I get the rest out fast?*

"Please. Let me finish. At some point, the man found his wife's diaries and gave them to the police. There was a trial, and the prosecutor claimed those diaries were a confession; that the wife had killed those poor kids. The wife was convicted of murder and went to prison in 1982."

"No. No." His hoarse voice drifted from her.

"But there's another version of that ending. One where the mom does not kill her children, because I mean, what mother would?"

She was so involved with the story she had missed the odor of fish mixed with irises, pretzels, and chocolate chip cookies baking at the stall in the far end, but once she stopped talking, the aromas filled her nose. Coffee, this being Seattle, overpowered the other scents, but she picked up the layers. Actually, the scents were pleasant on their own, but smushed together, not so much. She'd never noticed that.

Sitting this close to him, she also sniffed his stench. *Sweat and old pizza. Could that be?* She didn't want to scooch away and lose any chance to get him to open up, so she breathed through her mouth.

"Why are you telling me this? It has nothing to do with me." He half-smiled. "And, in case you hadn't noticed, I'm a busy man and need to get to my active day."

She chuckled. "Just a little more."

"OK. Finish."

"In this story, the deaths were not at the hand of a human, but from a bad gene, a mutation, in fact. Some researchers in Europe and the U.S. found that…a gene mutation was the likely cause…for why those children died. Not anything their mother did."

He jammed his furry hat on his head and yanked it over his ears and part of his face. His breath sounded like mucous had settled in his throat. He coughed into his hand, pulled a well-used tissue from his pocket, and wiped his nose.

"Not what happened. I don't know what you're trying to do, to confuse me, but that's not what they said."

Yes! She'd opened a crack and now wanted to wiggle her emotional equivalent of fingers into the crack and widen it. But she tempered her enthusiasm.

He leaned over, head in hands. "I don't know what you're saying. Genes and research is trash. Nothing like that happened."

"And you're right; none of this research existed twenty-five years ago. It's come up in the last few years. It's new information."

His forehead had gritty horizontal wrinkles and one huge vertical one between his eyebrows. He brushed the back of his hand over them. "So what? None of that matters. She's dead."

Is that what he thinks?

"No, she's not dead, but she will be soon. She's been in prison all of this time. But she's about to be executed."

"What? I thought she'd died not long after she went to prison. Good riddance, I thought. And now you tell me she's alive?"

"For a few weeks unless you help me."

"What does that mean? Not that I'm saying I know anything about this…this story you told."

Her adrenaline soared as she moved in for the final act. "We know that the girls…your two daughters…died from a gene mutation, for sure. They got it from their mother. The boys… that's a different case. They had a different gene, one that wasn't in the mom…."

He stared forward.

"Do you get what I'm saying?" His face was placid and his body slack. No tension. Maybe no understanding. "Wendell… uh…Berry. We need to know, or confirm, where the boys' gene mutation came from. Since you're the father, we assume it was you but need to test your DNA. There's no other explanation for those kids' deaths."

She stopped talking to let it sink in. Tourists wandered past, skirting his legs, which stretched out from the bench. Impatience nagged at her, but she smashed it. She'd done nothing this nerve wracking since her first mock trial in law school.

He spoke, eyes closed. "Why should I do anything for her? She killed four children. Plain and simple."

"You've got a right to be angry. But this is bigger now. More is at stake than just your children. Lots of families had children die unexpectedly, and many had these gene mutations. Knowing what killed Darrin and Brian would give you answers as well as others."

She stood again on a sharp decision cliff that fell off on both sides.

"I have no interest in that kind of thing. Nothing. Count me out."

She needed an additional act.

"I'll tell you why I'm interested. I talk about those other families, but to be honest, I'm selfish. I'm interested because…I had a brother who died early, like your kids. You remember Victoria's sister…Elisabeth? She's my mother."

He turned toward her, eyes wide.

"What if I have one of those gene mutations? If I ever want to have kids, that knowledge could affect my life. So, this matters to me." She took a quick glance for a reaction. Still nothing. "And since you and I are related, even if not genetically, I want to know what happened to your kids and to my brother."

He brought his hands to his face and leaned over. After ten seconds, she heard him take huge gulps of air and let it out in sobs, nearly silent, but heaving. Tears seeped out between his fingers.

What the—never expected this.

"Oh God. Oh God," he wailed. "Oh my God."

She scooted a little away from him, to make enough room to reach up and put her hand on his shoulder, patting his rough jacket. "I'm sorry. So sorry." She handed him a small pack of Kleenex. The tissues had African animal hide prints—zebras, leopards—but he didn't seem to notice.

"Thank you," he said, reaching for the tissues. "I'm sorry. Didn't mean to do that. You got me, though."

She removed her hand from his shoulder and looked again at the vendor booths.

He pulled himself to a straight position, feet directly under his knees. He could have been a child at a desk in the 1930s, straight back, hands on thighs, ready to receive a swift strike from a teacher.

"You want the DNA. You're asking me to prove I'm the reason they died?"

She leaned toward him again. "No, it wasn't your fault. No one's fault. It was random, a gene mutation you didn't know you had, if you do have it."

Head lowered, he tore the tissue into small pieces, and they drifted from his hand to the ground, becoming soggy in seconds. They stuck to the pavement and dissolved. He rubbed his shoe on them, so they vanished.

His voice was barely a whisper. "Married again after Vic… after she left. And had another child." He stared at his left ring finger's blackened nail. "Slammed a steel door on it a month ago…but when that child died, how could I blame another woman for that death? I was the common factor. Me. So I left. Tried to end it a couple of times, and now I'm here."

"Please don't be so hard on yourself. You didn't know."

"But I deserted her. And from what you say, I had the gene that killed them, not Victoria?"

"A gene mutation. One in the girls that came from Victoria. And a different one in the boys that may have come from you." She let a minute pass. "And if you let us test your DNA, we'll have answers. Finally."

Her practice of counting to ten wasn't working. She hit twenty and looked up at him staring at her.

"OK."

"Oh. Thank you." She reached over to hug him, but he pulled back.

"Not sure you want to do that. Who knows what's on me these days? My gold shower hasn't been working."

She laughed. "I am so grateful to you. You have no idea how important this is."

"I'm doing this partly for you. It's been a long time since I've seen someone fight so hard for this family."

Tears sprang, unexpectedly.

"Your folks should be proud of you."

If only.

"But let's do it before I become my normal ogre self again. And don't tell anyone what I did. It would ruin my playboy reputation."

I could come to like this man.

Chapter 47

Monday, July 3, 2006

Emma phoned Roy with the news as she waited for Dell to fill out paperwork at the testing clinic. "Success. He's getting tested. It turns out he had another wife, after Victoria. They had a child, a boy, who died of SIDS, or so he thought. Now he's thinking the gene mutation could have caused that death as well."

"We couldn't have done this without you. Good work."

"Thanks. We should get the results in a week."

"That's tight. Trial is upon us. And by the way, did you file the new Gleeson papers?"

She relished his praise, but it flickered by so quickly she had no time to savor it. *Hard driver, this man.*

"No, but I will."

"Be sure you do. I want them off my back. And yours. But you're pulling your weight on this Beringer one. Good job."

Again, crumbs of approval flitted past. *I'll take them.*

"And I need to search death certificates when I get back. I want to find Dell's other child and see what the certificate said."

"OK, and do it fast. Anything else?"

"I worry that he'll sink again, maybe depression."

"That's not your problem. Your job was to get the DNA, add it to the evidence for your client's case. You're not here to save the world."

"But I have a strange feeling. Maybe I should get him to come back."

"Remember I told you we don't do pro bono at Ivins; that we're not bleeding hearts? We're making an exception this time, but you can't save everybody. Forget him."

She opened her mouth but closed it. *Futile.*

"And oh, by the way, I've heard that Simmons is on the warpath for our experts. He'll want to discredit them, as a good prosecutor would. So be ready."

Simmons, of course. The man never quit.

She hung up as Dell dropped into the hard plastic chair next to her. "They'll send results to you," he said. "With permission to use them in court."

"Thank you again, Dell. Or Uncle Dell? How strange does that sound?"

He snickered. "Stranger than anything I've heard. Dell's just fine." He stood up and put out a hand, still grimy from the streets, even though he'd told her that he'd washed it for ten minutes in the restroom.

"What will you do now?"

"Back to my home away from home. I normally stay around Pioneer Square, but yesterday, I decided to check in on my buddies at the market. Lucky for you, I guess."

"Have you thought about returning to your old world? I could help—"

"Family means a lot to you. I envy you. Haven't had that for too long."

Her throat closed up. *Here's a man I met two hours ago, who saw that I desperately wanted a family, to be part of the one I have, and I haven't even fully acknowledged it.* "What'd you say?"

"That family seems important to you," he said.

"I've wanted to belong forever but never felt like I did. When my brother died, it seemed like the love my parents had just got soaked up into their grief. I never thought I was enough for them."

"Oh my God. I may have been a bad husband, but I can see what you're doing. If they don't see that you're saving them from going downhill, they're blind."

"I can't believe you think that. You give up your DNA, and now you tell me that I'm worth it."

He looked dumbfounded. "There you go again. Of all the crazy things you've said this afternoon, that makes no sense. You've pulled this scraggly family together when no one else could. After those kids died, I think we all scattered, like those stars in a nebula that spin away from each other. Know what I mean? And you've pulled the family back together."

She wanted to cry. This man, this gentle man, had such a big heart, and she wanted more of him.

"Why don't you move back to Surrey? Or to Snowville where my folks live."

He thumped his hat against his leg. "Can't go back. Too many memories. It means a lot that you asked. I wish I could do something for you in return—"

"You know you have. This test will make the case. I'm hoping Victoria will be out before too long. Thanks to you."

He left her at the door of the clinic. She watched him amble along Pike Street, touching the buildings' walls now and again for support. He never turned around.

Chapter 48

Wednesday, July 5, 2006

"Your best bet is the microfiche, down this aisle. Good luck."

Officer Caldwell saluted and left Emma in front of an old-fashioned microfiche machine in the country records office. Behind her, stacks of boxes dated from the 1950s. She pulled out boxes from 1983 through 1988, the five years after Aunt Victoria's trial. *That should cover the time when Dell's child with his second wife had died.* Three other people sat in front of the ancient technology and rolled the film.

The whirr of the spinning fiche from different machines sounded like orchestral tune ups: whirrrrrrr, stop; whirrrr…slow down…whirrrrrrr…stop; whirr, whirr, whirr. A quartet of micro fiche players.

After ten minutes, she found Charles Wendell Beringer, born October 15, 1985; died January 4, 1986. SIDS. *Poor thing. He hadn't even made it three months.* She slid her finger down the Cause of Death column. There was another SIDS death at the bottom of the page. She flipped pages: two…three, four…six… *So many back then.*

She froze. Evan Edward Simmons, born July 27, 1985; died February 8, 1986. *Simmons?* And there it was: Parents listed as Edward Michael Simmons and Marjorie Hopkins Simmons. Ed Simmons. *The Ed Simmons? My Ed Simmons?*

Maybe he isn't the tough guy he comes off as. Maybe there's a side to him that hurts as much as Aunt Victoria did, losing a child? This was several years after her case. *Maybe he changed? Softened? Should I give him the benefit of the doubt?*

Her phone vibrated. "Antigone? What's up? I'm in the archives building so have to be quiet."

"You're joking? What are you doing there?"

"A little research for the Beringer case. I'm back on it."

"Really? When's it on?"

"Soon. What do you need?" She didn't want to give anything more away.

"Are you up for the group bar crawl tonight?"

"Not tonight. I'm slammed."

"What are you finding? Anything interesting?"

Now was her chance to plant some information and see if it made its way to Simmons.

"Did you know Ed Simmons had a daughter who died young?"

Antigone skipped a beat. "God. No, how'd you pick that up?"

"I was scanning death certificates to learn about my aunt's kids and stumbled across it." *Does Antigone have a side that I don't understand or see? Why would she be on Simmons's side, anyway?* She waited for a reaction. Nothing.

"Nope. Why would I know anything about that man?" Antigone's voice went flat.

"I thought you'd met him?"

"Not really. Just listened to you talk about him. Are you sure about tonight?"

"No thanks. I've got a lot to do before the case opens."

An hour later, Emma walked into Simmons's office, where his assistant Richard Li intercepted her.

"I'm here to see your boss. I called a few minutes ago."

Simmons stepped out of his office. "Ah, Ms. Raddell. I hear you're now an archives expert?"

Antigone?

"I'll get right to it," she said. "You've tried so hard to get me to drop this request for a new trial. But now I've come to ask you to back off or at a minimum to ask for compassion."

He cocked his head. "I don't follow."

She had to find out if he was in the good guy column after all. She lowered her voice and leaned in.

"You, like Ms. Beringer, know what it's like to lose a child from something that you don't understand. It must have been awful for you and your wife. Going through something like that…it must have given you empathy for Ms. Beringer?"

Simmons's cheeks whitened, but his nose reddened. He made a fist of his right hand, on the desk. "What the devil are you—ah, the archives. But you think it was a daughter? Wrong."

Bingo. She'd caught the mole. But she had to follow through with her plan.

"Ah, right. I found your son's death certificate, 1986."

Simmons blanched, knowing he'd been caught.

"Going through that, you know how it feels, how Ms. Beringer suffered," she said. "That's got to put you on our team, on our side of things."

He leaned toward her and whispered, but his tone was harsh, not at all soft. "That is no business of yours and has no effect on this case. Emotions don't play well in the law. And especially not with me. You don't seem to know that."

The vitriol shocked her. *How could he be so cold? No emotion, no sign of compassion.* He really was a reptile, cold blooded. But she had to give it one more try.

"Oh, you and I both know that cliché reeks of duplicity. Of course, emotions matter. Don't be a hypocrite, pushing this case when you know you don't have a chance, when you know that the conviction was dubious. It's morally wrong, especially since you faced the same situation."

"There is nothing…*nothing* you can do or say that will make us back off." His eyes closed and opened as he hissed at her.

"That woman killed four children and confessed it. That's the law. That's our case. What my family experienced later has no bearing—"

"From what I can tell, you're going to present the same case that you offered twenty-four years ago? Or almost the same? What about the new evidence that says gene mutations have come into play here? What do you say to that?"

"Irrelevant in this case. I've seen your experts' depositions. Nothing we're worried about. Our scientists refute the research, but more important, the simple matter of the number of children, in one house, with one mother…it makes no rational sense."

"But the research might explain your son's death."

She felt smaller than when she'd walked in. *Is he gaining on me?*

"Ms. Raddell, you're out of line, again. And why do you think we have nothing new in this case? Or that I'm going to present it? Now get out of here."

Blindsided. She'd not considered that Simmons would have different information. *Or is he calling a new witness? Or will he have a different main presenter? That will throw Donohue off his game. Is Simmons beating us again?*

Chapter 49

Monday early evening, July 10, 2006

"We knew you could do it," Mom said.

Emma, Mom, and Dad, along with Rupert, clustered around the edge of Grant's kitchen while he fussed at the stove.

"Through this case, you've brought us together. And now I can't wait to see how you do in the trial." Mom hugged her, lightly, and Emma hugged back, a little stronger. Dad winked at her.

Grant handed out glasses of champagne. "Em? Champagne?"

"I'll pass. Want to be sharp this week."

"That's a first—not even wine?"

"You're grimacing," Rupert whispered to her. "What is it? We're celebrating your big case."

She leaned toward him. "Nerves. We still don't have the DNA results from the clinic in Seattle. They were supposed to be here today."

Her father joined them at the counter. He clinked his beer with Rupert's champagne glass. "You're ready for it, Lou." He squeezed her arm. "Victoria was floored that you found Dell and got him to agree."

"Final piece of the puzzle," she said. "Speaking of which, I'll call the clinic once more. They're open till 7:00 p.m."

"Thank you for calling, Ms. Raddell. I meant to call you today but haven't had a moment." The man's high-pitched voice sounded like a cartoon character. "I have your file here…somewhere…just a…ah. Here it is. Let me see.… Oh dear. I have some bad news."

The hamsters in Emma's stomach charged faster on that silly wheel inside of her. This person held the key to success or failure for her, so she needed to be kind, to be patient. *But blast it! Get on with it.* She sat on the toilet seat in the tiny bathroom that masqueraded as her private office at Grant's. Shadrach scratched at the door, his instincts to calm her at the ready.

"What's happened? I need those results. You promised I'd have them today."

"Yes, well. Technology is not always our friend, is it? And neither is the flu, which is slamming our office—"

"What's going on?"

"…Let me finish, please. I'm new here.… Our technician who does the tests was hit hard beginning of last week. The flu. He ended up in the hospital. He's still there and will need a few weeks of recovery."

"What does that mean? You can't shut your lab down because of one person?" She started hyperventilating and grabbed the sink's edge. *Breathe. Breathe. Slow down.*

"We've been talking about a solution for you, and we have one."

She felt her chest loosen. *A solution. Thank God.*

"We'll send the sample to our sister lab in Oregon and ask for the tests to be run there."

"And what's that mean? How long will it take?"

"They are backed up as well so we're probably talking several weeks."

Oh no. She slumped to the floor. "No. No, I need those results this week. For a legal case. A life and death case. Can't you speed it up?"

The artery in her neck throbbed, so she put her hand on it, trying to calm it down. This was a disaster. She'd failed. Failed Aunt Victoria, Mom, Roy Donohue. Everyone. She'd worked so hard to get things on track, and now…

"There may be another route. Are you able to invest some money?"

What's he talking about? I already paid to get these tests done. Now what?

"There is a lab, not fully on the up and up, but in emergencies, I used it in my old job as a backup. Are you interested?"

Her body was so limp she could barely hold the phone to her ear. *What choice did she have?* "Tell me."

The man squeaked out the information about the dubious external lab, run by some shady-sounding organization. The price for a single test was thousands more than what she'd paid. She couldn't justify it, let alone pay for it. "No. That won't work. Aren't there any other options?"

"No, sorry. I'm sorry about your case."

"You also ran a test for me, on my DNA. Did that get sidelined too?"

"Let me look. Give me a few minutes, I'm new at this system."

She wrenched herself back to sitting on the toilet seat.

Grant knocked on the door and opened it a crack. "You OK in there?"

"I hope to be. I'll be there soon." She listened to her monotone voice. *If he can't tell I'm in the dumps from that, he's not worth the effort.*

"Hey, you don't sound so good. What can I do?" He wrapped his fingers on the door and opened it enough to show one eye, scrunched up. "What's going on?"

"I'm on hold. I'll tell you later." *Maybe he is worth it.*

"Ma'am. Ms. Raddell?" Another voice came across the phone. A woman who could be a radio announcer, calm, clear, confident. "This is Dr. Wishbone."

Emma stifled a smile. *What a great name for a doctor.*

"I'm so sorry about all of this. The admin you just talked to is...it's his first day, and he's...frankly, things are a mess."

"You're telling me. Now who are you?"

"I'm the head of the lab. Our tech is out, as you heard, so I've been trying to track what's going on. I have some good news and bad news for you."

She felt whiplash. *Why do these people do this to me?* "I'm glad to hear about the good news but scared about more bad news."

"It turns out we found Mr. Beringer's test."

She lost all sense of ability to sit upright and was too weak to be glad. She leaned over onto her thighs. "That's great," she whispered.

"We can run the test on Thursday and get it to you that evening."

"No, that won't work. I need it on Thursday morning. Any way to get it earlier?"

"I could try—maybe we could get it done on Wednesday, but it would be late, maybe by 9:00 p.m.? I'll try to get them sooner for you, but it would be a stretch. We could overnight them Wednesday night?"

Another setback. "No, that's risky. I'll drive over to get it."

"All right. I could meet you at the office. We close at 7:00 p.m., but if you come, I'll wait for you."

"But what's the bad news?"

"The bad news is that your DNA test is missing. I can't tell if it was done yet or if it's just waiting. There were two orders with almost identical names. So, they may have been swapped, mixed up. I just can't tell. But the bottom line is no results on your test."

Chapter 50

Wednesday morning, July 12, 2006

Heat and humidity, mixed with the scent of anticipatory sweat, blanketed the visitors sitting on the wooden pews in Judge Andrew Masco's courtroom on Wednesday morning. The window air conditioners in the eighty-year-old building grumbled, trying to stay ahead of the July heat. None of that helped Emma's queasy stomach and pounding headache.

Aunt Victoria wore a hint of lip gloss, and her wrist bandages were gone.

In the courtroom, Masco waved his arm. "I apologize for our antiquated system. While I love the history and beauty of this building, it rarely serves occupants well, especially in summer. We've provided paper fans, with Surrey County logos, to quash the discomfort."

Earlier in the morning, Emma had asked Roy about his light blue striped seersucker suit, which matched his pale blue and white eye patch. Atticus Finch in *To Kill a Mockingbird* had nothing on Roy. "Courtroom theater rests on logic, evidence, and performance. I wear clothes—and my patch—to convey a message that I'm confident. You'll find your own style."

"Ah. But with my grey suit today, I'll be roasting in the heat."

"Then show them you can maintain your calm composure in the face of blistering heat."

The jury sat in two rows to Masco's right: four white men, five white women, two Asian women, and one African American woman. One man was a nurse in the children's hospital but claimed he could be objective about the deaths of four children who had lived and died before he had been born.

Attorney General Ed Simmons and his assistant, Richard Li, sat at the prosecutor's table. Simmons moved his alarming lizard eyes toward her, and she shivered.

From the bench behind the defense table, Grant gave her thumbs up signals. Mom and Dad grinned like they were at a performance of a high school production of *Music Man* and Emma was the librarian. Rupert and Natalia had claimed the last row, with Marty standing next to Natalia. Rupert had told Emma on Sunday night that he planned to move into Natalia's and help Marty care for her. "Who knows how much time we have, but we want to spend it together. Family comes in many ways," he'd said.

Sweat dripped from the nape of her neck. She gulped her second dose of aspirin in two hours, hoping it would jar the headache from behind her eyes.

This portion of the trial allowed each side to show its intentions. Ed Simmons reviewed the key points for the prosecution: that they would offer the diary confessions, call a witness who would speak to the defendant's unstable mind, and refute the defense arguments about scientific data and content analysis conclusions. In addition, they planned to call Sir Lyndon Packerton from Australia, the renowned pediatrician who had cemented the earlier case with his memorable statement about so many children dying in one family being not only unreasonable but impossible.

Roy stood. "Your Honor." He buttoned his sear sucker suit jacket and bowed slightly to the jury. "We will present recently found evidence, unavailable at the time of the original trial. As you know, Ms. Beringer was convicted mostly on the circumstantial evidence of her own words in a diary."

Emma glanced at Simmons for some reaction. Nothing.

"The earlier case relied on 1,500 words of the diaries, out of 40,000 written over a decade. Fifteen hundred words." Roy paused.

"We will present a more thorough review of the diaries, as well as scientific research and testimony from genetics experts and data from around the world. Our argument is that a gene mutation, or two, played a role in the deaths of the four children, not any malicious action. We call for a not guilty verdict for Ms. Beringer."

The plan was clear. Now they simply needed to execute.

Chapter 51

Wednesday afternoon, July 12, 2006

Simmons's first witness was Sir Lyndon Packerton, who joined by video. He beamed in from a room lined with books, many with leather bindings in hunter green, maroon, or black with gold lettering. Diplomas and awards hung over his left shoulder.

Emma scanned the jury: four nodded as though Packerton made perfect sense, three took notes, and one young man in a black shirt and white tie whispered to his neighbor, the African Emma woman, who, based on her age, could have been his grandmother. The woman patted the man's arm. Judge Masco scowled.

"We need your full attention. The defendant deserves it."

Packerton came across as a sage grandfather. He put his spin on the unthinkable.

"Certainly, multiple children in one family die, devastating to families. But in my experience…in my fifty years as a pediatrician and doctor to hundreds, perhaps thousands, of families… there is always something in the house that explains the deaths."

Damn. He is good. The set design augmented his credibility.

"Dr. Packerton. Oh, forgive me, Sir Packerton," Simmons exaggerated. "You're quite the distinguished doctor. Could you tell us what household factors come into play in families where so too many deaths occur?"

"Ah. Many factors…like parental arguments, separated families, families that move house frequently, families that are in poverty. Women who are alone."

Aunt Victoria stiffened.

"So, you claim that when multiple deaths happen, the cause is contextual, not genetics."

"Certainly. It's sad, but those factors mean danger for children. Genetics has nothing to do with it." He leaned back in his wing back chintz chair and lowered his glasses to the end of his nose. "That is one's objective conclusion."

One's conclusion? How pompous.... She couldn't wait to get her hands—or Roy's hands—on this guy.

Simmons bowed to the screen. "No more questions. Thank you, Sir Packerton."

Roy buttoned his seersucker jacket and straightened his eye patch. "Good morning, Sir Packerton...or, I'm sorry, good evening?"

"No worries on the time. I'm awake and with you. That's all that matters."

"Sir, you have talked about the statistical impossibility of more than one child dying in a family. What did you mean by that?"

Packerton sniffed and wiped his glasses on his tie. "I have said that for a family with a background like the defendant's, one with two parents, relatively stable income, the chance of one death is 1 in 8,223. So, the probability of more than, of, say, two natural deaths in the same household would be unimaginable, or, in other words, impossible."

Two jury members gasped. Emma's shoulders sank in disappointment. He'd captured their attention and threw out a point that would be hard to un-hear.

"But you're assuming, are you not, that deaths in a family are independent of one another. Why could that be the case? Couldn't there be environmental or...genetic factors? Making the chance of more than one death more likely?"

"I cannot say that, you cannot prove it, so I'll stay with my original claim. One death could be an accident, a second a tragedy, but beyond that, it must be murder."

"But, Sir, at least consider—"

"That is my opinion. It was and still is."

Roy tried to ask questions three different ways, and Packerton's response was essentially the same. After twenty minutes of frustration on both sides, he gave up.

"That is all for now, Sir. Thank you."

An invisible whack hit Emma's chest. *Would they win again?*

Chapter 52

Wednesday afternoon, July 12, 2006

Just before Masco pounded the session into being, Emma slipped into her seat after ten minutes in the bathroom.

"You OK?" Roy looked concerned.

"I'll be fine," she said, but she didn't believe herself. *When will this feeling so wretched end?*

Professor Clinton Yee took off his University of Texas Longhorn baseball cap as he walked toward the front of the courtroom. He wore a red V-neck sweater over his white button-down shirt and a navy blazer on top of that.

"How can he wear all of that? In this heat?" Victoria whispered to Emma.

"From Texas and has not one ounce of fat on him," Emma replied.

Yee moved like a sprite, bouncing up the aisle to the witness chair.

"Thank you for joining us."

"You're welcome. You live in a beautiful city."

"We do. Now, Professor Yee, please tell us your full title and what you do at the University of Texas."

"I'm a professor of psychology and linguistics with a specialty in forensic linguistics. I analyze text materials from bodies of work, which could be lost literary texts, speeches, notes from criminals, and others."

"Can you tell us how that method works?" Roy stepped away from Yee and moved toward the jury box.

"Yes, of course. I use tools developed at the FBI and CIA to do computer analysis of text materials to generate what we call a 'psychological state of the author.'"

"And what data do you use, Professor Clinton?"

"I look at the types of words used, say the percent that are 'emotion words' versus 'boring words,' like pronouns and prepositions. It's like a fingerprint in words."

When he said that, Emma pictured a huge finger pressing on the back of her eye sockets. She closed her eyes for a second and opened them slowly. She could do nothing quickly this afternoon.

"And are these methods validated in some way?" Roy leaned against the jury box.

"Yes, of course. The methods and types of data have been used in studies published in numerous scientific journals. All of them peer reviewed."

"For those who may not understand what means, could you please the term 'peer reviewed'?"

Clinton tiptoed his feet and his torso to face the jury. "Certainly. Peer reviewed means that scientists from the same field read and assess the validity and reliability of manuscripts before they are published. Usually three reviewers—all specialists in the field of the submitted manuscript—read and review the study. They evaluate and then write assessments on whether the study and manuscript are acceptable for a journal. Usually, the manuscripts need revisions and changes to improve them before they meet the standards for publication. And just so you know, most of the scientific journals we submit our studies to accept less than 10 percent of the submitted manuscripts."

"So it's a rigorous process."

"Yes, indeed."

"Thank you. And now let's talk about Ms. Beringer's diaries. Did you review them, using your method?"

Yee ran his hand through his Andy Warhol haircut, peppered with grey. "I did."

"How much text did you analyze?"

"Our program examined all 40,255 words. That was the full set of her notebooks over ten years. Of those 12,012 words dealt with the children, their births, health, deaths."

"And to refresh all of us, how many of those words did the prosecution use, in the first trial, to argue that she confessed to killing her children?"

"The prosecution used 1,500 words."

"Out of, what did you say, 40,255? That would be about what percent?"

"Less than 4 percent. To be accurate, it's 3.7 percent."

Roy chuckled. "And what did you conclude, using those reliable methods you described earlier?"

"We applied those principles and reliable methods to the data, which was the full text of Ms. Beringer's diaries. To a reasonable degree of scientific certainty, in my professional opinion, I would describe Victoria Beringer, at that time, to be self-reflective, anxious, and honest."

Aunt Victoria sighed.

"And did your analysis...conclude anything about whether... about whether she intended to harm her children?"

She held her breath. *Here it comes.*

"No. I found nothing to indicate premeditation. No sign of hostility. And she wasn't devious and didn't try to hide her actions or her thoughts. In fact, the text showed deep grief. A woman who, in that grief, began to question everything around her, who she was, what she had done, even her memory."

Boom. *That should shake things up.* She flicked her eyes toward Simmons. Nothing. The guy was a statue.

"Are you saying she wasn't thinking rationally?"

"I'm saying she was in a state of anxiousness, and she questioned herself. But there's nothing to suggest a person who would harm others."

"Thank you, Professor."

Yee smiled. "Happy to help."

Richard Li stood up, buttoned his suit jacket, and smiled at Yee. "Here we are. Two Asians making good."

What's he doing? She glanced at the jury members. *Confused?*

"Sorry?" Yee looked taken aback.

Li winced. "Professor Yee, before we get to your technology… do you know how the diaries even became part of the evidence in the first trial?"

"I don't."

"Ms. Beringer's husband turned them in to the police. He read parts and decided she was harming her children. Even her husband thought she was guilty."

Emma's stomach ached, and she felt Aunt Victoria shift like she was seeking a comfortable position but couldn't find it. *What a low blow.*

She started to stand, but Roy jumped up first. "Your Honor…"

"I agree. Mr. Li, you're moving close to the edge here."

"I wanted our witness to know that he wouldn't even have those diaries to look at if it hadn't been for the defendant's husband. He was worried about his children."

"Enough of that, Mr. Li," Masco said. "You're pushing."

"Yes, sir."

Simmons crossed his arms.

Insouciant. He seemed too relaxed, too casual. She made quick eye contact, and he smirked. *Is he so self-assured? With some hubris thrown in?*

Li turned back toward Yee. "Professor, your technology is recent and sounds impressive."

"Thank you," whispered Yee.

"It was unavailable at the time of the first trial. At that time, the experts—like you, experts in text—did a content analysis to uncover the defendant's state of mind. Humans analyzed diaries, not a computer program. Humans, who were able to put the writing into a broader context. Those experts, twenty-four years ago, found that the diaries entries were, in fact, and let me quote here, 'obfuscation and lies.'"

Yee's eyes widened.

She reached under the table and clutched Aunt Victoria's hand.

"In fact, the experts thought Ms. Beringer was brilliant at what she wrote, making it vague enough to be read as guilt, or as she said, 'letters to God.'"

Emma sucked in a big breath and pushed herself up. "Your Honor? Another lecture?"

Li held up his hands in apology.

Simmons smiled, a real smile this time.

Definitely hubris.

"What do you say to that, Professor Yee?" Li asked. "Human interpretation versus a machine. Why should we believe your algorithms?"

Yee cleared his throat. "As I mentioned before, this is technology derived from the FBI and CIA, made to help determine a profile of whoever wrote the text. Of course, humans interpret the findings. The program allows us to analyze large texts of writing. In this case, I wanted to find out what sort of person Ms. Beringer was from what and how she wrote. We analyzed the entire diaries, not only the 1,500 words the prosecution chose, out of context."

"Ah."

What a performer. Li must have learned from Simmons, but he seemed to be overacting, pushing the limit. *Doesn't Masco see that?*

"This gives a better sense of the whole person, who was not complicated, who was not trying to hide anything. She'd probably be unable to deliberately write in a way that would make us confuse a confession with what she called letters to God."

"Or the full 40,000 words were a way to cover up and dilute the confession?"

Roy and Emma both rose. Roy shouted. "Objection!"

Emma glanced at Roy and sat down. He was the main chair, but she couldn't help herself.

"Sustained. Mr. Li, focus on your witness's testimony."

Roy dropped to his chair and glowered at her. "I'll do it," he whispered.

"Just trying to help." *Am I on thin ice…again?* She glanced at a smug Mr. Simmons.

No. You'll never win. Not this time.

"Yes, sir," Li said. "I'm finished, Your Honor. Li strutted to his seat, leaned back, and stretched his legs. Simmons leaned toward him and murmured. Li jerked upright.

"Simmons?" Judge Marco prompted.

"Your Honor, we'd like to invite our previous witness, who is now here and able to join us. Since he will speak to state of mind of the defendant, which we've just heard about from Professor Yee, it might make sense to bring him in."

"We have no objections, sir," Roy said.

"Very good. Please proceed."

Farley Beringer had shucked his lumber jack look, shaved, and donned a navy suit. He avoided Emma's eyes.

"Mr. Beringer, please tell us who you are in relation to the defendant," Simmons said, walking away from the witness box.

Give the man credit…. He knows how to do this. She begrudged Simmons but had to respect his ability to perform. This technique of moving away as a person spoke was one her law professors talked about. As you moved away from someone, she would unconsciously raise her voice so you could hear. Effective. And Farley complied.

"I'm Farley Andrew Beringer, brother of the defendant's former husband."

"And why did you decide to testify?"

"I saw what that trial, what the deaths of those kids, did to him. It destroyed him. She destroyed him."

Donohue leapt to his feet. "Your Honor, hearsay."

"Sustained. Stick to what your witness knows himself, Simmons."

"Thank you, Your Honor. Mr. Beringer, you are here. Not your brother. Not the defendant's former husband. Why isn't he here?"

"You couldn't find him. Hell, I couldn't find him. He's homeless, probably, on the streets of Seattle."

Emma grumbled and said, under her breath, "You didn't look hard enough."

"Thank you. Now, Mr. Beringer, can you tell us what happened after the trial?"

"My brother moved to Seattle, where I live. He stayed with me for about four months."

"And during that time, how did he behave?"

"He drank, he cried, he refused to leave the house. He stayed on the couch for days on end."

"Did he talk about what happened?"

"He said she destroyed his life—"

"By 'she' you mean the defendant?" Simmons twisted toward the defense table.

"Yes, sorry. I mean Vic. Victoria. His wife. At the time."

"Did he talk about her behavior toward the children?"

"Yes. He said she was secretive, that she didn't want him around sometimes. He wondered what was going on. Then he found the diaries—"

Emma heard her mother behind her gasp and say, "Oh God. Oh God."

"Objection. Hearsay. Not directly observed."

"Sustained."

"Let's slow this down," Simmons said. "Did he find the diaries?"

"No, his sister-in-law did. Elisabeth. She told Dell about them, and then he looked at them."

"What was his reaction to them?"

"He was horrified. Gave them to the police. They didn't do anything until the last child, Dot, died. Then they arrested her."

Farley glanced at Aunt Victoria. "Why, Vic? Why?"

Simmons raised his voice. "Mr. Beringer. Do not address anyone but the questioners or the judge." He turned to Masco. "I've no more questions."

Roy stood. "Mr. Beringer, do you think of yourself as a good brother?"

Farley cocked his head. "Of course, I do. He lived with me. I tried to get him through those awful times."

"You cared for him for three or four months, over twenty years ago?"

"Yes. And I was glad to do it."

"But it's twenty years since this happened.... How can you remember so much?"

"I lived through those awful months with him. I'll never forget."

Emma smiled inside.

"But you have no idea where he is now. How can you pass yourself off as a good brother if you lost track of him for so long?"

Farley opened his mouth and then closed it. "I-I tried, but he disappeared. He lost track of himself.... I mean he didn't stay in touch. I tried..." He dropped his head.

The buzz of insects and thump of two ceiling fans filled the quiet space. Aunt Victoria clutched Emma's hand as the fan ker-thumped four, six, eight times.

Roy gestured toward Emma. "Our assistant defense attorney found him in a weekend, and yet you don't know where he is?"

Farley glared at her.

"Mr. Beringer?" Roy stroked the smooth wood of the witness box.

Farley stood and pointed. "Victoria, why did you kill those kids? And hurt Dell so much?" he hissed.

"Mr. Beringer! Please sit down!" Masco waited until the crowed was silent, glaring around the room the whole time. "That's enough. Next outburst, from anyone, and I'll order you from the courtroom. Now, Mr. Donohue, do you have more questions?"

"Not at this time, sir."

"Simmons? Redirect?"

"No, sir."

"Then let's call it a day," said Masco.

Emma rushed to her toy car and headed to Seattle. *Dell's results should be ready.*

Chapter 53

Thursday morning, July 13, 2006

Emma slipped into the courtroom at 10:02 a.m. and handed a manila envelope to Roy. "Just arrived."

"Ah. The DNA results. Good work," he whispered and patted her on the back. "We couldn't have done this without you."

She let a tiny smile onto her face. Her race to the Seattle clinic the night before was worth it.

Roy invited Dr. Simon Albrecht, the geneticist in Natalia's lab and the defense's crown jewel, to the stand.

"Dr. Albrecht, you work in Dr. Natalia French's laboratory at Westminster University, one of the most renowned worldwide. How long have you and Dr. French worked together?"

"Nearly twenty years. We are immigrants. She arrived from Poland. I came from Germany."

"What is your role at the lab?"

Step by step, under Roy's guidance, Albrecht presented his, Natalia's, and the lab's credentials as one of the top in the country. He followed the Daubert standard, like he had with Professor Clinton: facts, methods, acceptance in the peer community.

"Sir, you know that Ms. Beringer's children died, all four of them, under the age of two. How would you categorize the deaths? What's the terminology?"

"That's right. There are two commonly used terms. The first is SIDS—sudden infant death syndrome," said Albrecht. "That applies to infants, under a year. A second term, SUDC—sudden unexplained death in childhood, refers to deaths of children over twelve months and under eighteen years of age. The four Beringer children were all under the age of two. That's a fact."

Emma moved her head slowly since she had remnants of yesterday's headache, but she wanted to take a measure of the jurors. Three shifted one direction and then another. Four looked bored. *Maybe they're lost.*

Roy skimmed his notes before walking to Albrecht.

"So the fact is that four children died. Now, Dr. Albrecht, let's talk about the research that emerged on gene mutations, which could have been a factor in the deaths. Could you please give us this information in the clearest language you can. You're the famous scientist, I'm a country lawyer, so please be simple."

The bored jurors grinned and stopped squirming.

"Yes, of course. First, please understand that the research was based upon methods generally accepted for research in this type of work, in medical studies. And also, the studies around the world were published in peer-reviewed journals at the highest level. The research itself, across several studies, suggests that gene mutations, linked with certain underlying conditions, can cause death in children, from infants to ten years old. Around the world. A gene mutation, identified as CALM2, has variants that affect several areas in the body—from respiratory to the heart. Last year—"

"Excuse me. May I interrupt you, Dr. Albrecht? I'm sorry. To be clear, you say that such unexplained deaths are now being studied in countries other than the United States?"

"Oh yes. Many."

"And you helped us contact some of those scientists doing research on the gene mutations, did you not?"

"Yes, I helped you locate the studies and find nine top scientists from around the world."

"Where were they from?"

"Three from the U.S. The others were mostly from Europe—Denmark, Spain, the U.K. Two are in Australia."

"Did you find the research equally valid and rigorous across all of these sites?"

"Yes, of course. They were as good as anything we've done in our lab."

Emma clapped her fingertips under the table. *Impeccable credibility.* The jurors who had lost interest reengaged.

"Thank you. And what did the researchers conclude after reviewing the research on the gene mutations of CALM2?"

"That it was highly likely that the gene mutations, along with some underlying health conditions, could cause natural death in children."

"You sent the research results to scientists worldwide to review the studies. In fact, sixty-eight researchers, once they saw that review and the research as well, signed a letter of support for retrying this case?"

"That's correct."

"And they asked that Ms. Beringer be released?"

"Objection. Your Honor, that's an opinion, not a fact," Simmons said.

Aunt Victoria glowered at Simmons.

"He's right, Mr. Donohue. Stick to your facts, not opinions."

Ouch. First wrong step Roy had made.

"Yes, sir. Now, Dr. Albrecht, what did that research mean for the Beringer children in terms of what gene they inherited? Without getting too technical."

"Specifically, DNA testing was done on Ms. Beringer and on heel prick blood samples from the children. What's called gene sequencing was performed to see if the children—and the mother—had any gene mutations. The particular one of interest is called CALM2. It's a rare genetic mutation that could cause diseases like cardiac arrhythmia and heart attacks. The two girls had that gene mutation."

"They had the same gene mutation? And what was that exactly?"

"They had one called CALM2 G114R. And this is where it is a bit difficult. When someone has an infection, the mutation prevents a type of protein called calmodulin from doing its work, from helping the heart work smoothly. The body is unable to bind calcium, which, in turn, can lead to cardiac arrhythmia.

If there's an infection involved, it's more likely to cause trouble. Both of the girls had infections before dying."

A single tear traveled down Aunt Victoria's cheek.

"Dr. Albrecht, you're saying the daughters had some underlying conditions—and infections—in addition to this rare gene mutation, and together, that led to the equivalent of heart attacks?"

"Essentially, yes."

Back on track. He's got it.

"Dr. Albrecht. You know that Ms. Beringer had four children. Two girls and two boys. You say the girls had this gene mutation…what did you call it? Let me look…."

"CALM2 G114R."

"Thank you."

Roy leaned against the jury box.

Good move, Roy. Standing at the rail, he came across as being with the jury, not talking to or at them. She'd remember that for future trials.

Two jurors at the far end of the bench leaned forward, elbows on their knees.

"Yes. Now let's talk about the sons. How did they die?"

"One died after twenty-four days. He'd been diagnosed with 'laryngomalacia,' or soft larynx. It's a floppiness of the tissues above the vocal cords. Normally the tissues in the airway open and close during breathing. In this case, when the child breathed in, the tissues moved toward the airway and obstructed air flow. The second boy died at eight months from an airway obstruction as well, which came from epileptic seizures and a disorder connected to his blindness."

Roy faced the jury box. "Dr. Albrecht, did the boys have the same gene mutation that the girls had?"

Two women jurors jotted notes.

"No. A different mutation. Biallelic rare missense variants. They're in the gene BSN, 1898M. It causes early onset lethal epilepsy in mice. There are no studies in humans yet, but the connection seems strong. And…both boys had seizures."

A juror gasped and put her hand to her mouth. "I'm sorry," she mouthed to the judge.

"Are you saying that four children in one family had two different gene mutations that caused their deaths? That seems beyond statistical comprehension."

"Yes, it does. So let's take the cases, two daughters and two sons. In my professional opinion, based upon reasonable certainty of medical research, the daughters died of a genetic anomaly, a mutation, complicated by underlying medical conditions—weak hearts. The gene mutation came from their mother."

"But the mother, Ms. Beringer, never showed any symptoms of heart problems?"

"That's not uncommon, according to the research findings. The gene mutation carrier can be asymptomatic."

He looked down. "The son's situation was different from the girls'."

He spun around. "Dr. Albrecht. To be clear. You're saying the girls had a gene mutation that was different from the gene mutation the sons had?"

Albrecht pressed his lips together in a tight smile. "Correct. The boys' gene mutation came from the father."

Go, Roy, go. Building this case, brick by brick. She nodded her head, keeping the beat of the throbbing inside. Boom. Boom. Boom. She twisted backward to see if Rupert was still in the back row. He was sitting on the edge of his chair and when he noticed her, lifted his thumb up and smiled.

She handed Roy a manila envelope.

"Your Honor, we present the DNA test results of the boys' father, Wendell Aaron Beringer. Dated July 12, 2006—"

Simmons sprang from his chair. "We've not seen this material. We object to its appearance now."

Roy bowed toward the judge. "He's correct, Judge Masco. We received these results late last night, after midnight, to be precise, and were unable to get a copy to the prosecution." He pointed to the envelope. "But we have a copy now."

Judge Masco shook his head. "You cut things down to the wire, Mr. Donohue. I'll allow it."

Simmons set his jaw and looked down. *Is he giving in? When we win, it will be sweet revenge, for Roy, for Aunt Victoria, for me.* She loosened her grip on the chair arms.

"Dr. Albrecht, what does the research, the peer-reviewed articles on this particular gene mutation, mean for you?"

"Again, to a reasonable degree of scientific certainty, in my professional opinion, the boys suffered death from the same gene mutation—different from what the girls faced—that was connected to underlying heath conditions."

The jury's fidget factor was zero. *Good work, Roy."*

"And, Doctor, are there similar cases of such unexplained and unexpected deaths around the world?"

"Yes. A pediatrician in Italy maintains a registry, informal, I grant you, of SUDs—sudden unexplained deaths in children. He collects data from pediatricians, researchers, and families. It started in 1979 and now has ninety-nine cases in the system, sixty-eight in the U.S. alone. So, yes, such deaths happen, sadly, around the world."

Could this get any better? He was on target, covered the bases he needed to, and was articulate and calm. She felt good, buoyant almost. But then she stopped. *"Don't get too big for your britches,"* Mom used to say.

"One more question, sir. Why is this evidence available now when it was not in 1982, during the first trial?"

"One word. Technology. We didn't have sophisticated gene-sequencing technology then. We used DNA to solve some crimes, but we couldn't do tests to find out what gene mutations existed. It gets better every day."

Roy returned to the table and sat, hands clasped, like he was praying. Emma leaned in front of Aunt Victoria and whispered to him, "Nice going."

"What it is?" Grant and Emma sat on his back porch again. "You look wiped, and it was a good day in court, right?"

Emma reached in her pocket for an email she'd printed out at day's end. "It's the Italian pediatrician, the man who started the directory of families with children who had died unexpectedly. He's tracked nearly 90 families over the last decade. He can't testify."

Grant snatched the paper. "A stroke? Poor guy."

"That puts us down to two witnesses—the content analysis expert and Dr. Albrecht, the genetics expert. The content guy was excellent. I just hope that Albrecht can be as good during the cross-examination."

"Is that all that's bothering you? We never finished our conversation the other night before Roy called. What's on your mind?"

She hugged herself, holding in wobbly courage. "It's still the gene mutation. I had the test done in Seattle, when I went to find Dell. No results yet—but I'm worried."

"You know I'm with you, whatever you find out."

She reached to embrace him, and he kissed her. *He's such a good man. Will I ruin things? But he deserves to know.*

Waffling didn't suit her.

"What if we had a child together?"

"That'd be fabulous! But maybe we get married first?"

"Are you asking?"

"Do you want me to?" He winked and began to kneel.

She pulled his hands up. "No, nothing like that, at least not now."

A hawk flew into the yard and scooped up a squirrel bounding through the grass. The squirrel screeched and fought, but the hawk flapped away, squirrel in its mouth. She recoiled and screamed, and Grant covered her eyes.

"What the—" Grant yelped.

"I'm going inside. That's too much for today." She returned to the couch for safety. *Life's too unpredictable. Why would I ever want to bring a child into it? Not now. Not yet.*

Chapter 54

Thursday afternoon, July 13, 2006

Edward Simmons, all six feet two inches of him, stood slowly and he wiped his right index finger around the front of his collar.

"Dr. Albrecht, thank you for being here."

Albrecht nodded.

"Before we get into the scientific content, here, I have a few more questions about you, your background and credentials."

"Certainly." Albrecht moved backward in his chair, getting comfortable.

"You said you came to the U.S. as an immigrant. Both you and your colleague, Dr. French. You're from…" He looked at his notes. "…Germany?"

"That's correct."

"And by that you mean East Germany, is that not true?"

Albrecht leaned forward. "Yes. I grew up in Berlin, and after World War II, it was indeed part of East Germany. I lived there until 1986, when I came to America."

Emma brushed an invisible fly near her face. Even though there was no insect, her neck muscles tensed.

Simmons lowered his voice.

"Just before the wall fell, yes. And if I have this right, you spent your childhood in a suburb of Berlin, where your father worked in a factory making munitions."

Albrecht rubbed his palms back and forth.

"You are correct, but I don't know what that has to do—-"

"In fact, your father worked for the Nazis. Correct?"

"People were forced to in those days. Why are you asking—"

"He was, your father, one of the more visible sympathizers in the early 1940s, was he not?"

Emma's feet went cold. *Is Simmons painting Albrecht as some sort of Nazi supporter?*

"I simply want to understand your background," Simmons said. "You are an expert, in gene research, and I wonder how you got there."

Emma's stomach gnawed. She leaned over to Roy. "Where's this going?"

Roy shrugged. "Let's give it a moment."

"Dr. Albrecht, you attended a well-known, scientifically focused university in Berlin and had a professor named Herr Professor Dr. Rudolf Strauss, who was a doctor during the war. And afterward you joined the…let me see…the Department of Health, which, of course, has a German name I can't pronounce." He smiled at Albrecht and chuckled. "I tried to learn German but gave up. Too many long words."

Albrecht grinned weakly. "It's a difficult one for many people, I agree."

"Well, you worked in the national Department of Health in a small unit."

"A very small and short-lived unit."

Emma gasped as an unexpected stab ripped through her chest. *What the—*

"Actually, it existed for twenty-two years, from 1948 till 1970. And you worked there…let me check again…from 1961 to 1970. Nine years."

Simmons looked at Albrecht, whose eyes were trained on Roy, pleading.

Roy stood. "Your Honor, where is this going? Dr. Albrecht has established his credentials, and his expertise in gene mutation theory. We don't need to return to East Germany in the 1960s. His most important research was done here, not in Germany. What's this about?"

Judge Masco looked at Simmons. "Your plan?"

"Just a few more questions, Your Honor, and you'll see our plan."

Masco lifted his hand in a dismissive move. "Go ahead, then."

"Dr. Albrecht, what was the title of your 'small unit,' in English please?"

"It's…it's difficult to translate. It was human studies. Genes in humans."

"You're being modest, Dr. Albrecht. Was the unit not called, forgive my bad translation, 'The Center for the Study of Human and Animal Eugenics'? Its researchers studied how to make improvements in humans and animals, in particular breeding stock, is that not true?"

Emma couldn't focus on Simmons, who looked wavy in front of her. Aunt Victoria gripped her forearm, digging her short nails into Emma's wrist.

"Oh, I 'sink' you are exaggerating. We tried only to understand 'gins' in the early days." Albrecht said.

Oh God. His accent is coming through. He's stressed. Blood bath. How did we miss this? She had asked what they needed to know from the experts, to avoid surprises. *How did we miss this? Roy'll be furious.*

"My dear Dr. Albrecht." Simmons stood in front of the witness stand, blocking Albrecht's view of Roy.

Roy shouted, "Objection. The prosecution is patronizing this witness."

"Sustained."

Simmons shrugged.

"Sir, Dr. Albrecht, your small unit continued the work the Nazis started before and during the war. And you were there, before the funding stopped. When you came to this country, you created a false *curriculum vitae.* You covered up your experience to avoid admitting this."

"I…uh…I…was little involved. Just a young assistant. No responsibility." Albrecht pulled his handkerchief from his trousers' pocket and ran it over the back of his neck. "No real responsibility."

Emma's head pounded more. *How can we save this?*

"Sir, it really doesn't matter. What you've told us is that the foundation of your scientific knowledge, your work, your reputation started with abhorrent research that is long disputed and disreputable. Making you the same. How can we believe anything you tell us?"

Roy jumped up. "Your Honor, maybe we have a recess. I think the defense needs to regroup."

"I'll say," said Judge Masco. "We'll be back in the morning. In the meantime, Dr. Albrecht, you are dismissed." He held his hand over his microphone, but Emma could read his words, "What a fricking day." Or something worse.

Chapter 55

Thursday late afternoon, July 13, 2006

"Absolutely not. Natalia's not up to it. It could trigger reactions that we don't want." Marty, Natalia's caregiver, placed his hand on her shoulder and waved a paper fan at her with the other as the group squeezed into a sterile conference room.

"Natalia's our only chance." Roy Donohue sat at the opposite end of the metal conference table. "She has to testify. They demolished Albrecht. I'm glad the jury heard what he had to say before that happened. Even though the judge will throw it out, they still heard it."

Rupert held Natalia's hand. "I agree with Marty. This case is important to you," he nodded at Roy, "and especially to Emma, but we can't risk it. We're talking about Natalia's health here. Now that she's in my life, I don't want anything to take her sooner than—"

"She's my responsibility, and I'll decide what happens," Marty said. His face coloring matched his red hair.

Bile crept up Emma's throat. Simon Albrecht's rout had drained her. No one deserved a slaughter like that, and they'd let it happen.

Natalia raised her hand, asking for silence. "I need no one to speak for me. I speak for myself."

The room hushed, except for the clang of an air conditioning unit in distress.

"Thank you." Natalia scanned the room. "I choose not to testify. Short answer."

Pow. No reason, no discussion, no analysis, no emotion.

"I know this is difficult, but could we talk about it?" Emma's voice sounded shrill.

Natalia took three deep breaths, glanced at Marty, and nodded. "I'm OK."

He grabbed a chair next to her.

"I'm furious. Simon's reputation was torn to shreds…in tatters…through nothing he did." She took breaths after every ten or so words. "He's my friend, my colleague, my co-researcher for twenty years. We shared stories about those communists who nearly killed us. Physically and in spirit. That man…Simmons…he killed my friend, figuratively."

Emma couldn't blame her for being livid. Hell, she'd strangle the man if she could. But the only way to right this wrong was to win the case. And Natalia was the only one to do that.

"Natalia, you have every right to despise the man," she said. "But we need you—to save Dr. Albrecht's reputation, to save this case."

No one moved.

"No. I cannot do it. That is the end." Natalia looked at Marty, who stood, ready to leave.

Rupert rocked back in his chair and then heaved himself out of it. "Let's go, then."

"Wait, please." Roy tapped the table. "Please tell me why you'll not help us."

"Oh, so many reasons. I can't speak clearly. I'm too slow without the assistance device and I sound like a robot when I use it. No one in the jury box would be able to understand me."

"You know, when someone listens to you for a few minutes, they forget how you sound and hear what you say," Rupert said. "And being slow isn't a bad thing. It shows thoughtfulness."

"Thank you for the vote of confidence. But that's not all. The jurors would pity me, and that is not the way to win. You need power and strength. What Simon had, until that *dupek* started talking."

Emma looked at Roy, who also had knitted eyebrows. "*Dupek?*"

"Ha. *Dupek* is Polish for graceless schmuck, or worse, if you know those words in English."

"Got it. You're right. That *dupek* ruined our case. But you can save it. You're credible, you're smart, you're empathetic. And the speech doesn't matter, as Rupert said, after a few minutes."

Natalia pursed her lips. "The most important reason, of course, is that I have not been involved in the latest research. Not directly, not in three or four years. I retired, and then…this, so I've only written about it, not done the work."

Emma nearly shrieked. "What? You know this research as well as anyone, including Dr. Albrecht."

"You're kind to say so, but I cannot. I'm sorry, but not me." Natalia turned her chair to face the door.

Emma felt her adrenaline sink. They'd have to forfeit; let Simmons win.

Emma hurried to block Natalia's exit. "One more question. May I?"

Natalia nodded. "Go ahead."

"Tell me about ALS. Is it caused by genetic problems? By a mutation?"

Roy, confused, said, "Emma, this doesn't—-"

Emma lifted her palm and stared at Natalia.

"Actually, that's what some research suggests," Natalia said. "Because it's an orphan disease, not many people have it, so it is hard to get research funding."

Roy and Rupert looked at her. She imagined their minds rushing to fill the gaps in her path. Her mind felt sharp. Finally.

"Then let's walk this through. If that's the case…if there needs to be more research on gene mutations relating to ALS, but it's hard because there aren't many people with this disease… wouldn't you be the *perfect* person to talk about the importance of research for other types of mutations? For other rare diseases?"

She watched Natalia's face move from passive boredom to eyes wide with recognition.

She laughed. "Well done. You make a good argument. Maybe it's time you looked into law school?"

Chapter 56

Friday morning, July 14, 2006

Judge Masco brought the court to order, and Richard Li stood.

"Your Honor, we ask that Dr. Albrecht's testimony be struck from the record. We showed that his credibility was in question, so his testimony is as well." He clicked a pen on and off until Simmons touched his hand.

"We expected this. Stay calm," Emma whispered to Aunt Victoria.

"So be it, Mr. Li. Jury members, please disregard the testimony from Dr. Albrecht from yesterday. I know how difficult that is, but for the proceedings to move forward, you must. Am I clear?" He waited for them to nod. "Mr. Donohue, are you ready to start again today?"

"We are, Your Honor, and call Dr. Natalia French to the stand."

Simmons placed his palm on the table and made a fist, scratching his fingernails along the wood.

Frustration? Satisfaction? Emma couldn't read the man.

Natalia's wheelchair purred as she motored to the front of the room. She was sworn in and apologized in advance for her slow speech.

"Dr. French, I'd like to go through some of the testimony yesterday about the gene mutation research."

Over twenty minutes, Donohue painstakingly reviewed key points of Albrecht's comments, all of which Natalia backed up.

Not bad to review. Emma liked hearing it again and suspected the jurors did too. The complex gene mutations, mix and match of children and parents—it was good to hear once more. *Back on track. One point for the good guys today.*

After Roy finished, Li rose, again.

The night before, during preparations, Natalia had admitted that if Ed Simmons was the one to question her, she would give him a piece of her mind.

"You can't do that, Natalia, as much as you may wish to," Emma had said.

"Just wait and see." Natalia smiled.

But in the courtroom, Li, not Simmons, stepped toward her. An assistant fussed with a projector, readying a PowerPoint slide deck.

"Thank you for being here, Dr. French. It must be difficult for you...and a challenge for the jury as well." He gestured toward the men and women jurors.

Impertinent. Emma scooched forward on her seat, ready to spring into action.

Roy whispered, "I'll do it if we need to."

"Let's look at the pattern of sudden unexplained deaths in children, in Exhibit 12A, which came from the registry you mentioned. From the Italian doctor, Dr. Busso."

"Correct."

"You'll note that the average age of death in these children, sudden and unexplained, is six years of age."

Richard raised his eyebrows and looked back toward Natalia.

Emma quivered. *What a brute. If she were a wild wolf, she'd tear him apart.*

"Yes."

Richard pointed to the slide.

"You'll also see that on average there is more than one incident, specifically a heart attack, in the SUD children. The mother, or a close relative, tends to be with the child when an incident occurs. And the deaths tend to occur while the child is under some form of exertion—exercise, running. How does that fit with the Beringer children? All were under two. The parents did not see other incidents before the children died. No exertion. No one witnessed the death. And Ms. Beringer was the first on the scene. This does not fit the pattern of cases in the registry."

Natalia blinked slowly.

"I'm sorry. Did I go too fast for you?" Li stood in front of Natalia, forcing her to crane her neck to see him. The courtroom visitors murmured.

Why isn't the judge all over him?

"My brain has no problem, sir. Just the connections to my muscles."

Judge Masco pounded his gavel once. "That's enough. Please eliminate the chatter in this courtroom. Mr. Li, maintain respect."

"Your Honor, Mr. Li is lecturing," Roy said. "Is he going to question Dr. French or give his opinion on statistics?"

"Speed it up, Mr. Li."

Emma peeked at Simmons, who had a smug smile. *Does he think he's winning? What gall.*

"Yes, sir." Li bowed slightly to the judge. "As I said, this information comes from the registry you referenced. How do you explain the Beringer children's deaths, given the data?

"I'm not an expert on the registry. But yes...the averages are different from this case. But they are averages. Ranges, which includes deaths at earlier ages as well as unwitnessed deaths, for example."

"Then perhaps the Beringer girls were 'atypical'?" Li persisted.

"Not if you review all the data. The age range of death age includes older and young children, like the Beringer ones." Natalia lifted her shoulders as she took deeper breaths. Her mouth drooped.

She's waning. Is Li dragging this on to tire her?

"Also, some deaths were unwitnessed, like the Beringers," Natalia said. "And…the boys had seizures before death. The parents saw that."

She leaned across Victoria to Roy and whispered, "He's misleading. We should show the actual statistics. And she's tiring."

"Not yet. Patience."

Patience. Her favorite not-favorite word.

Two jurors fidgeted with their paper fans. Another flicked open her notebook.

He's losing them. On purpose? Maybe to make her look bad?

Li continued, "But, Dr. French, is it not true that scientists are never 100 percent sure, and perhaps like lawyers, never can find 100 percent agreement?" He chuckled and looked at the jury. No one chuckled back.

"Yes, scientists disagree. Often. So, we use data to confirm."

"But if the data are wrong, the conclusion would be wrong?" Li turned toward the jurors again.

"Correct. So, we asked nine researchers, from around the world—"

Li spun on his heel. "And let me stop you right there, please. You say several of these scientists—"

"Researchers."

"Yes, researchers…came from outside of the U.S. Given that we have the best scientific research and people in the world, like yourself, why should we listen to what comes out of Denmark or Australia?"

Natalia glared at Li. "Mr. Li. How can you say such nonsense?" Her voice had turned raspy. "The U.S.…has not for years held a monopoly on scientific talent or output. Many sources show this…." She breathed slowly. "I reject your premise to dismiss research from the world."

Li ran his hand along the railing in front of the jury. Red blotches slowly blossomed on his cheeks, but he remained calm.

"I'm sorry if I offended you. We have to question everything these days. We cannot accept a finding because one expert says so. Excuse me. So, we'll accept that these nine people, all of good standing, agreed on the research."

Natalia's jaw muscles pulsed, and she looked to the back of the room, presumably for Rupert. Her expression never changed.

"Should I continue?" she asked.

Li held out his hands. "Please."

"...We asked nine experts who study this gene mutation family...for their scientific opinions. Each agreed that the Beringer deaths likely came from mutations and thought the case deserved a review."

Li looked at his shiny black Brooks Brothers wingtips and pulled eyebrows together, like he was puzzling over something.

"Dr. French. You talk of data, of statistics. But one other piece of information baffles me." He brushed his hand through his thick black hair.

Another theatrical move?

Natalia's shoulders sagged.

"How can a family have four children who died under such unusual conditions? Four? Sir Lyndon Packerton, a renowned pediatrician in Australia, puts it more directly." He bowed at the jury. "As you recall, he said, 'One sudden death is a tragedy, two is suspicious, and three is murder, until there is proof to the contrary.' Many years ago, he said that more than two unexplained, unexpected deaths of children in the same family would occur only one time in 73 million. Many scientists call that 'Packerton's Law.' How does that affect what the scientists decided?"

Natalia chuckled. "Mr. Li, you quote someone from outside the U.S."

"You got me." Li grinned. "But please answer the question. How is it possible for one family to have four children die so young and it not be suspicious? Sir Packerton tells us it's impossible."

Natalia looked at the judge. "Must I give a statistics 101 course today?"

The crowd snickered.

Way to go, Natalia!

"I have studied Sir Packerton's statements. His statistics are wrong. He extrapolates. He makes assumptions that crumble when examined. In short, I reject his statement."

Li tilted back, as if in shock, and scanned the jury for skeptical faces. Most remained immobile. He returned to the prosecution table.

Roy stood. "Excuse me, Your Honor."

Marco looked dazed, as though he'd been interrupted from something he was studying.

"Uh. Yes. Mr. Donohue."

"May I delve into Sir Packerton's comments?"

"Mr. Li, more questions?"

"Not right now, Your Honor."

Marco lifted his hand.

"Mr. Donohue. How long will your questions take? Dr. French has been on the stand for more than an hour. Perhaps we should break for lunch?"

"Whatever you think best, Your Honor."

Marco looked at Natalia. "Doctor French, you've given us your time and insights. Let's give you—and ourselves—a break."

Emma saw Natalia's face drain of color and feared she might not make it the rest of the day. If she caved, they'd be back at square one. So much for the good guys winning an easy one.

Chapter 57

Friday afternoon, July 14, 2006

"She's exhausted. How could you do this to her?" Marty slammed his fist on the conference room table.

Natalia, next to him, rested her chin on her chest, almost asleep.

"Roy and Emma, I know you're desperate for your case, but Rupert? You're supposed to be with me in looking after her interests. We have to get her out of here."

Emma placed a plastic cup of water in front of Natalia, who ignored it. *Has she lost the energy to even lift a cup?*

"I apologize," said Roy, "but we had to try. The case depended upon her, once Albrecht was out. She's the most capable and well-known scientist in this field. We had to try." He hunched over.

Rupert touched Natalia's shoulder. "My dear, you've done a brilliant job, but we can't put you back in there. Marty's right; it's too much."

Emma screamed inside. She'd pushed so hard for this case, for the people involved beyond herself, and now, it was over. *Just like that?*

"Just a minute," she said. "Rupert, you're a research librarian. There are scads of names on those studies that Natalia did. Aren't there any other people we could ask? How can you list twenty people on a journal article and not have twenty experts? There has to be someone—"

He sighed. "Alas, scientific articles list everyone as co-authors, from the lab technician to the top researcher. So, no, those other names aren't necessarily experts. Natalia's the big one."

Emma placed her palms on the wall and did a standing push-up. She pounded her fist, jolting everyone from a minor stupor. Emily D came to her.

In this short Life
That only lasts an hour.
How much—how little—is
Within our power.

"You're right," Natalia whispered.

"Yes, we must take care of you, first." Rupert stood.

"At least someone gets it," Marty said. "None of you will see what this took out of her tonight." He looked at the clock in the room. "Already two. We should leave."

Emma felt the tik, tik, tik that came to her in the prison. The case slipped away, a tik at a time.

"Stop, all of you…." Natalia's malaise had evaporated, and her eyes twinkled. "Marty, I'll pay the price…or rather, you will…but we cannot end. When has an ALS patient saved a legal case? It's too important to hold back. We must do it, for Ms. Beringer, for other women and families…. I will do this, only if Emma questions me on the stand."

Emma suppressed a yelp of joy and fought off her creeping nausea. *Excitement? Nerves? Or the pregnancy making a point at the perfect inopportune moment?* This was her chance to be a savior, to beat Ed Simmons. If only she didn't lose her lunch or her train of thought during the process.

Chapter 58

Friday afternoon, July 14, 2006

"Dr. French, I want to follow up on two points Mr. Li raised—Dr. Packerton's statistics and the slide from the Italian registry on sudden unexplained death in children."

Emma pressed her right temple, pleading for the pounding to stop. *Focus. Focus on Natalia.* "First, when you talked about Sir Packerton, you said 'people dispute his conclusions and statistics.' What did you mean?"

"If you took statistics courses, you know people manipulate data." Natalia slowed, letting her words hang in the air, as though each word took thoughtful energy.

"Researchers criticized Packerton on two points," she said. "First, the Prosecutor's Fallacy."

The judge laughed.

"I never thought about it like that, Judge." Natalia chuckled.

"What is that, Dr. French?" Emma swept her eyes across the courtroom. Ed Simmons scribbled. *Is he nervous, having Natalia back in the courtroom? Had they hoped to drive her away?*

"Prosecutor's Fallacy means that Sir Packerton's statistics are false...if...another explanation is more likely. Here, the idea of a child, or four, murdered in one family is so rare that the probability of another explanation is high, such as the mother is innocent." She breathed two deep breaths. "It's like a false positive."

"If I understand, you're saying that one incident, in this case murder of a child by its mother, is *so* incomprehensible or unlikely, that an alternative explanation, meaning death by natural causes, has to be more likely."

"Yes."

A couple of jury members made notes. She took that as a good sign.

"Thank you for that explanation…uh…" She reached for some papers and felt her thought slipping from her. *Come back. Come back….* Shuffling the papers gave her time, and she was back, partly. "You mentioned…uh…you mentioned that statisticians disagree with Sir Packerton in a second way?"

Fuzz filled her head.

"Correct. They question his conclusions that multiple deaths of children in a family are…what is called 'statistically independent.' That is, he thinks each death is independent and stands on its own. Incorrect."

Boom. Emma had to be sure the jury understood it. Another nail in Packerton's—and Simmons's—argument. She needed to go through this step by step. *But can I?* Her head pounded, and she saw Natalia in a gauzy haze. *Nerves? The pregnancy?* This was not the time to analyze. This was the time to act.

Natalia squinted, like she was asking if Emma was all right.

"Are you saying that deaths in a family are connected? Why do you say that, Dr. Albr…so sorry, Dr. French?"

Emma glanced at Roy, hoping he would see that she needed help, but he studied papers in front of him. *How can Natalia tell that I'm woozy, but Roy missed it?*

She saw Rupert standing in the back of the room, mouthing, "Are you OK?"

She gave him a blank stare.

"Events in a family are rarely isolated," Natalia said. "They are not discrete. We must consider family conditions that might make children more at risk, including genetics. With so many factors in common, the chance of a second death is more possible."

She listed from one foot to another, trying to quell the motion in her head, and hoped others didn't notice her unsteadiness. "I understand. But didn't Dr. Packerton also say family conditions affected deaths?"

"He did, but you recall…he disputed, never mentioned, the possibility of genetics. To say only that poor families or single mothers would be the cause eliminates an entire realm of possibility. That's the crux here."

"Thank you. And what about the directory from Italy? What does that tell you?"

"Dr. Busso's registry shows several American and British families with multiple deaths. At least ten. We cannot look only at statistics but must include context."

Three jurors sprang doubles, and Emma shook her head to rid herself of extra bodies. "And how might that affect Sir Packerton's statistics?"

Rupert stood up again. *At least I only see one of him.*

"Sir Packerton so often says that multiple deaths just are not possible. Something else has to be going on."

Natalia slurred, or at least Emma thought so, but she didn't trust herself. The three jurors and their doubles nodded.

"I agree that's outrageous. Now let's look again at the slide Mr. Li asked about."

Natalia tried to smile, but her mouth tilted up only a small bit. She was tiring.

"What do you know about…about the registry?" *Losing my train of thought again.* If this happened once more, Roy'd pull her out. *Focus.*

She stepped toward the jury box and forced the double jurors to vanish.

She caught Roy, pointing at his chest. "Me?"

She didn't respond. She couldn't quit now.

"How did Dr. Busso create this registry?" She gripped the jury box hand railing to stop weaving.

"Dr. Busso asked doctors of sudden unexplained death patients to send…medical cases and documents, notes. Some families sent information. He tracks the deaths, looking for patterns."

"And the patterns?"

"Most critically, he found no evidence of the so-called factors that our British colleague mentioned—no parental separation, no abuse of children or mothers, no poverty. Something else was at play. Genetics."

Emma walked toward the defense table and caught her toe, nearly stumbling. Grant, in the bench behind her, made a move, but she put her hand out, palm face toward the floor. "No," she whispered.

"Thank you for that background. Mr. Li also asked about average ages when a child died, the likelihood of multiple incidents before death, the likelihood that someone witnessed the child's incidents and death. How would you address his concerns, given the registry data? Let's take them one by one."

"Dr. Busso says…these are averages." Three words, one breath. Natalia's voice sounded anemic. "But he says 20 percent of children's deaths in the registry were under two, like the Beringer children. Not insignificant."

Aunt Victoria tilted her head, more engaged than during earlier testimony. *Courage, Aunt Victoria.*

"Many of the registry children were under two years old. What about the claim that children had multiple incidents, heart attacks, before they died?"

"Again, Dr. Busso reported that two thirds of children died during and because of their *first* episode."

Sweat dripped down Natalia's temple. Marty stood in the back. "May I have a tissue, please, Judge?"

Judge Masco fumbled on his podium and handed Emma a box of tissues. She passed it to Natalia, who wiped her face twice, and then handed the box back.

"Do you need a break, Dr. French?" Masco swung from Natalia to Emma, asking both.

"Fine, Your Honor." Natalia said. "Thank you for offering. I want to keep going."

She turned to Emma. "You asked me if parents witnessed heart attacks before children died. In Busso's data, 66 percent of cases and deaths had no *prior* symptoms. Parents did not see attacks coming." Natalia turned slowly toward the jury. "Just like the Beringer children."

The jurors were back in their own bodies, no duplicates. Emma's confidence returned, if not a calm stomach.

"Thank you, again. A last question. What about Mr. Li's assertion that most parents witnessed the deaths of children who died in an unexplained or unexpected manner?"

Natalia nodded. "As I said, two thirds of deaths had no indication a child was at risk. Also, Dr. Busso found that 25 percent of registry children died in their sleep. No witnesses. Like the four Beringer children."

"Doctor French, you've been helpful. Thank you."

She returned to the defense table with sweat dripping down her cheeks, fearing her mascara would make her look like a racoon. She wiped a tissue under her eyes. Sure enough, black.

Roy leaned in front of Aunt Victoria. "What's up? You're white as a sheet. Can I help?"

Emma closed her eyes and whispered, "At the break," and wrenched her focus back to the courtroom to hear the judge's voice.

"Mr. Li? Questions?"

"No, sir. Thank you."

Simmons stared at the table without expression.

Is he beaten?

"Then we'll move to closing arguments. Tuesday morning. 10:00 a.m."

Bang.

Chapter 59

Saturday morning, July 15, 2006

"Who knows what harm Natalia's testimony did? If jurors couldn't understand her, that's as good as nothing at all. Or maybe worse, they're irritated."

Roy Donohue faced a white board filled with notes for the closing argument and tapped a blue felt tip pen on his palm. He and Emma were alone in the office.

How dare he blame Natalia? Emma seethed. He was the one who practically bullied her into taking the stand. Sure, they had no other choice, but what a disaster. It was their responsibility, not Natalia's. Her roiling stomach and fuzzy head wouldn't let up.

The front door bell buzzed; a special delivery package was at the office front door. *On a Saturday? Could only be bad news. Didn't bad news always come at unexpected times, as a middle-of-the-night phone call or a special delivery on a non-business day?*

"Excuse me. I'll be right back."

The package's return address was the Seattle clinic. She rushed to the restroom. She needed privacy, feeling her now-regular morning sickness about to hit.

The contents had to be the results of her DNA test, the results that could change her life. She ripped open the envelope, raced through the cover letter, and gagged.

"We are sorry we do not yet have the test results. It pains me to write that our sister lab in Oregon has misplaced your test. They have scoured the incoming tests but are unable to find them. We need another sample. The good news is that our lab is fully functioning again, so we should have the results in a matter of days. Please call to set up an appointment."

What the… Am I jinxed? With the pregnancy plodding along, week after scary week, she needed to know whether she might be a carrier. And now this. She'd go to Seattle tomorrow, do the test on Monday, and try to get back in time for closing arguments on Tuesday, because she had to present. *Who else could make the case as relatable as I can?* That meant convincing Roy.

"Emma? You in there? Are you OK?" Roy knocked on the women's room door.

Of course, I'm in here. No one else in the building. Who else would it be? "I'm here."

"Is everything all right? We need to finish this argument."

She lumbered back to the conference room, sinking to a chair. It was 11:00 a.m., and she wanted to be in bed.

"Roy, we need to talk about who's presenting the close."

He studied the white board. "Nothing to talk about. I am."

She tapped her trusty No. 2 on the table. "I think I should."

He rubbed his cheek under the eye patch, which today was sunny yellow with pale blue stars.

"There's no question. I'll do it. You've done a brilliant research job, I'll give you that, but you're clearly not ready for prime time. I only let you question Dr. French because she demanded it. Discussion closed."

Rage moved up her body. At least the headache was gone, even if the stomach buzz was not.

"As a matter of fact, I had considered asking you to close until that disastrous session. You and Natalia completely confused the jury."

"How can you blame her? You pushed her to do it. She was exhausted. No wonder she slurred her words. That was your decision. You sabotaged it."

His glare sent knives into her chest, and she deserved them. She had poked the bear again, this time smack in the face. *Brace yourself.* For some reason, though, she felt she was ready to take it.

"How brash you've become. I agreed to take this case, pro bono, and asked you to be on it, when I didn't have to. The partners were against it, you know. And this is how you show gratitude?" He slammed the door as he left.

Well, Emma, you've really done it this time. Probably a good thing he left before she said anything else. Now she had to decide what to do about the closing argument.

Stay and help? Give up on the closing? Or fight for doing it?

Tap, tap, tap. The pencil was almost worse than the tik, tik, tik, tik sound.

Every step of this case had been a fight. *Why stop now?* She'd fight to present the closing. *What do I have to lose?*

Emma stood at the whiteboard, making circles and arrows between words. Roy slipped into a chair.

"Apologies come hard to me," he said. "But I owe you one."

"Neither of us can claim the high road today. I'm sorry I've been impertinent. Excitement maybe? But I need to watch my manners."

"Both of us." He reached out his hand. "Are we ready to get to work?"

She hesitated. "May I make my plea for doing the closing first? If you disagree, I'll accept it, but I'd like the chance."

"You remember your pitch you made about taking the case? That was what I expected to see in court yesterday. You were precise, driven, and clear. Do that now. If I agree, we'll have time to prep."

Should I tell him I'll be away Sunday and Monday? Not yet. Get the job first, then figure things out.

"By the way, do you know about the 'fidget factor'?" Roy asked. "In the 1880s, I think, a man named Francis Galton came up with what he called a 'measure of fidget.' He watched people during a large lecture and counted how many times people fidgeted per minute. The more they fidget, the less they're paying attention. What you want during this closing is a zero-fidget count. Got it? Grab my attention and hold me by the lapels for the whole thing."

"There's a way to make me nervous." She laughed.

"See, by laughing, you're halfway there to feeling confident. Now go for it." He settled in his chair.

"Since you like the short version, here goes." She stood up straighter. "…This is a case of a woman who was the victim of a miscarriage of justice. She was accused, tried, and falsely convicted of four deaths. While the jury did the best it could and the defense and prosecution used the information and investigation methods available then, we are two decades beyond those times with new research and new evidence. And that called for a new trial."

She pictured herself capturing the attention and the hearts of the jurors.

"Good. Good. Keep it tight."

"This case made three points for the acquittal of the defendant, Mrs. Victoria Beringer. First, Ms. Beringer's children died as a result of underlying illnesses and gene mutations, different in the boys and girls, but mutations, nonetheless. There was no murder, no crime. Just a sad tragedy."

Take a breath. He's engaged, nodding.

"Second, with more advanced analysis methods, her diaries, the primary evidence, showed a distraught and anxious woman, not a murderer."

"Keep going."

"Third, this case has depended heavily on recent research to unlock the secrets of these gene mutations. The research work can exonerate Ms. Beringer and give closure to a broader community of families who lost children in unexplained, unexpected deaths. Other convictions could be overturned because of this knowledge. In addition, and perhaps equally as important as the defendant's acquittal, is the information future parents could gain on whether they carry gene mutations that could be harmful for their potential offspring. Ms. Beringer carried the deadly CALM2 mutation but had no symptoms. Just as parents can learn the health conditions of their unborn children through sonagrams, DNA checks going forward would save trauma later."

"Nice."

"I'm not finished.... You don't know that Ms. Beringer is my aunt. So, the children who died were my cousins. You also do not know that my parents, sitting behind the defendant's table, lost a baby, my brother, before the age of two. Just like the Beringer children. That means one or both of them may carry a faulty gene. That means I could. I've been tested but do not know the results. Should I have children one day, I'd like to know whether I carry a gene mutation that could kill my babies."

Roy's mouth opened. "I...uh...I don't know what to say, what to think."

"I have a little more."

He gulped coffee. "Geez."

She couldn't remember feeling this strong, this certain, in a long time. "This case is about one woman, yes, and finding a way to exonerate her. But, given what I just said, this is about more than one person, one family. It's about giving women—all women—the information they need to make decisions that affect their lives and the lives of those around them. Giving them the chance to be tested, to find out what their future might hold."

He clapped.

"Just to be clear. This is all about a bigger issue than what we initially thought when we began this journey. Everyone has missed that point so far. It's time to show them how important this case truly is."

"That's awfully personal, and, as powerful as it could be, it's too risky."

She stared him down. "I disagree. It's relatable. Parents and would-be parents will get it. By putting it into a bigger context and a personal one, they'll understand better. It's my aunt's life we're dealing with. I want all the fire power I can use."

"Well, it's strong, I'll give you that. And…OK, against my better judgement, let's try it. Now let's get this organized. You've got work to do."

And less time to do it in than you know.

Chapter 60

Tuesday morning, July 18, 2006

The night before closing arguments, Emma raced back from Seattle. Dr. Wishbone had taken her sample at 3:30 p.m., earlier than expected. But the toy car broke down on the city's outskirts, and she spent the afternoon, into evening, at a foreign car repair shop in Issaquah before getting on the road again about 7:00 p.m. Five hours of night driving to Surrey left her jittery at dawn.

But she felt better than Ed Simmons looked.

Simmons rose slowly, like an old person with back problems. "Our case is straightforward, easy to understand, and unimpeachable in terms of the reasons we argue that the defendant remains guilty of murder, as she was twenty-four years ago. A cold-blooded killer of four innocent children, all under the age of two.... And yet..."

He slipped his right-hand fingers into his suit jacket pocket. "And yet, we see the poignancy, we see the sad waste of a life, over these last two decades."

Emma braced. *Could he be backing down? Showing some humanity?*

"During our preparations, we discussed how to be compassionate for this woman, given her long sentence in prison."

He turned his torso slowly, looking at each jury member.

Emma's breathing slowed. *What is he doing?* He sounded almost conciliatory. *Had my visit swayed his conviction after all?*

Simmons approached the jury box and leaned on the railing. "Yes. We discussed this long and hard." He stared at Aunt Victoria. "Yet in the end, we decided a crime of this heinous nature demanded a serious look once again, a sober review of the evidence, old and new, to determine whether this woman…" He pointed at Aunt Victoria. "… committed these murders. We believe she did."

Aunt Victoria looked so angry, Emma feared she might spit on the table.

He'd planted false hope and then dashed it, like killing baby seals in the ocean. Offering a hand of generosity and then slapping it. The man was bull's pizzle, as Shakespeare would have said.

"So, members of the jury, ladies and gentlemen, we moved onward." He flipped a sheet of his legal pad, ran his finger down it, and placed the pad on the table. "The defense team has offered some evidence, or as they have said, some 'research.' This research was reviewed by scientists, some who they have found, some who we found. Unfortunately, scientists do not all agree on what the research tells them. In fact, the various scientists disagree about the evidence's importance and whether it confirms the reason for the deaths."

Punch. Once again, Simmons twisted words. Making hash from fresh, clear ingredients. *The evidence was not lacking in agreement, at least not from legitimate scientists. It was his group of rag-tag losers….* This would confuse the jury, and she'd have the job of clearing up his mess. She had to focus, or she'd miss whatever else he was going to lie about.

"…fortunate to have access to many scientists who also reviewed…"

There he goes again. I could scream.

"…While we agree that the technology has allowed for more information about the gene mutation, we continue to put before you one simple, memorable fact, substantiated by one of the foremost doctors in the world."

God. Again. The sound bite heard around the world.

Simmons paused.

Does he expect the jury to repeat the blasted Oscar-Wilde-wannabe slogan, like it's a sports tag line? Excruciating.

"How is it possible for four children, not one, which is a tragedy, not two, which might be plausible, but four… four children to die in the same household? That is beyond believable."

Simmons halted, looked toward the judge and again toward the jury.

"Four children. Under age two. How could a mother do such a thing?" He shook his head.

Playing this for all it was worth, and if she was honest in her assessment of the jury, some of seemed to buy it. Several nodded, and the rest stayed riveted on Simmons. He was crushing the measure of fidget.

"Of course, we took other aspects into account. The diaries offered a confession, in the defendant's own words. That comes from committing an act that leads to guilt. And remember, in all four deaths, the defendant found the children. Allowing opportunity for harm."

A boulder landed in her gut. Fuming, she grabbed the chair arms. Roy sat passively. *Does he expect Simmons to trip up?*

Simmons walked into the center of the room and faced the jury, like he was holding court, which he was, in a way.

"And last, please recall that one diary entry said, 'stress made me do terrible things.' That entry alone shows awareness and confession. Professor Yee said she was anxious, and in deep grief. Of course, she was. Grieving for what she'd done. Her children died, and she used those diaries to cover up what she did."

Outrageous. He simply used the same argument from twenty-four years ago, refuted the new evidence, and dragged back those trite slogans, which were, unfortunately, easy to remember. She fidgeted, from anger, not boredom.

"Ladies and Gentlemen, this crime is one of the worst I've encountered in decades. I was involved in the original case two decades ago and was horrorstruck that a mother could injure, let alone murder, her children. Too many deaths. Far too many."

Three jurors lowered their heads. A man on the end looked at the ceiling, as though seeking inspiration.

Victoria squirmed. "Evil man," she whispered. "He did this last time. I want out of here."

"It's not over yet." Emma leaned over. "Courage."

"That's long gone. I just want the fortitude to get through this."

"Therefore, we argue for a guilty verdict. For too many deaths…" He bowed. "Thank you for your attention."

Boom. A sledgehammer whacked her. She'd known it would come, but hearing the words repulsed her.

"Let's take a fifteen-minute recess," Judge Masco said.

During the break, Roy grabbed Emma by the shoulders. "Are you able to do this? You look pale again."

"Nerves, I'm sure." She slathered on some lip gloss. "Is that better?"

"You've got this. Use the fire in your belly like you did the other day. But don't overplay those personal comments. You'll have a killer finish…oops, bad word choice." He chuckled.

"If I don't jump down Simmons's throat first."

"Judge Masco, Ms. Raddell will give our closing argument," Roy said.

The judge raised his eyebrows. "Are you sure, Mr. Donohue? She's rather new."

Emma took that to mean "inexperienced" and shifted it from the angry part of her brain to the "let it be a challenge" part. *I'll show him. And Simmons. And the jury, of course.*

"She has our full confidence." Roy sat.

"Thank you, Your Honor," Emma said. "I may be younger than other counselors, but I'm fully committed to this case and want to win it for our client."

"Please make your argument, then." Masco lifted his hand to welcome her.

"Ladies and Gentlemen of the jury, thank you for your time and attention to this case and this closing statement. We'd like to summarize what you've heard, help you interpret it, and last, ask you for a verdict of not guilty."

The jury settled. No fidgets, yet.

"This case concerns a mother who was accused, tried, and convicted of crimes she did not commit. This miscarriage of justice demands to be rectified, and that is what we sought during this trial. The problem with the previous trial was being in uncharted land. Granted, the prosecution, the defense, and, of course, the jury, did their best with the information and investigation methods that were available then. But technology, information, and ways to analyze have moved forward, and we must adjust."

Still no fidgeting, but simply blank faces. No real connection.

"In 1692, women were tried as witches in Salem, Massachusetts. To test their guilt, villagers used the 'swimming test'—women were tied up and dunked into water. If they floated, they were charged as witches, and many were hung. If they sank, they were presumed innocent, but by then, they were dead, so…not much vindication. We no longer use the swimming test as a method of investigation of guilt or innocence…."

She saw skepticism creep into two faces. *Move on, Emma. Don't let them wander.*

"Now what does that have to do with our current case? Times, techniques, and ways of investigating have likewise changed in this case."

The skeptical faces relaxed. She imagined Roy's voice: "Good, good. Keep the energy up."

"I will review the case in four main points that argue for the acquittal of Ms. Victoria Beringer." *No turning back now.* "First, Ms. Beringer's children did not die because of anything she did to them. Instead, sadly, the children died as a result of the interaction between various underlying illnesses and gene mutations. The boys had respiratory illnesses and a gene mutation related to epilepsy that caused their deaths. The girls had cardiac arrythmia, serious heart problems. They died of heart attacks because of those conditions and another gene mutation. The bottom line is that Ms. Beringer did nothing to contribute to those deaths. They were horrible, serendipitous accidents of nature."

Take a breath. Slow down. Are they with you? She checked each jury member's reaction. Six seemed satisfied, but two looked perplexed. She needed to repeat what she'd just said in a different way. Back into the breach.

"Now, that sounds complicated, to me at least. Let's break it down so everyone, including me, understands it." She stopped, like she'd just remembered something. "Have I told you I have a smaller than average sized brain?"

Heads perked up. The judge tilted his as if ready to stop her tangent. She waited for Simmons, but he sat still.

"Your Honor, I do have a reason for this small side street."

Masco nodded.

"Several years ago, I was driving, and suddenly, something like mud covered my right eye. I rushed to the eye doctor, who called for an MRI to check my brain. Hint—never get an MRI on a Friday. It ruins your weekend."

Several in the courtroom snickered.

"On Monday, the neurologist said there was nothing wrong with my eye but that my brain was 'smaller than average.' But he said Einstein's brain was too, so I was in good company."

More snickers. She had them.

"The moral is that I use my small brain as an excuse to read through, hear again, learn about something more than once, usually three or four or even seven times. So, indulge me as I review this science once more."

"Ah. Thank you," Judge Masco said. "Proceed."

"All right. Let's take the girls, who died of heart attacks. Different ages, but both were asleep and under age two. The autopsies showed their hearts weren't operating normally. Because no one knew about the gene mutation, there was no chance for early intervention. Combined with weak hearts, the mutation pushed the girls to their deaths."

The skeptics nodded, back in the fold.

"The boys had respiratory trouble and epilepsy, and that, coupled with the gene mutation, likely caused their deaths. I realize the chance of something like this happening is quite low, as the prosecution argued, but it happened, nonetheless. There were scientific reasons for the deaths. They had nothing to do with Ms. Beringer's actions."

Aunt Victoria's mouth tickled a smile.

"Now, the second point is Ms. Beringer's diaries. The prosecution has claimed they showed confession. Not so. Using advanced analysis methods, unavailable at the time of the initial trial, we showed that her diaries instead revealed a woman who was distraught and anxious, but not a murderer. Professor Yee, you'll recall, analyzed all 40,000-plus words, not just the 1,500 the prosecution focused on. More data, more information, more accurate conclusions."

Heads nodded. She reached in her suit pocket for her Scottish lapel pin.

"Third, this case has depended on research by scientists around the world who study these dangerous gene mutations. Their work, replicated numerous times, is the key to exonerating Ms. Beringer. But the research is useful in other ways. The research and the directory in Italy have helped bring closure to a broader community of families who have lost children in unexplained, unexpected deaths."

Simmons jotted notes, flipping his yellow paper as fast as he seemed able. *It's hitting him. And they don't have a clue what else is up my sleeve. Sit tight, boys.*

"Uh… In other countries—in Australia, Austria, and Chile—parents are on trial for the deaths of their children, in cases very similar to this one. Scientific evidence will help acquit them. Previous convictions could be overturned because of this research and knowledge. And, if Ms. Beringer is exonerated, that would help those cases in Argentina…no sorry, Australia and Austria. Getting my A's mixed up."

Her head had begun to swell. Her thoughts felt fuzzy. *Don't look at Roy, or he'll pull you off. What's going on?*

"Excuse me for a minute. Let me just check my notes… ah. Yes. In addition to the impact that an acquittal could make for people elsewhere in the world, there's another even more important consequence of this case. The future."

Don't trip over your own feet.

"What about parents or future parents? Don't they want to know about their unborn children, about any possible diseases? Deadly gene mutations? Just as parents wish to know the health conditions of their unborn children through sonagrams, doing DNA checks going forward would save trauma later."

She coughed. *Can I go through with this? You made the decision. Now just execute.*

"Is everything all right, Ms. Raddell? Do you need a break?"

"No Judge Masco, thank you for asking, though." She needed to drop the final zinger. But her heart sped up, and she worried her words would too. *Breathe.*

"Ladies and Gentlemen. I raise this last point about the future, about knowing about these mutations for future generations, not to only understand what happened in the past. It's important for a number of reasons. Some of them very personal…to me."

By now the fidget count was zero. No one moved. A notebook or phone dropped on the floor. "Oh shi—" someone whispered.

"Order!" Judge Masco surveyed his domain.

"Thank you, Judge." She turned to the jury. "Ladies and Gentlemen, you do not know that Ms. Beringer is my aunt."

She heard gasps from the jury and from behind her, in the courtroom.

Simmons sprang to his feet. "Judge! This is a huge conflict of interest. How could the defense allow—"

"I agree, Mr. Simmons. We need a recess and to excuse the jury. Please be ready to tell me what this is all about."

Roy, Emma, and the prosecution team, met in the judge's cramped dark office. Emma stood.

"The conflict of interest alone is enough to throw the whole case out!" Simmons let his voice verge on shouting.

As if he hadn't known about this all along. *Hypocrite.*

Masco nodded. "I agree. So please tell me what this is about and why you should be allowed to give this closing?"

"Your Honor." Emma stepped toward his desk, next to Roy, who stood and offered his chair. She shook her head.

"Mr. Simmons is correct that under normal circumstances, it would be inappropriate for a relative to be part of this case. But I did not know of this woman's existence, my aunt's, until April of this year. My parents had never spoken of her, I had never met her, and I had no inkling that we had a relative in prison. So, she was a stranger to me. Under those circumstances, I met her, learned about her case, and have treated her like any other client. But, of course, over the course of the last few months, I've learned about the gene mutations and the effect this family and on other families. Such health issues are personal, and I want the jury—parents or parents to be—to understand that."

Masco swiveled his chair away from the group and rocked. "I'll allow it. But watch your step."

Chapter 61

Tuesday afternoon, July 18, 2006

On the way to the courtroom, Emma slipped into the restroom to think. *Now I have to decide how far to push….* This was about so much more—the power of science, the vindication of other families whose children died in unexplained ways, and the need for women to have information to make a life-changing decision. So much more than one murder.

She pressed her palms to her eyes and heard Natalia's voice in her head: "We can't hold back. It's too important to Ms. Beringer, to women, and to families."

This was a career maker—or killer. *I should find out now so I can plan for a new career if I need to…. Travel agent? Veterinarian? Or stay with law?* If she bombed, she'd be a crack-pot pariah in the profession.

A knock on the door jolted her. "They're starting," Grant said. He hugged her as she walked out.

Masco nodded at the jury. "I've ruled that Ms. Raddell's relationship to the defendant is not a problem for this case."

Courage. She'd told Aunt Victoria to stay strong; now she needed to follow her own advice. She noticed her shoes were scuffed. *How'd I miss that?* She breathed in and out for a count of four and looked at the people she had to convince.

"A few minutes ago, I told you that Ms. Beringer is my aunt, and her children were my cousins."

The ceiling fans swished in the hushed courtroom.

"You also don't know that my parents, sitting behind the defendant's table, lost a baby before he turned two in an unexplained death. Like the Beringer children. That means one or both of my parents carry a faulty gene. And…so could I."

One of the jurors placed her hand over her mouth.

Clearly not a sign of fidgeting. More of horror?

Masco leaned forward, gavel in hand. "Ms. Raddell?"

"Judge Masco, if my aunt had known about the gene mutation, she might have acted on it. This affects more than just this one case, more than just one family."

"Proceed. With caution."

In her mind, she saw the red line on a cliff. The problem with cliffs was not knowing how far down the leap would be. She doubted this would be a small jump.

"Thank you. As I said, I've been tested but don't have the results. I'll admit, I'm racked with fear. Should I have children one day, I'd like to know whether I carry a gene mutation that could take my babies too early. Just as parents learn the health of their babies through sonagrams, using a gene mutation test could be part of normal checkup. It would save trauma later."

Several people in the courtroom gallery muttered, but the jurors remained rigid. *Am I offending them?* She stroked her belly lightly and stepped toward the jury box. The jurors had no idea she was about to light a firecracker.

"Why do I worry about this gene mutation so much?" She looked toward Roy. Aunt Victoria gave a tiny nod. "It's because…I'm pregnant."

The courtroom burst into cacophony. Sounds of "Oh my God" and "NO!" and a single "What the hell?" echoed through.

Judge Masco pounded his gavel three times. "Silence! Order! Now!"

The room quieted to a low rumble. Several jurors' faces had paled. "What just happened?" one said.

"Recess. All of you," Masco pointed to the lawyers, "my office. Now."

As they left the courtroom, she glanced at Mom and Dad and Grant, all of whom sat motionless, mouths open. "Sorry," she whispered. Aunt Victoria smiled.

At the judge's office, Roy yanked her arm. "What the devil were you thinking? That's way beyond what we talked about? You've probably lost the case."

"I had to; they have to know the anguish this puts on peop—"

"You're done for. No more excuses. Even if Masco says we can continue, you're done speaking."

He walked into Masco's office before her, not holding the door for her. Ed Simmons grabbed the handle before it closed and held it open for her.

"Very creative." He smirked. "I doubt it will get you there, though."

She strolled into Masco's chambers, feeling more relaxed and like herself than she thought possible.

Chapter 62

Wednesday morning, July 19, 2006

"The jury will please disregard the final personal statements made yesterday by the defense. The comments do not directly relate to this case and the evidence provided. I know it's difficult to unhear something, but that is what you must do."

Ed stood up. "Your Honor, we call for a mistrial. The jury has heard information that you wish them to disregard, which, of course, is not doable. The chance for a fair interpretation and conclusion by the jury is impossible."

"There will be no mistrial, Mr. Simmons," said Judge Masco. "This case will reach its conclusion, without the jury being influenced by the outburst of the defense."

Masco reached for his paper fan. "In a few moments, this court retires, and I will send the jury to deliberate on its verdict. But first, let me remind you of a few instructions. Please disregard the testimony of one witness, Dr. Simon Albrecht of the Genetics lab at Westminster University. You have also been asked to disregard the defense's final personal comments to her closing argument. Once Ms. Raddell veered beyond the evidence review, she moved outside of her purview, and you should dismiss those comments."

As Masco's words sank in, Emma's heart thudded. *What was I thinking?* She'd shattered her efforts to make a difference in this family, for this case. Masco had ripped the core of her argument away from the light, forcing the jury to remember only the possibly confusing information about gene mutations. No emotion allowed. Now the jury would never understand the broader importance of this case and why it went beyond Aunt Victoria.

She heard Masco's instructions through a blur and closed her eyelids over burning eyes.

Chapter 63

Wednesday, July 19, 2006

"I can't breathe. I need to get out." Emma faced Roy across the metal conference table.

"We can't leave. The press is swarming."

"I…I should say I'm sorry about pushing the personal stuff…but I just can't. It was important."

"Maybe to you, but you probably tanked the case. I should have refused to let you do that, so I'll take responsibility. But I'm not sure you would have listened anyway."

She sniggered. "You're probably right. And in the process, I bought myself a reputation as lunatic. Who'll want a lawyer like that?"

"You're memorable, that's for sure."

She shoved a legal envelope across the table to Roy.

He skimmed the handwritten notes. "What is this?"

"I didn't want to show you this, but now it doesn't matter. My notes about Simmons. You know how he seemed to know everything we were up to and was always one step ahead? A mole in the office fed him information. I didn't say much, but it was enough. About some witnesses, the juror who was bribed. He knew it all…and so did Antigone. I thought she was trying to be helpful. I'm so naïve still."

Roy's eye drilled into her. "One of ours? Are you serious? Here's our mistrial."

"I don't want a mistrial. But I can't push anything at this stage. Your call. But you might need to have a heart-to-heart with our colleague."

"I'll heart-to-heart her right out the door."

The courtroom clerk tapped on the door. "They're back."

"It's only been two hours? Is that a good sign?"

Roy scrubbed his cheeks with his palms, urging some color into them. "Probably not."

The courtroom rose when Judge Masco entered and remained standing as the jury filed in.

Emma looked at the jurors. One glanced at Aunt Victoria and looked away. Another scowled. *Anger? Distaste?* The young man twisted a black ring on his finger and squinted at the floor. Emma looked at Simmons and saw Antigone, sitting behind Richard Li. *Traitor.*

"Be seated, please," Masco said. "The record will show that the jury, the defendant, and both sets of lawyers are here. Mr. Clerk."

"Case Number 976, State versus Ms. Victoria Knox Beringer, charged with one count of manslaughter and three counts of murder in the first degree."

"Thank you." Masco faced the jury. "You've reached a verdict?"

The grandmotherly African American woman rose. "We have, Judge."

Roy, Emma, and Aunt Victoria stood. Emma's knees trembled against the chair seat.

After the judge read it, the foreperson opened the sheet of folded paper, but it shook in her hands.

"Members of the jury," said the clerk, "how do you find the defendant, Ms. Beringer, on the count of manslaughter of Darrin Thomas Beringer?"

Emma stared at the jury foreperson. In another world, she looked like a good baking partner. But today, she pleaded with the woman in her head.

"Not guilty."

Emma's insides felt like jelly. Aunt Victoria gripped Emma's hand. Babbles from people seated behind her mixed with some buzzing in her ears.

"And how do you find the defendant, Ms. Beringer, on the count of murder in the first degree of Brian Anderson Beringer?"

"Not guilty."

The courtroom gallery commotion built. Mom whispered, "She's done it. She's done it!"

"How do you find the defendant, Ms. Beringer, on the count of murder in the first degree of Fiona Mary Beringer?"

"Not guilty."

Emma squelched Mom's commentary in her head. *"Don't get too big for your britches." Doesn't apply anymore, Mom. I'll get as big as I want.*

"And finally, how do you find the defendant, Ms. Beringer, on the count of murder in the first degree of Dorothy Mabel Beringer?"

"Not guilty."

Gasps filled the room. Someone in the back clapped.

"Can't believe it."

"She did it. Couldn't they see that?"

"Somebody should pay. This is wrong."

"Order," Masco barked. "Let's poll the jurors to see if they agree."

Each did.

"This is your true verdict. The defendant is free to go."

Aunt Victoria lowered to her chair like a lump of dirt and wept.

Roy cradled her as Mom and Dad reached across the railing to hug Emma. Grant stood back, waiting his turn. Emma didn't want to look at him, expecting to see judgement, shock, or something worse in his eyes.

Suddenly, she felt a stab of pain and rushed from the courtroom. She made it to the restroom just as she felt warm liquid leaving her body, flowing down her legs. "No! NO!"

Chapter 64

Friday evening, July 28, 2006

Emma let Grant push the glider on his back porch. It screeched, startling the two hummingbirds around the feeder. They zipped away but returned when they sensed no danger. The luminescent red and green feathers sparkled in the dusk light.

Emily D #1680 came to her, unasked for.

Sometimes with the Heart
Seldom with the Soul
Scarcer with the Might
Few—love at all.

"God, Emma, why on earth didn't you tell me?" Grant pulled her closer and held her like he'd never let go.

She let the swing move back and forth for a full minute, gathering strength and words. "I didn't know myself how I felt about it all until the miscarriage. In that moment, that awful moment, I realized I wanted to be part of a family, my own family. And that I want to have a child one day. And not because I need to prove something, to offer something 'more' to Mom and Dad. I see that I'm enough, just me, and I didn't know that before."

"And you didn't want to include me in all of this pondering?"

A bolt of pain shot through her chest. She stopped breathing to let it settle.

"I'm sorry to hurt you. Really. But I wasn't ready. As I said, I couldn't articulate any of this until very recently. And…we were—we are—still new to each other—"

"What changed?"

"Thanks in part to you always being there for me, to almost losing Shadrach, and to finding my way back to my family through Aunt Victoria. For the first time in a long time, I feel hope. I want love—and transparency—in my life. And you're the core. With my parents as well. And I think I can do it. This case forced truth into the sunlight, made us confront things that should have come up years ago. I'm glad I could be a part of that." She squirmed. "Sorry, this sounds cheesy."

"Not cheesy but a bit out of the ordinary for you—the strong, silent type. You know I have your back. And I hope you know I love you, almost as much as Harriet." He winked at her. "Seriously, what else can I do?"

The chest ache melted and instead, simple warmth flooded her. "Nothing, Mountain Man. This helps, just to tell you."

He slipped off the glider and got down on one knee. "Let me do it this time." He reached for her hands and kissed them.

She felt lightness in her limbs that she'd not had for months. "I'm ready this time."

"Emma, you crazy dog lover and savior of families, will you marry me?"

"Only if you let me eat expired processed food once a week."

Chapter 65

Saturday, July 29, 2006

"Let's have some tea and sit."

Mom carried a tray with five glasses, five iced tea spoons, and the West End Penguin ice bucket, and Emma opened the screen door to the back porch.

Dad, Grant, and Aunt Victoria rocked on the porch. The group talked, laughed, and grieved for the child Emma had miscarried on the last day of the trial. Devastated, she withdrew for days afterward, but gentle Grant drew her back into life. The day the trial had ended, he'd asked her to move in with him.

"How does Harriet feel about fish? You'd have to take the full package—Shadrach and me, but also Hildegarde and Augustus, our newest fish family member."

He laughed. "I'll take whatever creatures you bring as long as you're leading the pack."

But today was for the human family. They talked about the summer heat and how good it was to have Aunt Victoria with them.

"I got the test results," she said, killing the congenial buzz. "And I wanted to tell you all together." Grant squeezed her hand.

"Emileen, no matter what you tell us, I'm sorry blew up at you. You have to make your own decisions about children," Aunt Victoria said. "No one else should tell you what to do. I only wanted to protect you from the sorrow your parents and I went through. But it's also part of life."

"I know you care, and that's why you did it. But relax, I don't have the gene mutation. I'm fine."

With that, the group of five rocked in sync.

Afterword

Research marches on.

In March 2023, the international journal *Science* published an article (DeAngelis and Hofmann, 2023) that suggests zebra fish have a capacity for empathy and that it can spread through a social group, especially when it comes to fear. So maybe Emma was right about those fish companions after all.

Also, a bigger headline recently appeared. The Australian case that inspired this book made headlines (*Science,* 2023) when it was reviewed, given the new evidence from the gene mutation research. Kathleen Folbigg, imprisoned for over twenty years, was released and pardoned.

References:

DeAngelis, R.S. and Hofmann, H.A. "An Evolutionarily Ancient Signaling Pathway Mediates Emotional Contagion." *Science* 379 (March 2023): 1186-1187.

"Scientists Help Free Imprisoned Woman."*Science* 380, no. 6649 (June 9, 2023): 994.

Acknowledgments

Special recognition goes out to *60 Minutes Australia*. In August 2021, the program burst open the decades-old Australian case and set me on a path to create a similar story based in the U.S. More recent episodes in late 2021 and 2023 continued to cover the case.

A recently published book, *The Big Folbigg Mistake* by John Kerr (2022), also added pieces to the puzzle.

Kristen Wise and Maira Pedierra talked me off the ledge more than once. Thank you both.

Zora Knauf and Lisa Poisso, thank you for the editing help, from the start to finish. You both have made me a better writer.

Thanks to Hildy Ayer, Linda Clark-Santos, Kira Dale, Lisa Hales, Justin Henderson, Elizabeth Mabbutt, Elisabeth McKetta, Gary Raney, Angeli Weller, Hal Van Woert, and my dog, Matisse, who never talked back on our walks.

And always, thanks to Tony Olbrich, my best friend and partner for decades.

Meet the Author

Distinguished Professor Emerita at Boise State University (USA) and a former Adjunct Professor at Aalborg University (Denmark) and at the National Economics University in Hanoi (Vietnam), N.K. Napier teaches strategy and creativity, coaches executives, and leads the Boise State Executive MBA residency to Vietnam.

Napier co-created and hosted *Idaho Business Matters* on NPR's local affiliate (Boise State Public Radio), was a regular guest on KTVB Channel 7's *Noon News*, and wrote for *Forbes Vietnam*. She continues to write columns for Psychology Today and the *Idaho Statesman*. Her long-time work as a teacher, researcher, and writer has led to several awards, including a Medal of Honor and a Medal of Friendship in Vietnam.

After thirty-five-plus years in the academic and research world, N.K. Napier is embarking on something completely new: fiction writing, which offers her the joys and challenges of being a beginner again, with opportunities to do in-depth historical research and fact-checking to create fun new worlds and characters.

Hello,

I sincerely hope you enjoyed reading *A Case of Too Many Deaths* as much as I did writing it. If you were enticed by Emma's thrilling courtroom drama and medical investigation, I encourage you to share your thoughts with other readers via a review at the retail outlet where you purchased the book.

Please visit my website at NancyKNapier.com so we can connect and you can learn more about my previously published books as well as my upcoming projects.

As a thank you for reading *A Case of Too Many Deaths*, I am excited to include a sneak preview of my next mystery novel:

> What happens when a naive curator from Vietnam discovers an art crime that affects both her own family and her country? Thuy, a proud thirty-nine-year-old assistant curator in Hanoi, Vietnam, loses a long-sought-after job but then gets the chance to mount a major exhibit at her museum, which could vindicate her. The exhibit will show lost paintings of Vietnamese artists that a collector in France has offered to the museum. Four of the paintings are by her famous great-uncle, whose reputation has been critical for the family legacy for decades. But, right before the exhibit opens, she's faced with the possibility that some of the paintings are fake. She must find out if they are, why they are, and who's behind the scam.

More to come,
N<N

Made in the USA
Middletown, DE
27 September 2023

39556167R00194